Platinur

Every Mother's Son

A novel set in Helmand, Afghanistan
By
Pelham McMahon
© 2014

'Camp Bastian has been a place which has sustained operations, providing everything from bottled water to fast air support. It's been a place to do your laundry, and for guys who were stationed out in the forward operating bases to come back to, for a bit of normality, to get a shower and a shave and a cup of coffee.' Lt Col Laurence Quinn. 2014

'There is something meaningful in that first hug: every returning soldier will tell you the same. It speaks of her gratitude for your return, it shouts with relief that her days of fear and worry are over: it is the moment when your aching body can at last relax against the softness of her loving breasts, as she surrenders herself into your hungry arms. Your heart sighs with relief and your eyes shine with tears of joy, until you remember those who were injured and those who had died.'[Platinum 10.Ch29]

ISBN -13:978-1500439767

ISBN – 10:1500439762

Dedicated to my own hero Joseph Brian McMahon

RA & RAF 1939 – 1997

To the two sons of Vera Dev who died of their wounds.

And to all who served in The Afghanistan Conflict of 2001 – 2014

As well as all those who loved them and who bravely prayed for their safe return.

With thanks to the following

I have not been to Camp Bastion or to Camp Leatherneck. But through the eyes and ears of the following people, who valiantly wore their helmet cams, spoke openly and sometime defiantly as they were filming and who after several years of consistent broadcasting on YouTube, I saw and heard the historical backdrop for my novel. Then there were others whose books I read and the many media commentaries I found in the press, plus visits, and phone calls that have supported me throughout this project, some more dramatically than others, but I make no distinction between them. All have help to give bones to this fictional story.

To all of these I give thanks

Adam Aziz, Battlefield Sources, BBC, Ben Anderson, the British Army, British Forces News, Captain Lauren Phipps TA, Carla Prater, CNN, Danny Knap, Devil Dog, Discovery World, Dr Christopher Bowman TA, Doc.central, Documentary Central, Doug Beattie, Fox News, Funker 530,

General W. Cardwell 4th, Julia Gibbs, ITV, Journeyman Pictures, Julien Hensey, Laurence McGinty, loteq101, Major Bill Steuber USA, Mark Roberts, Michael Mosley, Negat Centre, Newsbreaker USA, NurdR4G3, On Target, Only Documentaries, Pte David Wylie TA, Pte Michael Lewis TA, Paul Orton, Peter Mitchell, Lieutenant Colonel Laurence Quinn, Ringsight91, Robert Ham, Sam Simpson, Seagame Kahking, Sky TV, Super Docs Today, Ian McNett USA Marine, War Storyful, And Zeb Lockerman.

This is a work of fiction and some place names were invented to aid the story. The roles played by certain individuals in the story, cannot be attributed to any known serving soldier or medic deployed.

A Useful Glossary

Alpha = used by MERT workers to indicate severely critical level of injury.

= Also the letter A in International radio call signs.

ANA= Afghanistan National Army

Baad = Afghan method of payment in kind, for a debt, often with a daughter given in lieu.

Bergen = Largest British military rucksack

'C' = controller of the British Secret Intelligence Service, known as the SIS.

Celox = Gauze that effectively helps blood to clot quickly, used extensively on the battlefield

CH-47 = Chinook Helicopter

Cookhouse = British Catering and eatery

CP or Check Point = satellite bases of between 12 and 50 men

CSM = Company Sergeant Major

Dead Zone = area safe from attack by the enemy

D-FAC = American Catering facility

ExFil = rapid departure for American medical rescue helicopters

FLO = Family Liaison Officer

FOB = forward operating base large and well manned by several hundred men.

Fusiliers = Infantry soldiers, foot soldiers

'General Order Number One' is a USA military command to all service personnel stationed in a War Zone. Some call it the 'No sex please we're soldiers' rule because it forbids all romantic and sexual fraternization between the sexes; even between married couples serving in the same arena.

Golden Hour = the vital first hour after injury

HLS = Helicopter Landing Site

Humvee = High and wide Multi-purpose Wheeled Vehicle

ILBE= 'Improved Load Bearing Equipment.' [American rucksack]

ISAF = International Security Assistance Force

ISO Can = A Cargo container to the British

JTCA = Joint Tactical Air Controller

Lieu-ten-ant = Americans use the original pronunciation

Lef-ten-ant = British pronunciation of Lieutenant

5

MERTs =*Medical Emergency Response Teams* on Chinooks and in ambulances

MRE packs = foil wrapped, ready to eat food, for when patrolling away from camp.

NVD = Night Vision Device

'Op Minimiser' = the tannoyed signal that all communication with the outside world is to stop, because a Soldier has been killed. It is done to protect the relatives of the dead.

PB or Patrol Base = usually about 60-100 men and acting as half way house to FOB

Platinum Ten = the first ten minutes after sustaining an injury.

PRR = Personal radio

ROSO G1 = a Military advisory service

Sinking Air = the air that is forced below a hovering helicopter by its own blades, causes dust storm around the Chopper and can be dangerous.

SIS = Secret Intelligence Service [former MI6]

TOC = Tactical Operations Centre

Vauxhall Cross = HQ MI6

Contents
Acknowledgements
A Useful Glossary
    Chapters

Platinum Ten

Chapter One

Recalled **into Service**

I knew the first time I saw Lieutenant Guy Williams of the Lancashire Fusiliers speaking to Private First Class Alice Holford, of the American Army, that they were in love.

My name is Matthew Fleming, no relation to the famous Ian Fleming. I began my military career with a life in the Navy and ended it as Commander Fleming of MI6, but time has changed things in the Service; these days I would be considered a bit of a fossil. I am quite literally too old to undertake assignments alongside the SAS, as I did nearly forty years ago, but I had left the service with a bit of a reputation. I was judged to be good at photography and excellent at assessing political situations when submitting reports, which would usefully aid the judgement of politicians and senior staff in the military. In other words I could write a comprehensive assessment without costing the Service too much time and money. It always comes down to money, but on this occasion I think it was about the lack of money. Gordon Brown had none to spend; the Army Chief of Staff was on his back wanting more, much, much, much more, than Gordon had in his already depleted treasure chest.

I must have seemed a suitable candidate for the role of classic fall-guy! Whether that was due to my command of the English language; thanks to Mum and Dad, both English teachers and my excellent English teacher, Mr Thornley, the Head of English at my local grammar school, I'll never know. We pick up language bit by bit and from a multitude of sources; beginning with nursery rhymes and fairy stories until through a lifetime of books and media influences, we settle for the words with which we are most comfortable. Dartmouth Naval College probably added to my command of the English language and now I'm man enough to be grateful for my education, and for my military training; it has all made me what I am today.

The beginning of this story goes back before the day when I stood in the mustering area by the gateway of Camp Bastion, watching a young couple of soldiers obviously trying to look indifferent to each other, while their body language screamed out their passionate longing to be in each other's arms? I knew about passion, then and now for I have been married to Cathy these past many years, and we are happily settled down in a beautiful part of Cheshire named Lower Peover. Cathy and I are unencumbered; there are no children, neither of the two-legged boy/girl variety, nor the four-legged doggy/cat variation. Consequently we are enjoying a vibrant early retirement, take our holidays in France, and enjoy gardening, entertaining, and yes, I'm still, in my retirement, an enthusiastic photographer.

Although forever obliged to respect the Official Secrets Act, I consider myself relatively well behaved for an oldie, if somewhat of a boring one. Well, that is until after three pints in my local, The Bells of Peover, then I enjoy recounting some of the crazier moments from my military life, which my best friends, both retired senior policemen, enjoy; until they try out-bidding me in a verbal rivalry, which leaves the wives and others listening in, either gasping with laughter or accusing us of exaggerating. I suspect the latter is the more truthful judgement. Yes, I am given to a touch of verbal diarrhoea in my attempts to entertain others, and sometimes it is useful to blind others with words, especially when the truth or the science doesn't add up to much.

There is no way that Cathy and I could have foreseen the request that came from the PM. I was summoned to Vauxhall Cross by 'C', the controller of the modernised version of MI6, also known as the Secret Intelligence Service, who upon my arrival in his office, looked at me with a stern face, and cautioned me that I was still under the Official Secrets Act, before hurrying me to Number 10 Downing Street.

The year was 2009 and as everyone will recall, the PM was in trouble, his popularity was fading in many quarters, not least with the military. Things were heating up out in Afghanistan and too many senior people were joining the discontent being voiced from within the lower ranks, and complaining about the lack of certain very expensive equipment, and now the Prime Minister was being troubled by even the well-polished top brass, the four-starred generals and the field marshals, who were demanding yet more helicopters.

"They don't seem to know how much a helicopter costs," he said with a shake of his head and a worried expression on his face. "I can't find any more money for helicopters, new boots maybe, but helicopters? No! They must have forty-eight helicopters out there, by now. If not, what have they done with them? Find out and tell me what is going on, please, Matt."

There he was, Her Majesty's Prime Minister Gordon Brown, calling me Matt, and begging for my help. In a strange way I felt sorry for him; the whole world was short of money and Gordon was no different; the whole country was strapped for cash.

"You're handy with a camera, Matt, and quite frankly the Treasury is stretched to the limits with this war. You're good at writing reports; know how to work undercover, and oh, well … can you still ride a bike? I believe it is a good way of getting about out there, and it saves on petrol. You can, good! Ride! Do what you will, but assess what is going on. Check out the complaints and just get me the answers, either with your camera, or with a sufficiently detailed report for me to be able to put it before the Cabinet, by the end of the year. This year, please, Matt. Do you hear what I'm saying, Matt? It's one year to the next general election!" I said yes! I must be mad!

Chapter Two
Camp Bastion, a Monday two weeks later

Fred stood at respectful attention at the top of the ramp, looking out over the apron of the airfield, he saw the lines of troops with heads bowed, and forming a guard of honour as the hearse drew up. In the silence only the noise of the pall-bearers steps could be heard. It was a sombre moment as Fred watched the coffin draped in the union flag, being gently carried up the ramp of the plane, to be reverently lowered onto the table he had prepared. Behind the coffin the clergy followed and stood to one side, while the pallbearers and Fred lined up on the opposite side. All stood to attention during a short Memorial service. The army chaplains spoke words of Thanksgiving and blessing for Corporal Henry Black, a British marine. He had been killed by a roadside bomb just 36 hours previously.

Corporal Black had been killed a week before his twenty-fifth birthday, the only son of a widowed mother and all the talk in the camp was of the failure to save him. His death was believed to be an unnecessary death. It had stirred up even more complaints about the lack of sufficient rescue 'birds' and the contentious arguments along the lines of, 'could he have lived if the Golden Hour had been adhered to?'

Then as the chaplains walked reverently away from the solitary coffin, followed by the marching pall-bearers, Fred closed the ramp and signalled to the pilot that they had completed their sad duty. It was time to leave Camp Bastion and if they were to achieve all their connections as booked by the Joint Tactical Air Controller, they needed to set off without delay. The timing for the journey home was set for the flight to arrive promptly for the repatriation ceremony at 1330 hours local British time.

Hidden in the tomb-like cavern of the C130, nobody saw Fred reaching into his Bergen to find his personal tribute to Corporal Henry Black. Placing the small wreath of poppies on Henry's coffin, for the duration of the journey, Fred then prepared himself to spend most of his time sitting quietly reading, as if keeping the young soldier company throughout that long sad time. It would make no difference to anybody that he behaved with such reverence before the coffin and the remains of a dead soldier; but it was symptomatic of the respect felt by soldiers for their fallen comrades.

As the last echo of the C130 died away over the miles and miles of the Helmand desert, Camp Bastion had quickly returned to normal after the *Op Minimiser* had passed.

But back at home, every mother held her breath until she knew for certain that her son was safe, for every soldier is every mother's son, no matter when, no matter where, he is fighting and dying. She holds her breath in fear of the footsteps coming up to her front door and the Bell being rung by an officer's hand.

The human telegram, 'Mrs Black may we come in?' Pause a moment and imagine her feelings she cannot escape the truth, when her son's regimental officers are standing respectfully on her doorstep.,

****

Lieutenant Guy Williams, grateful that for once it hadn't been one of his fusiliers killed so needlessly, would spend the best part of that day out on patrol with the '5 Platoon A Company' of the Lancashire Fusiliers. It was one of those dreaded six hour foot patrols along the banks of the river, which runs through the heart of Helmand Province.

As he watched his men walk cautiously, spaced out and in single file behind the point man, the searcher sweeping the ground with his hand-held IED detecting equipment; Guy Williams was focussed on their safety. He scanned a horizon that promised little in the way of possible protection, should the Taliban attack them. The unspoken fear that accompanied each man on every foot patrol was matched by their courage. He watched his young fusiliers, as they faced up to the possibility of being blown to pieces with every step taken. He felt it was his duty to appear unafraid; to pretend he was as unflappable as Spock on the Starship Enterprise, 'boldly going where others feared to go,' regardless of his personal safety. *But I'm as afraid as all of them*, he said to himself; not to be afraid was to be foolhardy; fear made you cautious.

But with every day out on patrol, it increasingly seemed to Guy Williams that fate was somehow warning him, telling him that soon it would be his turn. The best way of describing it, he told his American sweetheart Alice, was that a weird feeling

15

kept coming over him, which said 'you're a cat who has had eight lives and the next time, it may well be your ninth and bingo, you're dead!' His deep-seated consciousness of the inevitability of death kept him awake at night, and lectured him with unnecessary scruples during the day. It seemed to be constantly shouting at him, 'It is your turn to die!' It would repeatedly overcome him, to the point that he almost wished it would happen. *Never wish for anything*, his foster mother had said, *and then you won't be disappointed.*

Walking back through the gates of Camp Bastion at the end of the patrol and listening to his men, he realised that he wasn't the only one in the platoon with such feelings. Discipline helped him contain his own feelings about the dangers facing the soldiers fighting in Helmand, his officers friends all came back from foot patrols shaking their heads and trying to cope with the deep seated fear of losing another man. But there was no Officers' mess in Camp Bastion and he seldom met up with colleagues and friends from Sandhurst days. If one was out on a six hour patrol, another would be up country on a twenty four hour patrol. He missed his peers from his training days. Lieutenant Guy Williams had a soft heart behind that look of efficiency, and perhaps it was because he was in love that he was super sensitive to his Platoon members and their feelings.

He listened to them. He absorbed all their hidden fears and sensed their bravery behind the joking and the camaraderie.

As Bryn Jones, one of the youngest and bravest of the young soldiers in his platoon, barely nineteen, said quietly to him, "I keep thinking, 'is it my turn?" and Phil Ayres who at twenty-one and a seasoned veteran of Bosnia, Iraq and now on his second tour of Afghanistan, said, "I've put it into my head that I'm already dead, sir. That way it won't make any difference to me." Guy tried his hardest to encourage the more nervous men. He had no choice but to encourage them, regardless of his own feelings; his boys and men were dependent upon him for their own safety.

Williams was known as a staunch believer in, the fighting man's principle of; 'look after the man on your left and the man on your right; and they will look after you.' Others might interpret it as the spirit of 'a band of brothers', but Guy felt it went even deeper than that; it was a trust that gave the soldier a reason to go on fighting. He once said, "If there's no cause, why fight!" The cause, he believed, was the man standing beside you. Trust your brothers in arms, yes, they all did just that, but the very suddenness of the IEDs made them the most traumatizing of weapons. Lieutenant Williams would years later describe the war against the Taliban as the 'Invisible war'. You could not see the Taliban and you could not see the IEDs.

That day those six hours on patrol had seemed endless, and as the day had dragged by, he found he was imagining how it had been for the family and regimental colleagues of Corporal Henry Black. Trying to concentrate on the job in hand, Guy had been glad when their six hour patrol was over, without incident. "All safely gathered in!" he said to himself.

They had got back to Camp Bastion alright, all alive even though dirty and tired. Time was then spent sitting in a circle, as they cleaned their weapons and debriefed at the same time. There was a great show of brushing off the dust and dirt not only from their weapons, but also from their clothes and their boots, before the men headed off to the cookhouse for a hearty meal. Most of the men hated the cold pre-packed MRE meals issued for time away from base camp. At least the cookhouse was up and running, and hot food was available twenty-four-seven; it was reminiscent of home. There was always the 'plenty of meat and two veg' variety of meals, the curry and the pasta as well as the all-day breakfast, another favourite, not least for those who lived the upside down lives of permanent night duty, for the war did not sleep, the enemy did not sleep; in truth it was under the cover of the night sky, that the IEDs were planted. But for now he just sat and watched his men as they enjoyed eating and chatting in the cookhouse. He sensed their muscles and nerves could relax and for a while they could escape the heat of the Afghanistan desert, because at that time most of the Camp Bastion cookhouses provided a modest amount of air conditioning.

Williams remembered his first tour two years previously, when Camp Bastion was a mere shadow of its ever growing present size. He had been nothing more than a second lieutenant in those days, and his responsibilities then, in the Fusiliers First Battalion, were nothing like as onerous as they were now. Looking back, he could count each fatality and devastating injury endured by the regiment. The strength of the enemy was still largely unknown, and the Taliban were still extending their use of that roadside bomb, into the fields and empty compounds the ISAF soldiers had to search.

Today everything around him seemed to grow larger and larger by the day. Camp Bastion was expanding daily. First with hundreds more cargo carriers arriving with supplies, then with prefabricated units hurriedly erected inside the expanding perimeter wall, much of it consisting of Hesco blocks stacked three high and creating a barrier as much as thirty feet high in some places, to offer shelter from snipers. Yes, there was a sense that the very size of Camp Bastion sheltered you; there was the possibility of down time and restorative sleep, within its walls. Compared with other smaller FOBs often no more than a few hundred men; or the patrol bases with maybe sixty to one hundred men if you were lucky, Camp Bastion definitely felt like a town in which you could hide. But the CPs, the checkpoints, often with less than twenty men around you, made the thought of being at Camp Bastion seems like being in a safe-haven.

But this was a time when the area of the Afghan desert that was Camp Bastion, was still growing, as it played host to parasitic satellite camps settling around its hub. By the time a halt was to be made to its growth, there would be three Camp Bastions within its walls, as well as Leatherneck and Shorabak. In fact the original base, when seen from the air, would appear to be swallowed up by its neighbours, and the airfield became one of the busiest British airfields, ranking alongside places such as Gatwick, in its importance and capacity. Planes could land and turn around in as little as an hour.

Following promotion Guy Williams felt the need to evaluate his first months as lieutenant with the growing responsibilities it imposed upon him. He felt the differences that were currently affecting his men now, most notably the fear of being injured and stranded until you just bled to death. The war had reached a point which allowed for a fairly accurate assessment of the threat to ISAF troops and the troops response to that threat. He believed he needed to counsel and encourage, for top of the list was the anger his platoon felt towards how they were instructed and controlled by the rules of conflict in fighting the enemy. There was a fairly universal feeling amongst all the troops that they were fighting with their hands tied behind their backs. On the one hand they were not allowed to fire their weapons unless the enemy was attacking first; the parameters of warfare as set by the Geneva/Hague Conventions were fine; providing the enemy can read them and abide by them. What good is a written military convention to the illiterate? And every officer serving under the ISAF knew that the Taliban did not respect the modern rules of warfare.

Added to these deep-seated feelings, there was the anger felt at the many public outcries; so frequently stirred up by the media at that time, condemning the military for failing to achieve targets set by those behind desks in Westminster or Washington! And the continual frustration when the men on the ground felt they had to wait too long for the birds to come and extricate them, at the end of difficult patrols or when the shout was, 'Man down!' What good was a directive which said the injured must be transported to safe medical attention within a 'golden hour' when there was no bird swooping in to collect and care for the wounded?

'More Helos needed,' was an oft repeated complaint; especially when there was an injured man to be airlifted to the hospital. Minutes mattered then, ten minutes maximum to stop the bleeding, sixty to the hospital, if they were lucky. Guy sat silently listening to his men; better to let them complain to each other, and then when they phone home the annoyance might be forgotten, and their phone calls with the ones they loved would hopefully be life-affirming. Satellite Communication was all very well, but they were in a war zone and the enemy was listening in, all were aware of that problem. How many loved ones longed for a phone call? He reached for his locally purchased Afghan mobile phone, should he ring, should he text her? It was late.

"Oh Alice, I'm sorry, can't get to you tonight."

Yes, that night, because of the time spent with his men, Guy had abandoned his wickedly delicious clandestine meeting with his American sweetheart, Private First Class Alice Holford. Whenever he was on base, he would try and sneak a few moments with her, late at night and under cover of darkness. Checking his watch, he realised that it was too late to let Alice know, she would be in bed by now; he just knew she would have realised and got herself off to bed.

Eventually he went off to his bed himself and found some peace dreaming of Alice and the day they had first met. The dust had been blown up into a cloud that stung the eyes, when Alice who had been walking with her head down against the grit in the atmosphere, had crashed straight into his chest; naturally he had put his arms around her to stop her falling; Alice had looked up into his face and oh, how they both believed, for ever after that; that it was truly 'love at first sight'. That was months ago and how he ached for her, how they both hated the American Directive Number One!

Chapter Three
Cheshire to RAF Brize Norton, England, Monday

Preparations had been conducted in secret and were over too soon. I had to face up to leaving my comfortable home and my loving wife: the day had arrived.

I was as ready as I could ever be, after such a hurried briefing about the list of places and people I was to photograph, the assessment of an intended gas pipeline, I believed that was the real reason for this mission, but they insisted it was about the need or not for more helicopters, which was worrying the PM. My cover story was explained and my contacts details given in an e-mail from C. Travel details were given. There was no turning back Commander Mathew Fleming RN Rtd was back on duty.

I had written my will, as instructed, and lodged it with my solicitor. I had my official photo taken, the one they print alongside the announcement of your death. I tried to look proud to have died for my country, but the result was one of a wooden boredom with the whole procedure, and I naturally hoped it would never have to be used. Then I had to remember that I was travelling undercover as a freelance American War Correspondent, which 'C' believed would fool those living on the Camp Bastion site, and it might just allow them to be more open in their criticisms and complaints if they thought I was working for an American TV company.

'C' had mused upon the anonymity I could achieve by posing as an American. "People always astound me, the way they believe reporters only report about issues that affect the reporter's country. You arrive dressed as a Yank and to everyone there you will be a non-combatant Yankee!"

"If you say so, Sir, but I don't speak Yankee!"

"Then keep your mouth shut, shoot the lens, and listen to what the English are saying."

That seemed reasonable. But my mind said, *I'm going into a war-zone and I'm just not the right age to die. My fitness level says I could live to a hundred; so at fifty nine I'm technically a shade over middle-aged, in my book at least. Still, I'll not have to face the enemy, no, I'll be fine.* Gradually I settled any fear inside myself to a reasonable belief that I could succeed and should accept the assignment. I can't claim that I no longer speculated upon possible scenarios of being shot or wounded, for on the whole I preferred the idea that a little fear goes a long way to retaining a sensible level of caution.

The day before I set off I spent two hours on a borrowed bike, it being twenty years since I had last used one for more than a few minutes of showing off. My legs were going to kill me, was my assessment of that exercise. A hot bath in loads of bubbling Radox followed that ridiculous attempt at following the PM's suggestion of riding around Afghanistan on a bike; then dressed and ready to treat the wife, we dined out at The Bells of Peover with our friends and ended the evening extremely jolly, being teased about the no-alcohol rule which I would be facing. Well, I had told my nearest and dearest where I was going. I described it as a photographer's dream holiday to record Camp Bastion for posterity. Neil, the landlord, suggested that he might be bankrupted by my departure and ceremoniously presented me with a bag of wine gums, with the proviso of a safe return or else! The ribbing went on until ten o'clock, when Cathy extricated me with the announcement that I was on a five o'clock alarm call.

****

Now all I had to do was say goodbye to my darling Cathy, it was to be a short mission; I should be home within weeks. But I could tell my wife, my beloved Cathy, didn't believe me; I had waffled too much, I was borderline drunk and she was shaking her head as if to say, 'Just stop it!' I argued against her fears. "How bad can it be when the most important question was, Commander Matt Fleming, can you still ride a bike?"

Cathy hit me then, playfully, enough to make me respond with an assault upon her person that delighted her and satisfied me; a memory I was to find myself grateful for, as in the coming weeks my mind and body ached for the delights of her supple loving body. She slept on as I quietly dressed, and I left her asleep, gently placing a red rose on the pillow beside her, before turning to leave. With careful steps I moved to the bedroom door; turned for one last look, before shutting it as quietly as I could manage. I knew how she hated goodbyes; I suspected she was half awake and just didn't want me to see her tears.

Mine came as I drove the hired car out of the driveway and headed towards Chester. I call them tears, but they never rolled down my cheeks, just irritating moisture that clouded my vision. Moist eyes, something that has bothered me as I've aged, but where was the toughness of forty years ago, when I could set off on dangerous assignments without a doubt about my ability to succeed? I hardly dared think about the weeks ahead; truthfully, I felt real fear, I acknowledged my lack of fitness, I knew my nerves were no longer made of steel.

Glancing in the rear-view mirror, I recognized that my looks were gone, wrinkles were there, and the eyebrows had that bushy look that comes with age. There was redness to my face that probably came from time in an early retirement that had given way to almost daily visits to my local, The Bells of Peover. Fortunately I was a great walker and had kept my weight down to eleven stone, retaining a slimness that suited my six foot height. Yes, with luck I could possibly pass for an American. To my drinking buddies I was Matt; however, much the rest of the world still recognised me as Commander Matthew Fleming RN Rtd, even if to the Foreign Office and its Secret Intelligence Service, the one that used to be called MI6, I was no more than a number; 'Operative 395, retired'.

Yes, that's me, just a number on the old MI6 records. When you work for the government, that's what you do; pretend to be James Bond when you are nothing more than a dogsbody who is trusted to do the job however unpleasant it turns out to be; but without any glamorous double 'O' to your name, even though you're controlled by someone referred to as 'C'.

To the outsider looking in it must all seem as if this would be a fantasy of a job. I suppose it might be, unless you ask yourself, how important is a state secret? Who decrees it is a state secret? How necessary are the Official Secrets Act and all the trappings of international control?

I was a long way from the answer that cold spring day, knowing I would not see my beloved again until I had fulfilled my mission. No, that should be, unless I 'successfully' fulfilled my mission! Then I may return to my beautiful home, and hopefully live a quiet life.

Firstly, I was to report to RAF Brize Norton, ready to fly out on board a transport plane. It was an overcast and damp day when I arrived there the evening before my flight; and found myself being escorted to the camp commander's office.

Throughout 2009, RAF Brize Norton was the main base in the United Kingdom for transporting goods and personnel to the war in Afghanistan. Occasionally RAF Lyneham was called upon to help, but for the most part, in that year it was RAF Brize Norton doing the donkey work. That the general public only seemed to register its military role during the repatriation of the dead from that conflict, was perhaps a healthy fact, for it allowed the work of the base to continue without pressure from political groups. There were no nuclear issues clouding the transporting of the different weaponry or supplies that had to pass through its hangers; therefore no rat-tail camp of protesters hindering the approach to its gate.

That morning, I had left home in my best brown cashmere jersey and corduroy trousers, looking every inch the perfect English gent with a Crombie overcoat and carrying a battered leather suitcase. I arrived at RAF Brize Norton looking every inch an American war correspondent.

This was achieved away from prying eyes, after a stopover at a recruiting base near Chester, where I was kitted out for my journey by a middle-aged female Liverpudlian named Betty, a TA worker in supplies, who seemed to be highly amused at my story. I said I was filling in for an American who was off on a secret mission and I had to stay with the Yanks in Camp Leatherneck.

"Can you imagine they've no room for me in Camp Bastion?"

She sniggered at that; "Bad planning if you ask me," before going on to give me the parcel that had arrived for me. As I opened it and began sorting its contents, she kept me amused with a commentary that helped put me at my ease; at least I would know what to call all the items included in the American idea of necessary protection and comfort when in a war zone.

"This is described as American gear of the 'Universal Camouflage Pattern', not full combat dress, but just enough of it to make you appear a Yank, sir."

"This tee-shirt is a bit of a muddy colour!"

"This is the soft combat trouser, and this the jacket and soft cap, which apparently is called a 'head' although watch out, sir, the Yanks call the bog the head! Anyway, sir, the Yanks wear this grey stuff and out there, we Brits wear more beige colours, so you can easily tell the difference, sir, between the armies. All shades of greyness and no glamour attached to the Americans!"

"Thanks, I'll remember that, I suppose beige is suitable for us Brits!" I said with a snigger.

I thought she'd never stop talking; apparently she was from Liverpool and she seemed so content with life that I had to forgive her. The boots I was given had a thick synthetic sole, and knowing the terrain to be covered, I was grateful. Especially when Betty announced, "Just be grateful you've got Yankee boots, our boys do nothing else but moan about our version." Then in the second package that had arrived for me, there was also a complete change of clothes, some special underwear that fighting men wore when out in the combat zone, an enormous backpack, which the clerk had listed as an ILBE, not as a Bergen.

"Isn't this a Bergen?" I asked.

Seeing my puzzled look, her stream of consciousness continued without a pause, as she said,

"That's a British Military name, sir, but the Yanks call this size an ILBE. Don't ask me why, laddie, don't ask me why! And this smaller backpack they call an assault pack. As far as I'm concerned the whole lot are kitbags! You get one of each. Torch, yes, another rule is always being visible at night, when moving about the camps. Oh, yes, you'll need several water bottle pouches to attach to your webbing. You can also have a bag to carry extra water if you want, I'd recommend it, sir, if I were you. It's hot out there and you can easily get dehydrated if you are to be out for any length of time. Oh, and this is another help for when moving around the camp in the dark! It's a high visibility belt; they call it a glow belt! I like that one, don't you? I think all school kids should wear a glow belt."

I laughed and realised that I would need to acquaint myself with endless words used by Americans. I smiled to myself as I thought of my wife's favourite musical and started to hum, 'You say Pota-to and I say Pot-a-to,' well, naturally my Scouse lass began singing along with me. It was very relaxing and a great deal of the unobserved tension that had built up inside me began to disappear, and I found I didn't mind her chatty nature. But seriously, I was astonished as the pile grew with every conceivable item for my comfort. Even down to an American-made bar of soap and an American brand of toothpaste. That merited the comment, "Perhaps you'll get teeth like American film stars, sir, you know, like tombstones, sir?" Before I could answer she laughed and uncovered a white plastic container.

"A tub of 'Wet Ones' for when there's no water to wash with, sir!" This came with a giggle and a sly wink as she rubbed her bottom, and finally a selection of items that were to become my signature symbols; I was now to all intents and purposes to be an American war zone correspondent.

Even Betty became serious when we opened a box labelled 'computerized' equipment. There was a Nikon d300 and to my great joy a small black piece of plastic that was in fact the marvellous Olympus WS-331 digital voice recorder. 'Small enough to hide in a pocket and just record the differing points of view, just in case you need it', said the note from the quartermaster. Other equipment included a selection of lenses and a Nokia e71 satellite phone. I dreaded the cost of it all, thinking to myself; *Sorry, Gordon, you could've got another bird with the money being spent on my gear!*

"You better not lose any of that, young man!" said Betty with a wagging finger, "Probably cost more than a rifle!"

I agreed with her and she set me up in a corner to get changed. After which Betty helped me pack my ILBE and assault pack ready for the off. My 'English' clothes she parcelled up for me with the promise to keep safe against my return. I was almost sorry to leave the depot, but I wasn't going to chicken out now. Bless her, Betty saluted me and began singing, "There'll always be an England and England will be free, if England means as much to you as England means to me." I was laughing as she waved me off, I would remember Betty often in the weeks ahead.

Were they truly dragging me out of retirement; as they had said for one last time, just to take photos; any old fool can take photos, why me? How little I knew of the reality of my mission. Was I really getting too old to see through the lies being piled up, to explain my presence in a war zone?

I left the hired car at the pre-arranged garage at Wootton Basset; it felt as if I had cut an umbilical cord; now I was completely an American who was getting into a taxi to arrive at RAF Brize Norton at 1700 hours.

At RAF Brize Norton I was escorted to a briefing by the station commander. He was a friendly chap, and invited me to dine with him in the officers' mess. I cheerfully accepted and we both had a healthy dinner of steak and vegetables with a pudding of a traditional English apple pie and custard. I was to be billeted for the night in a dormitory block used for travellers who were to have early morning flights. Warned that I was to be up before dawn, I didn't accept his invitation to relax in the officers' mess. We said 'Goodnight' and I left him with his whisky and soda, while a young corporal showed me to my room. Was I mad? No alcohol at Camp Leatherneck; should I have stayed for one last drink? Reason told me sleep was needed; the journey was going to be bad enough, without adding on a hangover.

****

In the married quarters, Fred prepared for bed and as a religious man, a churchgoing Catholic, he had sat quietly praying for the repose of the soul of Corporal Henry Black, for his sad family and friends. It had been sunny when the C130 had safely landed exactly at 1330 hours. Once there, the whole of RAF Brize Norton had come to a respectful silent shut-down, for a quarter of an hour, until the repatriation was over. The soldier's family, waiting at RAF Brize Norton, were comforted by the presence of military personnel from the camp itself, and by the family liaison officers who would be with them throughout the next days and weeks, to help organise the funeral. They would also be available to advise and help, long after the funeral was over, as anxieties about married quarters and widows' pensions were heaped upon the head of those who were grieving. Families would receive letters and explanations would be given, both from commanding officers and those who knew and loved the one now being repatriated. But, on that day, all a parent, sibling and spouse would want is time to grieve and time to feel the pain of their loss, in a quiet and dignified silence. That they would never knew of Fred's prayers for their beloved boy; did not bother Fred, he had his faith and he knew his prayers for all the dead soldiers helped him cope with the stress of his job.

Fred Dickson had gone home to his married quarters with his instructions for the next day, in his pocket. He had only briefly glanced at them; an American war correspondent? Fred thought to himself, *someone to chat with!* It pleased him, and for once the thought of the flight made him happier than usual; Fred was your basic chatty man! After a good night's sleep, he returned early the next morning to the runway and what he thought of as his plane, his bird, for his usual Tuesday flight back to Afghanistan, with a new load of supplies which would, as always, include several empty coffins and a new supply of the Union Flag. But wonders of wonders, this Tuesday morning his check list of the cargo had an unusual addition: an American war correspondent, listed as Matthew Fleming. Oh boy, chatty man had company

Chapter Four
Camp Leatherneck late on Monday Night

Alice lived in Camp Leatherneck, which was within the massive perimeter walls of Camp Bastion, yet was also growing independently of Camp Bastion; it was like a walled city attached to the side of another walled city, however, it was somehow united in a common purpose and affection for Bastion's amazing air strips and hospital.

At Camp Leatherneck, the site was being extended to house thousands more American personnel, and as a result, Private First Class Alice Holford, along with other military clerical staff, had to factor this important detail into the demands of their ever-growing clerical duties that assisted the day to day military manoeuvres, as well as the aftermath of battlefield deaths and their concomitant repercussions. It was a constant battle to cope with the demands of a perpetual building site, set in a war zone. It just went on day after day, new block by new block, longer roads and bigger stores, and everyone irritated trying to remember where to go to get to their bed because everything looked the same. It usually took the newcomers several days to find their way about; if you made a map, it was out of date within twenty-four hours.

The word 'dust' was the one most frequently on Alice's lips as she cursed its intrusive invasion of her clothes, her boots, her eyes and ears and especially when it blew into her mouth, if perchance she had the audacity to try speaking when the dust was dancing in the air around her. For most civilised people the images of building sites are of mud; in Afghanistan they were of bone-dry, penetrating reddish dust hanging in the air.

It was late and still no text from Guy, she could guess why. Now she could add to the irritations of that particular day, the disappointment of a day without as much as a glimpse of her beloved.

Sadness seemed to swallow her up as if evil spirits were seeking to destroy her. The British may have lost one; but the Americans had lost three men that day, and nobody spoke of the other ISAF losses. Alice felt the death of every soldier regardless of his ISAF rank. Other issues affected her, the dreaded the sight of so many Afghan children with their limbs blown off by IED's, being brought into the Hospital. The British hospital was like all the ISAF hospitals, prepared to assist as many as possible, regardless of nationality or age.

Yes, it was difficult being in that war zone, especially if you were as tender-hearted as Alice Holford. Why she had joined the American Army her parents never understood. Had she not got a beautiful home, had they not given her everything she wanted? They never noticed how lonely she had been, an only child growing up on a vast farm, miles from the nearest neighbour. The army gave her friendship; many of the nurses over at the hospital had become good mates during the five months of her tour, which was now only half way through.

Her boss, General Mike Raven, had kept her on her toes, dealing with the sorting of times for the repatriation of those who had died that day, and for memorial services to be held at the Camp, not even the building projects were allowed to interfere with respect for those who had died in battle. The memo to all in charge of the platoons had to be circulated and the ceremony at the American Memorial site organised.

Then there were preparations for the replacements. "You lose a man, you lose a fighting machine," was the General's comment to Alice as he chivvied her on, to get the replacements flown in within twenty four hours. *Men in, men out and men in again*, was her motto when trying to keep pace with the frantic turnaround of soldiers that was Camp Leatherneck. She had to deal with endless phone calls to organise new billeting, the billeting officer had got herself pregnant and been sent back to the States. Alice thought to herself, *Please, more staff, just one billeting officer would help or two or three or four!* But she knew the building work must be completed before more soldiers could be flown in, unless they just slept on the floor as they were often obliged to do when outside the Camps and FOBs. To Alice it had become a Catch Twenty-Two situation, made worse by McNaughton.

If only Captain Gwen McNaughton would get off her back. It wasn't as if McNaughton was super-efficient; half of Alice's troubles came via the chaos the older woman made of her own duties. Others, in the outer office of General Mike Raven's headquarters, often felt sympathy for Alice, realising the Captain was jealous of the younger woman. The theory was that it was probably due to the familiarity which existed between Alice and the General. Was McNaughton trying to cosy up to the General? Alice thought not, because she was aware that McNaughton was more interested in a certain Captain Sheila Taylor back in the Marines HQ in San Diego, California. There was probably more truth in the theory propounded by other girls living and working on the base, that McNaughton hated Alice's pretty looks when contrasted with her own heavy-smoker/heavy-drinker/over-dried-up sun-baked skin and lined aging face. The Captain looked at least ten years older than her natural age.

Then in the middle of the afternoon there had been trouble with the quartermaster, stocks missing, and the proof was needed that it wasn't necessarily a member of the military staff. If it was a non-military worker or Afghan, who, what and how to control the problem?

To Alice the awareness of the good Afghans allowed her not to tarnish all Afghans as evil monsters to be killed or imprisoned. She liked so many of them, finding them helpful and friendly and some even respectful of women. Not all Afghan women wore burkas, yet Alice acknowledged that all behaved with courteousness towards her and the foreigners living in their country. It troubled Alice that the Taliban and other extreme Tribal chiefs were often reported as being violent towards their wives and daughters. She cringed when told of young girls forced into marriage, dying in childbirth and sometimes murdered by their own parents. There were moments when she wished she was anywhere but in Camp Leatherneck, until she allowed her thoughts to wander around her dreams of marrying Guy Williams. All day with no time to sneak out and see if he was still about, her heart ached; she knew she was in love.

It was gone eleven o'clock at night when she finally sat down on her low comfortless camp bed, slowly untying the laces before pulling her boots off her neat feet. She was a small woman, barely five foot three, and she was noticeably well-shaped as a woman, to all the men watching her, with their lonely hearts and missing home. Some would say she just looked sexy; certainly her blonde hair and her sweet-faced 'girl next door' smiling beauty was manifestly obvious to the men living and serving in the American section of the base. It was even more apparent to the British Lieutenant Guy Williams, based in Camp Bastion.

Stuck for now in a rickety box of a billet, she knew that she would be moved to more comfortable quarters eventually; but this night the thought of her simple camp bed and the possibility of six hours sleep was all the comfort she needed. *'Sorry Guy,'* she thought, *'I will try and see you tomorrow, I'm done in, I must go to bed, my darling love.'*

The hope that tomorrow would bring a few stolen moments, behind the British NAAFI with her beloved, was her only happiness. *'Lord don't let anyone die tomorrow, I want to see Guy.'* It was always impossible during an Op Minimiser, for then regardless of the vast size of the camps, it constantly felt as if all and sundry had returned to the apparent safety behind that perimeter fence, and they seemed to throng the back alleyways, where the lovers could secretly meet.

She and Guy had got very clever at finding blind spots, away from perimeter arc lights and the constant circulation of human traffic, for those treasured moments, to indulge in the comfort of each other's arms. It was balm to their war-weary hearts. There was, however, a problem; both were breaking the law with their romantic meetings, it was a punishable offence according to the USA army regulations, for those in war zones; Army Directive Number One.

Maybe it was childish, but Alice wanted to believe it didn't matter because Guy Williams was not an American soldier. How wrong she was and how they were discovered, would always make both Guy and Alice shudder at the memory. For now meetings were relatively smooth, both had access jeeps and their simple routine was to alternate between the camps, and various spots too far distant for people to witness their rendezvous. But this Monday night it was not to be and so, tired and still hungry, for she had missed a proper meal twice this day, all she wanted now was bed and time to dream.

Typical, just when bed seemed within her grasp, sleep had to wait a while longer, because she heard her name called and going to the zipped entrance to the billet, she was handed a sealed envelope. The young soldier charged with the circulating of sensitive mail around the offices in the American section, was apologetic. Gary Smith was one of those young men who spent his life trying to ingratiate himself with his superior officers; his ambition was to gain a quick promotion, thus he believed it was his duty not to delay delivery until morning, even though when he saw her tired pale face he felt bad, he could see the exhaustion on Private First Class Alice Holford's face, yet he knew she would deal with the matter and not spoil his chances of a word of praise for his efficiency; she would not get him into trouble. Alice had that effect upon the young troopers, she was reliable and they all knew it.

If only the letter had been from Lieutenant Guy Williams. But she knew the missive was not from him, she recognized the scrawl, and it was definitely not from Guy. The disappointment was intense.

What now' was her next thought as she tried to read the tightly written script, which was on official notepaper? She had never enjoyed handwritten missives; like most young people with a university education behind them, the computer and a printer had replaced any affection for a fountain pen or ball-point.

The note was from General Mike Raven, the Camp Commandant; her boss, oh dear, she knew that somehow or other she must get control of her fatigue and read, digest and then destroy the half page document. Those were her usual orders, when written messages were sent via a courier, unless instructed otherwise.

"Okay, Mike, I just kind of hope you had a long leisurely dinner, because I was typing while you were eating! Couldn't this wait till tomorrow? What now?" she said as she switched on the bright table light, that was on her minimal sized desk; a Heath Robinson contraption, created by a stack of upturned fruit boxes. Like all the soldiers, Alice had improvised the homeliness of her space in the four-person cabin she lived in as her quarters. Although this was her first tour to Afghanistan, Alice had taken advice from girls returning from there and so with some foresight, as she had prepared for this deployment, Alice had packed her large ILBE with some canvas hanging shelves, a metal container that acted as her 'lockable safe' and a collapsible clothes maiden that allowed her to keep her second uniform protected from the eternal dust of the desert, by hanging it up inside zipped protectors; but, a desk? Nothing had come to mind that she could suitably transport in her luggage, hence the raid on the camp kitchens and her now useful, but rickety desk made up of wooden fruit boxes topped with a plank of stolen wood from the quartermaster's workshop.

A laptop, printer and letter rack sat side by side with the small powerful lamp. They might be out in the desert, but with such an embedded military site, there was no way the generating of electric power was going to be allowed to fail. The camps were riddled with generators providing power, which also permanently added to the noise of the camps. After a while you ceased to notice the buzz in the background of your life. You regarded it as a symbol of the comfort light allowed you. Certainly it made Alice feel safe when noises outside disturbed her rest; she could always hopefully switch on a working light.

Looking round at the other women reading or sleeping, Alice Holford knew she would not be disturbed, so she scanned the sheet onto her laptop. Then using the zoom, the page was enlarged to Alice's satisfaction. Suddenly General Mike Raven's illegible handwriting was capable of being read and hopefully understood.

"Holford, a special assignment; you are to oversee and facilitate the work of a British war correspondent who is working more or less undercover. He arrives tomorrow. I have ordered a billet for him. He has strict orders to fulfil several tasks, absolute discretion on this; his British contact is Lieutenant Guy Williams. Call into my office sometime tomorrow and I'll fill you in with the details."

Marvellous! "How about his name, rank and number, I think I could do with them. Or, how about telling me what time this mystery man is due to arrive! I wouldn't want to be late with the bunting for a British contact for Lieutenant Guy Williams now, would I?" she muttered to herself as she deleted the words on her laptop, before tearing the paper into a myriad of pieces. Looking at the pieces, Alice thought, *well, I'm not going to eat them*, as she took them and flushed them down one of the heads, set inside a block of Portaloos.

Another job to cope with, but the contact! Great, it was to be Guy Williams! The thought of that happiness allowed her to sleep well, in spite of the constant noise of the camp, the snoring of the other women, and her own growing curiosity about her new charge; she made herself sleep dreaming of her British soldier.

The wind blew hard, but she slept on, not hearing the flapping of the camouflage canopy fastened over the prefabricated units, which in the dawning of the day made the camps look like beige sand dunes covering nondescript mounds of indeterminate shapes, each so disguised to hide their functions and importance, when viewed from the air.

Chapter Five
Camp Leatherneck 0700 hours' local time, Tuesday

The next morning, very early before breakfast, Alice found General Mike Raven alone in his office and ready to enlighten her about her new responsibility.

"Good morning, Sir. What's all the mystery about this Englishman arriving today?"

There was an obvious familiarity in the manner of their conversations whenever they were alone. Alice Holford and Mike Raven came from the same Mid-West town; they both were from farming stock about eighty miles south west of Springfield, the capital of Illinois, and if in fact you had searched through their family trees, you would have discovered the relationship between them. Mike was her uncle on her mother's side of the family and he was not only fond of his eldest niece; he had told her mother, his sister, that he would keep an eye on her as far as possible.

"But I can't guarantee anything; out there things happen instantaneously, and I can't have Alice following me around all the time."

As it transpired, Private First Class Alice Holford was assigned the role of gofer to General Raven. It was a highly prized position. The English would just say she was similar to a batman. Alice would dispute that categorizing of her job, would describe herself as the General's dog's body, even on occasion describing him as a slave driver. But on the whole she was happy enough. He was family, he was part of her reason for enlisting, hadn't he told her four year old ears, hundreds of bedtime stories of his young soldiering days, the places he saw, and the fun he had had with his fighting buddies. He had never married giving as his excuse that he never had time to go off base and look for a 'gal!' When his cheeky niece was old enough to tease him, she offered to go on line and find him a bride. The laughter was always real between Mike and her, but he kept his counsel and his many secrets from Alice.

She suspected that her uncle had used a very dishonourable piece of nepotism to secure her as his gofer. He hadn't, but his sister and niece believed he had, and were grateful for his imagined protection. The truth would have worried her mother even more; her daughter was assigned to the post to prevent her working too closely with the rank and file. "She's too good looking for her own good," had been the reason Captain Gwen McNaughton had given for choosing to place Alice with the General. Captain McNaughton was tired of having to lose staff because they had broken Directive One, got pregnant and been shipped out. For the General it was a delight, because having his niece near him allowed him to tease her mercilessly. A few moments of light relief in his busy days; he was smiling as he spoke,

"So, kid, this is very important. This guy is somehow going undercover to catch drug runners or some such, and so you can guess why he's here."

"The poppy, the harvest is in?" Alice said with a sigh.

46

He was still teasing her in the way he rolled the words around his mouth almost as if singing a Negro spiritual, and waving his hands Al Jolson style.

"Yep, de poppy, de poppy, de goddam poppy; everybody loves de goddam poppy, except me, dear Lord, dear lord dear lordie, lordie lord!" He had a beautiful tenor voice and Alice always loved listening to him, even when as now he was teasing her. He sighed and laughing, he looked straight into Alice's blue eyes as he continued, "Who knows, they might be too busy to fight, you never know!"

"They'll still be fighting, Uncle, you know they will."

"Ah well, whatever he's here for, you can bet yer bottom dollar we won't be told the truth. I've asked billeting to put him in with officers and I've told them, you will be his Mother Hen or Goose, or whatever the Brits expect. I believe he will be here for between three to twelve weeks. But, young lady, if he goes off camp you are not to drive him. Do you understand me, Alice? Do you understand me, gal? If he leaves the base, Corporal Hudson can do that. You okay about that? Tell me you are not still sweet on that particular guy?"

"Negative sir, Hudson and I, well we sort of agreed the war was more important than getting really serious."

"Good, good! Time enough for that when you get back home. I wouldn't want you sent back to your mother in disgrace, now, would I?"

47

The General paused for a few moments to study Alice's face; deciding his meaning had hit home, he turned and sorted through some papers looking for a name.

"Ah, yes, right, here it is. Now, this guy, this Lieutenant Guy Williams, over in Bastion One, he's your contact; have you met him before?"

"Yes, sir!"

"Oh? What's he like?" His frown told Alice that the General was curious.

"A good soldier, he saved someone's life."

"That could mean he's foolhardy."

"No, I'm certain he's not like that. The men like him very much and I thought he was, well, intelligent."

"Oh, did you now? How come you ..."

"He was..." She stopped and seemed to need to turn her head away from her uncle. She couldn't say what she wanted to say to him when his uniform clouded her awareness of him as a dear uncle. He looked so very smart; she had to remember that he was now her boss. He wasn't the kindly man who had played tag and who had squirted her with water from the garden hose, and who had always given her sweets at Thanksgiving. He was now a stranger in a smart uniform. Regaining her courage, she closed her eyes before she turned back, and blurted out in one continuous stream of information.

"He was ... kind of ... talking to some guy at the hospital, I was there, remember?"

It was something Alice did when unsure of her words; she would hesitate and say 'kind of' in the way

48

that some youngsters constantly say 'you know.' Taking another deep breath she went on,

"You had sent me to check up on Captain Brandon, and I overheard him, the lieutenant, talking about some of the fighting that had gone on that day, and how he … kind of … believed that it would be better to put our money into education, and the man he was speaking to said things like 'the bloody natives' were beyond teaching and well, Lieutenant Williams … kind of … spoke amazingly about his ideas for teaching people who had never been in a classroom. I was so impressed. He saw me listening and when the other man left, he came over and was very kind."

Eventually Alice paused for breath as the General studied the pink cheeks and embarrassed look on his niece's face and he said,

"Hoo-rah, was this before you ditched Hudson, or after?"

"Before, sir, it was some time ago."

Nodding his head, his smile said he understood. His kind heart decided not to tease her anymore today. Hopefully it was no more than a distraction the girl might find exciting, she looked a bit peaky some days, and today was one of them. On the other hand she wouldn't have much chance to get cosy with a young handsome Brit, if he kept his niece busy with the old boy coming in from RAF Brize Norton. But all the same, Mike Raven decided he would keep an eye on Alice; he didn't want her being sent home for breaking the Direct Order against sexual activity when in a war zone. Only the week before two women went home pregnant, and with their careers facing a doubtful future. He stepped closer to Alice and hugged her before pulling her nose and, speaking almost playfully, he cautioned her.

"Listen, kid, dream away, but don't break your heart over an Englishman, however plausible he is, and no doubt I'm certain he's as you would say, '… kind of… better looking than Hudson!' Well, your old uncle is just saying, be careful, that's all I'm saying. Be careful!"

By now Alice was blushing and the General was chuckling quietly as he said,

"Run along, Alice. You phoning home today? Give my love to your mom. Go on, smile! Get Fleming sorted for me, there's a good girl. Keep him and his secrets out of my hair." With that he laughingly rubbed his hand over his almost bald pate.

Alice was still blushing as she left General Raven's office; if any of the staff in the outer area noticed, they discreetly looked away and let the young woman hurry off to do her duty. Well, all except Captain Gwen McNaughton, who followed Alice from the office and called her to attention.

"Holford, where were you last evening? I went looking for you, the other soldiers were there, and they tell me you never got back before eleven. Why?"

"I had to eat and I chose to eat in the Bastion hospital cookhouse, Captain." A blatant lie, Alice had no choice, she couldn't confess to have been waiting for a rendezvous with Guy Williams.

"What were you doing over there? Answer me, what were you doing over there?"

"I'm friendly with some of the nurses, Captain."

"Oh, how come?"

"The General often sends me over there to check on the injured, Ma'am, and the English girls are very friendly. They often invite me to eat with them."

"That better be all, Holford. That better be all! From now on I'm going to watch you more closely. Bed by ten; we might get a better day's work out of you if you spent less time socialising. Do you understand me?"

"Yes, Ma'am."

"Dismiss!"

With that the Captain turned and went back into the office and Alice went off to find a jeep. She had breakfast quickly and then got texting. It took very little effort to reach him, and set up a meeting. Both of them had local Roshan phones with the appropriate SIM cards, all purchased from a local market and only used for their two way conversation, she kept that phone inside her uniform. The one for use with her job was in a breast pocket. So far she believed no one had realised that she was using a second mobile.

Ten minutes later, she jumped into the General's jeep and had raced to an area near the hospital. If anyone asked, she knew there was at least one injured US serviceman she could say she was checking, at the request of her boss.

Guy was on time, he was dressed in a sweatshirt and fatigues, but no jacket or protective vest, he was on base and feeling safe, and for once he had a legitimate reason to meet up with his darling girl. He hopped out of his jeep and stood beside Alice's left hand drive vehicle; his right arm moved to rest along the back of the driving seat. Before long she felt his fingers pressing into her back and as they spoke, he gently moved them as if to transmit a silent message of love. Alice hardly noticed what was being said; this was neither the time nor the place for romance, it was too public; and the very need to control it was powerfully significant to both of them, but her body reacted to the pressure of his hand as his index finger drew circles across her spine. The tingling was shooting messages along every nerve in her body and she couldn't move for fear that he might stop. She turned her eyes to his and he read all the longing deeply embedded in them.

"I love you," was whispered under his breath.

Suddenly her heart was full of pain. Uncle Mike had seemed to indicate that he suspected she was in love, he knew his niece too well; Captain McNaughton was coming down on her. Alice knew she was breaking military law, and needed to be circumspect and not make Guy's life difficult; it would only take a word from General Mike Raven to Brigadier Henry Fulton of Camp Bastion, and the young lieutenant could be shipped back home.

They talked on and after ten minutes, Alice looked at her watch; she must go before she said anything too personal. Unable to kiss him goodbye she steadied her gaze as she said, in a raised voice that could be heard by some nurses walking past,

"I'll sure look after him, Lieutenant; just let me know when you need to see him. I expect he'll sleep first; they usually do after that journey. We could arrange to meet tomorrow after he's had a rest."

"That would be good," said the Lieutenant quite loudly, before glancing around to make certain nobody was within earshot, before whispering,

"But no flirting with him! Remember promise me, ten, tonight behind the stores?"

She raised her voice again,

"Oh, he's come ...,' then she thought better of it and lowered her voice once more, "... out of retirement so he sounds old. Anyway, I think we need to be careful, my uncle knows about us, I'm certain he does!"

Guy was feeling her nearness everywhere inside his mind and body and he knew he would be hurting if he didn't boldly say something.

"Darling, we will be careful. Ten o'clock, please, I need to kiss you and this is killing me. I'll wait there all night if necessary."

"Be careful, if you get sent home, I'll die."

"Sweetie, I'm the one who might die; their snipers are every bit as good as ours."

"I know and it frightens me. Do be careful, I love you so much."

"I must go, Alice, we've got another six hour patrol in half an hour. But, I must see you tonight; because Wednesday and Thursday we're out on a forty-eight hour patrol. I'll be late back and the turnaround will be a nightmare, since we are out on a goodwill visit to Karvelk early Friday morning, which means, I won't see you until Friday night! Oh darling girl, smile to keep me going, come on, smile!"

She had set the ignition even before he had removed his arm and with only half a smile, and without looking at him, Alice drove off, leaving him standing there. She thought her heart would burst; patrols were when the guys got killed. The world outside the wall was all IEDs and snipers. She drove around trying to look as if she knew where she was heading; but it was solely to give her time to recover from the panic rising up inside her heart. As for Williams, he hardened his jaw, put his hands in his pockets and sauntered into the hospital as if that had been his destination all along. Anyone observing him at that moment would not have been able to judge his feelings about Alice Holford. Although he knew even for himself, they were not for examination at that precise moment; problems in his platoon were more important and demanding of his attention than the forbidden love he had for Alice.

"Duty first," he said to himself as he straightened his spine and pulled his shoulders back.

Brigadier Henry Fulton had been standing with the British Surgeon Commander Peter Wallis just a short distance away and, witnessing the movement said, "He'll go far, a good fusilier and good leader of his men, and a good looking lad as well. I've often wondered about him, he doesn't seem to be the most confident of the young officers."

Surgeon Commander Peter Wallis nodded his head as he agreed with him.

"Who was the girl he was speaking with? Pretty little thing."

"Well, she's American I can tell you that much."

"Pretty, though."

The two men finished their conversation and greeted the approaching lieutenant.

Guy Williams had gone through university on a cadet bursary, and after Sandhurst had quickly reached the rank of Second Lieutenant. A modest man, but ambitious enough to take time over his education, and to carefully avoid some of the excesses indulged in by many a spoilt youth, he was determined to ascend up the military ranks. His ultimate dream was to get to be at least a two star general. He wasn't going to let any squaddie spoil his chances of promotion, he needed help with his platoon; he accepted that, but he could not fathom why it was happening. Yes, there had been a lucky day when he saved an injured guy, who had been shot. Since then there had been incident after incident and in the past, on his previous tours of duty in 2004 and 2006, several deaths, but he could not see why his platoon had been so disadvantaged then, nor why he had seemed luckier this time around. If it was due to his own skills as a leader of men, he was unable to pinpoint either the 'what,' or for that matter the 'why'. And the replacements seemed beyond his control. Admittedly one of them was slightly older than he was and a staff sergeant; but rank is rank and he still could not get the discipline he wanted from them.

Surgeon Commander Peter Wallis greeted Guy as he entered the hospital and reassured him that Private Bryn Jones was fit to go back to his billet. "Job done, it was just a boil in a very awkward position, which needed careful lancing!" said Peter Wallis with a grin on his face.

The Brigadier complimented Guy on the platoon's current safety record, but suggested with a guffaw that boils usually mean, 'the privates weren't washing the privates properly!'

Laughing, Guy collected his platoon member, young Bryn Jones a farmer's son from North Wales, whose dad could understand his son being a loyal soldier of the Queen; had not Her Majesty had her wedding ring made out of Welsh gold? On the way back to their quarters at Camp Bastion, Guy was laughing as he told Bryn that he was duty bound by order of the Brigadier to tell Bryn to wash more thoroughly!

"Truly, Bryn, now the old man wants you to wash more thoroughly!"

"Understand, Lieutenant, sir!" the young man said, pronouncing it the English soldiers' way. Nobody could ever explain why the English say 'Lef-ten-ant' and the Americans 'Lieu-ten-ant'. Living as they did on such a vast area with several camps existing side by side, yet all ostensibly speaking English, the differences in uniform and speech were the two main distinguishing marks. Skill as warriors was universal, who could say which force was better than another; unless you took into account the quality and number of weapons and the birds in the air?

They laughed and relaxed and enjoyed telling the rest of 5 Platoon that Bryn's balls were now the cleanest in the camps.

Chapter Six
RAF Brize Norton Tuesday 0630 GMT

Punctually that morning, I boarded the plane, and nobody would have recognised me as anything other than an American military man. I wore the flat topped soft cap with its hard peak, known as a 'head' to American Marines, it was in the same multi-camouflage pattern; my name reduced to 'Fleming' was sewn to the space above my breast pocket. I carried no weaponry, no protective helmet or vest, but I was reliably informed that any such need would be sorted out upon my arrival at Camp Leatherneck.

I made myself as comfortable as possible, knowing that a journey of nearly four thousand miles was ahead of me. For take-off I initially strapped myself into a solitary row of seats set against the side of the fuselage. The whole plane was essentially a cargo plane and seemed stacked with boxes of supplies. Apart from the crew up front and a load master keeping an eye on the cargo; I was the only other person on board. I had been briefed to settle down and doze or read.

We were due to arrive late afternoon at Camp Bastion airport, it being nearly five hours ahead of us time-wise. Someone had advised me that the flight was a through flight with no stop off at either Akrotiri in Cyprus or Kabul the usual airbase entry into Afghanistan. Being unsure of the flight catering, and reasoning that it was many years since I had travelled in a military capacity, I had sensibly equipped myself with a flask of hot coffee, sandwiches and other tasty titbits, all stashed in my smaller assault bag, along with reading material and my laptop. I knew I would have to keep myself entertained and comfortable during the flight, but the book I had with me was to be instantly rejected; the noise of the plane was too intrusive. As it transpired Bert, the load master, was to wander in and out during most of the flight. He claimed that he had to check the cargo; I would say the tedium was his real reason. There was nothing new for him, except my presence. Somehow or other he produced some hot drinks; then he would sit beside me, munching on his own rations.

Bert was talkative. He questioned me about being a war correspondent and I lied with beautifully constructed yarns about my time in Bosnia. He was talkative and I let him talk, so that in the end I learnt a great deal about the conflict in Afghanistan from him; and to be honest it filled the time, so that I also was never bored. My sympathy was real, when I realised he did the trip twice a week, often having in the return journey cargo those killed in the conflict. When I asked him how the men responded to the numbers killed, he talked of the monument with a cross on top.

"Look out for it, when some poor guy has been cut down there is a vigil around that cross and it's like they are going to his funeral, only they are not. But it helps them, they can somehow say goodbye and then they have to go back ready to face the enemy, walking out through the gate not knowing if the next vigil will be for one of them. The Yanks do the same, in their own way. It's peculiar to this war; they pay their tributes in their camp. I mean, in Bosnia we didn't have time, most of the time."

"Bosnia; was that also your war?"

"Yeah, it was an ugly one for me; I was young and was in for the so-called making the peace time; mostly digging up the dead. Nasty, whole villages lost all their menfolk. Bad one, that!"

I nodded and just said, "Yep, a bad one!"

Bert was a family man and his obvious awareness of the pain felt by the families who would be waiting back at RAF Brize Norton was tangible. I came to like Bert; he seemed to be a long serving military man who still had a heart and still had a belief in his job. His mental strength matched his physical prowess and I admired him for his loyalty. He was a for 'God, Queen and Country' warrior through and through.

Inside my head, I prepared myself against harshly, judging the soldiers I was about to meet, at the various sections at Camp Bastion. Their days and nights were filled with the threat of injury and possible death, and yet the world expected them to show kindness, gentleness even, to the non-combatants, especially the children, living in the war zone.

I thought for several moments of the stories of children used as suicide bombers and realised that I wouldn't be surprised if I found some men were hardening their hearts towards even the children, in the region.

Chapter Seven
Arrival at Camp Bastion

"Camp Bastion has been a place which has sustained operations providing everything from bottled water to fast air support. It's been a place to do your laundry, and for guys who were stationed out in the forward operating bases to come back to, for a bit of normality, to get a shower and a shave and a cup of coffee." Ltd Colonel Laurence Quinn said years later in 2014, when the camps were about to close, but here I was arriving in early 2009. Growth was very much in evidence.

Arriving at Camp Bastion I waited until Bert said it was safe to move, then heading towards the back of the plane and walking down the ramp, dodging soldiers already unloading crates onto lorries, I was hit by the dusty atmosphere and the brightness of a desert setting sun. It was not initially blisteringly hot, just so much warmer than expected; the feeling of that dust was similar to that which you get when out in a gritty peasouper of a fog; it enveloped you in a cocoon that acted as a blanket to keep you warm, yet it grated on your skin with varying degrees of sharpness. It was made worse by the squaddies, as they moved the supplies out of the plane at such speed that the enormous pallets crashed down the ramp to land on the desert soil of Afghanistan, to throw that dust up until the breeze caught it and spread it further and further. Dust was and remains the strongest memory of that day. Even so I had time to look about at the seemingly endless row of helicopters of all shapes and sizes; at several quite large transporter planes either loading or unloading, what I don't know, I just didn't pay much attention to what was being moved in and out of various planes. Turning my head I saw what looked like a cabin that might be a waiting room. Then there was an air traffic control tower just as if it was at a normal airport. Well, it was just that, as busy as several British airfields and before many more moons had passed it would count as the sixth busiest British airfield. I could believe that, having seen the number and size of the parked planes loading and unloading, the Hesco and the concrete blocks forming the perimeter and the open vistas seen wherever there was wired fencing. It all looked barren beyond the camp, but I could see in the far distance some observation towers, I was to learn they were intended as early bird warning posts. Even as I looked out at that dusty plain with the evening sun changing the colours from a golden glow to a hideous beige barrenness, I felt the evil that was beyond my sight. The words of my boss came into my mind; "You cannot see the Taliban, but they can always see you."

I rummaged in my pockets for the shades I had been given by Betty, with instructions to wear them when out in the sun. I put them on as much to shield my eyes from the dust, as from the glorious setting desert sun, now in a blood red sky beneath brush strokes of black and midnight blue, as it lowered itself into the far horizon. I then found the piece of paper with instructions concerning my missing escort. A glance at my watch told me we had landed ten minutes ahead of time, so I sat on one of the waiting crates and I had finished the Evian water I had in my luggage, by the time a jeep drew up with a rather dishy-looking female in the driver's seat.

"Commander Fleming?"

"That's me!" I replied with what I hope was a smile of gratitude at her arrival. Strangely, I found myself eager to get out of the low direct light coming from the setting sun and the dusty heat, which was already warming me up. I had stripped down to my tee-shirt and even that was little relief. Looking about I saw military personnel I recognised as British, they were beige coloured, as predicted by Betty, with full fatigues and loaded Bergen's, walking as if they were unaffected by the heat; I realised that they were carrying anything up to and sometimes over a hundred pounds in weight. I on the other hand was already bathed in sweat and glancing down, I saw the vast wet stains spreading through my tee-shirt, front and no doubt, my back, as well as under my armpits. Climbing in beside the driver, I again gave my name.

"Matt Fleming and you are?"

She turned slightly and as she took her right hand off the left hand drive steering wheel, I was able to read, Holford.

She smiled and for a moment I felt dazzled by what Betty had called, American teeth, as over-pristine as fine Sevres china. I did not grin back too widely, suddenly I was conscious of my aging tea-stained gnashers; it was a mere half grin. But give Holford her due, she continued to smile and chat as we journeyed across the airfield to a gap in the wall that was to lead into Camp Bastion One, according to a notice set beside the gap. Her focus was entirely on the busy traffic racing across the vast spaces that existed between the main body of the camp and the airfield. I was fascinated by the activity all around, when all of a sudden the noise of helicopters coming in to land was superseded by the sirens from ambulances, as they raced to meet the incoming wounded.

"We're on 'Op Minimise'," Holford said in a voice that assumed I knew exactly what was going on. My face must have indicated something because I was frowning.

"You can't contact or phone home."

"But if I wanted to text the wife; I do every day?" I said, still looking puzzled. Was I over-playing my ignorance? If she thought so, this delectable creature played along with the pretence.

"All news in or out is blocked until the next of kin are informed. You will be told when it's safe to use your phone. It probably won't work until you've gotta new SIM; I'll show you where tomorrow, you'll need it to keep in touch with me, I'll text you more often than not when you are on Base. It's quieter, and quicker, and it's more private. Do you know what I mean?"

I sat with a heavy heart; life goes on relentlessly and death is always at home in a war zone, but to have arrived to find a man down! I felt as if I had been wounded myself and every quote imaginable raced through me. What was it? Who was it? Who said something like: yes, it was John Donne, who said,

'Any man's death diminishes me, because I am involved in Mankind; therefore never send to know for whom the bell tolls; it tolls for thee.'

I sat wondering how the soldier had died. How many more were injured. Remembering Bert's description of the monument, I remained silent as Holford drove on for nearly three miles, towards the American sections of Bastion, known as Camp Leatherneck. The noise of the MERTs could still be heard in the distance. Helicopters and military planes were overhead, people were everywhere, and yet there was a feeling of being alone in a strange vast world of purposeful business. Did it all lead to injury and death? Was I going to come out of this alive?

"I didn't realise that Camp Bastion is in reality more like a town than just a military base."

The moment I said it, I knew that sounded crazy, because I was lying just for the sake of conversation. I had already seen maps and photos enough to know what lay ahead. I had wanted to talk, that was all. Speech would help me relax; I wanted to cope with the strangeness and to begin to feel at home. If Holford thought I was trying to flirt with her, I didn't care, she was meant to be looking after me; anyway I had to be at least twice her age! She probably thought I would have to be on Viagra, if I wanted a romp. Suddenly she cut into my mad thoughts and said,

"Right, you've sussed it. Four miles by two, and will eventually hold not that much short of thirty thousand people. You'll get given a map, when we eventually get you to the office. I'm told that the whole site is as big as somewhere called Reading. Mostly you kind of live in the section assigned to you so don't get too worried about getting lost. You could run one and a half marathons around the perimeter of this place, only I would advise to use the internal side of the wall; fewer snipers! And yes, we have Pizza Hut and KFC and the PX, while the Brits have the NAFFI." She smiled at me as if to reassure me that I would feel at home, then she added,

"There are other sections, there's Bastion Two and Bastion Three. Never mind Leatherneck and the camp for training the Afghans. The good locals run a weekly market; I'll show you, that's where you'll get a SIM card and you'll find it is kind of a good place to buy gifts for back home, only there are no straw donkeys, this is no Spanish vacation!"

She laughed at her own joke. Her voice sounded friendly and I felt the beginnings of a sense of a return to normality and of welcome, if it was possible to feel welcomed into a war zone. For a start I felt my uniform was different from some of the personnel we saw, as we passed through areas that were obviously cordoned off. Snaking around behind high walls created from concrete sections that looked reasonably solid and were topped with barbed wire, I also noted how secondary protection came in the shape of hundreds of shipping containers stacked to differing levels and endless dirt-filled Hesco blocks, all big enough to stop at least incoming sniper fire.

At last I relaxed enough to laugh myself, I couldn't help thinking; *is it in the haircuts or is it in the body shapes?* The British soldiers seemed built for a game of rugby; but when we came to a wall that indicated a divide and we passed into the section of the site labelled Camp Leatherneck, it seemed peopled with American Football players; all six foot four and slim-hipped, but broad shoulders visible beneath their UPC combat gear. Some with shoulders so broad you would have been forgiven for believing they were wearing football shoulder pads, ready for a match at the New York Yankees' stadium. There was a markedly different visual between those who worked out and those who didn't. Yes, they were fit, their biceps said so and you knew instantly that this was the American zone of the camp. Size-wise I felt I stood out as an undersized wimp; until I suddenly remembered I did blend in as my American combat gear was now cloned on everyone I saw about me. Silly, I know, but was it the upheaval from my beloved home where I was the tall one, the physically strong one that was making me feel insignificant beside some of the American men walking past the jeep and casually saluting?

I wasn't certain what was expected of me, so looking at my escort I was given a signal that said, 'Salute', or did she mean acknowledge, so I just raised my hand towards the cap on my head and hoped it didn't look too disrespectful.

Holford was chuckling.

"Don't worry, most of these are squaddies, they have no idea who you are. So, now, this is where you will be staying, the newest bit of an American section now called Camp Leatherneck," then Holford further informed me, "and it's large enough for our needs and small enough for getting about on foot; unless you would like a bike?" She was still laughing and again it came with a snowy white smile that had caused me to wonder yet again; were all Americans so blessed with teeth the jealous British call *tombstones*? Then I berated myself for wasting thoughts on such a childish concept and put the matter down to lack of sleep.

I looked at Holford and asked wearily,

"I'm done in, any chance of a sleep?"

"Sure, you get given time to acclimatise, sir. That's first; we all –k know what it's like travelling with cargo."

I noticed that the poor girl had a hesitant stutter every time she said the word kind; it came out as a 'k-k-kind' of hesitation, as if she was unsure of herself. Maybe it was a nervousness that hinted at an awareness of her junior rank in my presence.

"You do? Thank God for that, I'm feeling ashamed that I've just not coped as well as I used to; It would be tiring even in a 747 at my age!"

She laughed, and I liked her laugh. For a moment I wondered if I would ever find out her first name. We drew up beside a Nissan type structure that was covered by a dusty beige-coloured camouflage canopy; well, I assumed it was such. Then she surprised me by saying rather kindly,

"It's been k-kind of quite a day for you, and well, I k-kind of guessed you would like to hit the sack! Oh, I don't blame you; a rotten journey, especially if it's a cargo plane, and then we do find the temperature difference does upset some people. I believe England is cold, compared with this. We do allow for acclimatization, so don't worry, time for a kip. Here are your quarters, sir. You don't have to share at the moment; the men are up country out on patrol at a FOB."

I must have looked puzzled, because she immediately said,

"A Forward Operating Base, sir. And there is a shower in the washroom over there,"

With a smile still on her face, she pointed to what looked like a row of cargo containers; it was apparently a block of shower cubicles.

"We have to make use of everything," she added laughingly.

I deliberately smiled and tried to put her at her ease by asking where the loo was.

"Over there, Sir, that type of *Portaloo* is what the Brits call the Karzi, or the loo, some of our guys tease them calling it the crapper. Truthfully best to do as the Marines and just say the 'head' or as polite ladies say, the bathroom!"

Then there it was again, a difference between us, it was a strong hint of a drawn out vowel sound as if an 'r' was inserted into the word bath.

I wasn't certain, but I think she had cottoned on to the fact that I was bemused not only by her accent, but also by the differences between us with regards to our vocabulary, because she tried to moderate her American accent as she said, "So cool off, have a shower, eat when you need to; you'll find I've left some food ready for you and the bed is made up, OK? Sleep as long as you want to, otherwise have a walk about, you can't get lost and I'll be back to collect you, tomorrow morning, say eight hundred hours. The Camp Commander expects you after you've had breakfast. So there you go, hit the sack and sleep well!"

It was rather sweet of her; I smiled and said with a cheeky grin,

"I would kind of like that!" Suddenly she burst out laughing at my clumsy attempt to sound like her.

"Good night, sir, hope you sleep well."

With that and a friendly wave she drove off, and I stood for a few moments just looking about at the activity around me.

Holford had deposited me and my Bergen, sorry I really must think and feel as American as possible. I dropped my ILBE and assault bag outside the zipped-up entrance to a rigid tent, visible beneath the overhang of the camouflage canopy, and then I watched as Alice drove away into the far distance, without any further ceremony. Glancing about, I realised nobody was taking any interest in me. They were all too busy, but the light was amazing and suddenly the camera man inside me kicked off, and even before I had got inside the billet, I had dug down into the ILBE and found what was to become my trusty d700. Click, click, in rapid fire I just hoovered up the images before me. One after the other, snapping the light hitting the outlines, catching the red colour of the setting sun casting a rosy glow over the myriad of silhouettes, the lines stretching left and right into the far distance, the moving figures, walking, cycling, driving jeeps, driving weirdly shaped vehicles that spoke of war; and then all of a sudden the sun disappeared and I was left in the darkness, at last the rapidly developing darkness encouraged me to seek the shelter of my billet, just as arc lights lit up the scene outside.

Picking up my luggage, I set about getting my new life organised. First things first, a trip to the loo, that was an experience! Reminiscent of the Portaloos used back home at rock festivals and the like!

Then before unpacking I ate; grateful for the food, a flask of hot soup, over-filled sandwiches that reminded me of the cartoon character Dagwood with his multi-layered high sandwiches, followed by a choice from a bowl of fruit. The bottled water was warm and tasted unusual, perhaps it was because of the heat, it had neither the flavour of boiled water nor the slightly plastic taste of bottled water. I'd read up about the bottling plant that the British had built here the year before, and I knew that this was one of its products, a square bottle to stop it rolling about.

Deciding a shower was one method of cooling down; I went out to the ISO can which Holford had pointed out as the shower unit, to sort out where and how to get a shower.

Everything was clean, and by now I was too tired to have cared if they hadn't been pristine. Surprisingly there was no element of air-conditioning in the rigid tent-like structure that was housed beneath the camouflage canopy covering, and was to be my home for the next few weeks. The space was adequate for four men to live in comfort, with two sets of bunk beds. It was more comfortable than I had expected. There was very little storage or for that matter floor space, but the lower bunk bed was well padded with a deep mattress and to my surprise I had bedding rather than a sleeping bag. That fact alone told me I was being treated as a civilian visitor, in spite of the uniform disguise. Fatigue precluded any attempt to dream; it was so hot I lay half naked on top of the bed, but as I shut my eyes I remember it was the face of a pretty young American that was the last memory of the day, or was it Liverpool Betty singing, 'the first time, ever I saw your face?' Sleep came quickly, and when I woke it was to a feeling that finally my fatigued muscles had relaxed enough, and I could face whatever lay before me with a degree of equanimity.

Chapter Eight
Camp Leatherneck behind the D-FAC

Sitting in his jeep, reading by the glare from a bright flood light and from his helmet light, Guy Williams was finding it difficult to concentrate on the memo from his commanding officer. Every now and then he stopped reading to look at his watch. It was already an hour over their suggested rendezvous time and Guy was feeling nervous. The wind was blowing and so he had put the canvas roof up. He liked that, it gave just a little more protection from prying eyes.

When Alice walked round the back of the D-FAC she was relieved to see he had waited. It had been a trying time; overwhelmed with questions from various platoon leaders as to who or what was the mysterious newcomer. Once again she had hardly had time to eat. But it had been useful; because it had highlighted for her just how the personnel at the camp had a curiosity, that if she wasn't extremely careful, could trip her up over Guy and their frequent meetings. Thus she approached the jeep slowly, looking about to see if they were being observed. Watching in the wing mirror Guy was puzzled, and as soon as Alice jumped into the passenger seat, he asked her.

"Honey, what's wrong?"

"I can't do a thing without some busybody commenting on it and just now they were kind of all over me like a rash. I think I'm gonna go mad in this place." He put his arms around her and kissed her. It was a satisfying kiss and he lifted his head up to gaze into her eyes, turned a deep blue by the shadows around them.

"I love you," was all he could say.

"And so do I," said a deep masculine voice from the tall man now standing beside the jeep. His back was towards the arc light, thus making it difficult for the young lovers to see the face of the stranger.

A cold fear ran through Alice and she cried out, "Please, leave me alone."

But Guy just said, "Damn you, Norcross; this is none of your business."

"Evening, Lieutenant!" was all Norcross said before hitting the side of the jeep and walking quickly away.

The silence was almost deafening, until Alice realised her breathing had become more laboured as she tried to calm herself.

"Who was he?"

"Norcross, from my platoon and he's a bastard. He's one of the four I had to report to the Brigadier and that's why our SIS man is coming to be embedded on your side of the fence. What's his name?"

"Commander Matthew Fleming."

"That's the guy! I don't know what the MOD is up to; I've been told to act as if nothing's happening."

"But, I don't think I've ever, ever seen that Norcross man. No, never, never, never! How can he say he loves me?"

"The whole world is in love with you, my darling. Aren't you the most beautiful girl in the world, and you're sitting in my jeep and I'm just about to kiss you again, ready?"

Alice was laughing so much it all became a clumsy groping kiss that left her face wet and glowing as his mouth wandered away from her lips, to every sweet curve of her beautiful face.

It was twenty-three hundred hours before he dropped her outside her billet. In the dark, neither of them noticed Norcross hiding in the shadows.

Nor did they observe Captain Gwen McNaughton standing beneath the awning outside the back of a newly erected American D-FAC, enjoying her final cigarette of the day and saying to herself, "Got yer, Holford."

Chapter Nine
Wednesday, 5 Platoon Patrol Helmand.

It was an hour before sun up, when Lieutenant Guy Williams gave the order for 5 Platoon A Company of the Lancashire Fusiliers, to move out on a forty-eight hour foot patrol in the open desert area of Helmand Province. It wasn't his first time leading a platoon on such an extended foot patrol, here in Afghanistan. It sounds so easy to say, 'No more than a weekend away' but this was different from the Brecon Beacons or a yomp in Germany, this was Taliban country and he felt anxious.

Besides which, he missed his former leader, now promoted to captain, and serving with another platoon. Guy had been advised to lean on his Staff Sergeant, Gareth Hughes, to give him any necessary advice and support. Hughes was a relatively unknown member of the Lancashire Fusiliers; he was considered a loan from another regiment as a temporary replacement for one of the young men injured by an IED, who was currently being rehabilitated in England.

"Lean on your experienced men," was a directive Guy had been given in his Sandhurst training days, "Make them part of the team, so they understand the exercise and can help lead the troops."

That seemed like a good idea, but Hughes had arrived with three other experienced men and Guy had initially set them up as a section in the platoon, so as not to disrupt the loyalties already existing in 5 Platoon.

Johnstone, Norcross and Lewis seemed to follow Hughes around, almost like puppy dogs. Guy was uncertain if this was a good thing, but in the weeks they had been with him, Guy found them distinctly odd and had even sought advice from the Brigadier. He'd been instructed to just keep calm and observe their behaviour, and report back if things got worse.

"Make a note of it, if it will help you. Just don't get too anxious, in the scheme of things, group loyalties usually begin in the four man sections," counselled Brigadier Fulton, the camp commander.

Guy had to be satisfied with that, for now.

The twenty-four members of the patrol boarded a Chinook and before being flown to the area assigned for their foot patrol, they were flown in a sweep over the whole of Camp Bastion and Leatherneck. It was a frequently used decoy tactic; used by the Air Force to confuse those Taliban known to be watching the airfield.

Once he was settled in the Chinook, Guy tried to focus on his map reading. They were to go to an area sixty miles south of Camp Bastion, where a number of compounds formed what had originally been an independent village, and which now needed to be cleared of the Taliban, to allow the villagers to return. Guy and many of the foot soldiers who came through Camp Bastion, found the Afghanistan people charming, if somewhat unsure about the presence of ISAF troops in their country. However in Helmand the

Taliban had taken hold and their rule had been stressing too many of the local people. Therefore the idea was to sweep though and, having killed or captured the Taliban, return the area to the villagers, many of whom had run away and were sheltering in caves, in the mountains. Some villagers had sought shelter in neighbouring settlements or in the numerous vacated compounds that littered the desert.

The vastness of Helmand, three times the size of Wales, but with only half the number in the population, and most of them working as farmers, meant that settlements were widely spaced across the landscape. Access to water seemed to be the determining factor for choosing a place to put down roots, and many farmers built large compounds with differing sections for cattle and for growing food. Spaced out across the wide flat plain of Helmand, the compounds were numbered in a disorganised pattern.

On this day 5 Platoon had to clear compounds 61 to 65. Often rescue pilots found it difficult to read maps, which had all the compounds numbered with the pattern deliberately confused because they followed the lines of the geology of the site, rather than the pattern formed by the logical development of the buildings, at the site. For that reason many platoon leaders on the ground, like Guy, carried a large piece of red cloth, which could be spread out to show the best medevac position, should they need to get an injured man back to the hospital at Camp Bastion. It was safer that lighting flares to signal to a helicopter, smoke could be targeted from a mile away, if not further.

In the twenty-four man group, Guy had a medic, a wireless operator, and twenty one fusiliers of different ages. The youngest was just nineteen and the oldest; rightfully present, was Staff Sergeant Gareth Hughes. In the helicopter the noise made conversation impossible, and most of the men sat in silence, dozing on and off during the half hour flight.

They were dropped off a couple of miles from the first compound to be cleared, known as Compound 61, and having been set down, after sorting out the order in which they were to lead off, they managed to space out behind the lead scout, known as the searcher, who carried his IED detector.

In the first instance it was Craig Lewis, one of the men in the Staff Sergeant's section, who had volunteered. He had a conscientious respect for the job in hand; he had his rifle slung over his shoulder because he preferred a two handed method for holding the detector as he walked with his eyes down constantly searching the ground for signs of disturbed earth or vegetation which might indicate the presence of an IED. Right behind him was Johnstone with his SA50 ready to defend his colleague; as they worked their way through quite a few fields of waist-high poppy plants, and then across several dried out streams. It became obvious to Guy that he needed to rotate the searcher because it was a tiring and stressful task. Using the PRR to warn the troops to stop within a dip caused by a dried out stream, he suggested they sat for a moment and had a drink of water. Lying low, leaning against their backpacks, the men were reasonably safe from snipers. All the men were glad it was spring because the last time they had come along this route they had been completely exposed; the streams were full of water. It was a universal problem for patrols during the winter, when snow fell in the mountains and there was an overspill, the streams ran high and there was nowhere to hide, the water being freezing offered no long term shelter. But it quickly evaporated during the spring and summer when temperatures could rise to above the forties, then there was little water left to feed down into the main river, the source of water used to irrigate the Green Zone that runs through the middle of the Helmand province.

The men sat and cooled off, ate and drank and some even just had a cat nap. When ordered up again, as they continued Lieutenant Williams arranged a change over after twenty minutes and less than half a mile was covered because of his caution. Knowing that IEDs were often planted out as a protective ring around compounds, Guy was especially alert as they drew near to number 61. So careful was the searcher that it had taken nearly half an hour to cover that distance. Two men stepped forward and again, after yet another while, the Lieutenant pulled them off that duty, and sent two new men to lead the file of soldiers, walking spaced out behind and in single file, with their weapons at the ready. Guy had the medic and the radio man to the rear of the file. Morale seemed high, *so far so good,* he said to himself.

It may seem to us looking back at their slow progress, that it was a leisurely way to walk a few miles. But the new enemy was the IED. There were thousands of them easily hidden and the cause of more death and injury than can be imagined. The use of a single metal detector at the head of the foot patrol, did not guarantee safety, the Taliban had got wise to the changing tactics of ISAF soldiers and began using less metal in the IEDs. Some lucky platoons had access to sniffer dogs, but not Guy's platoon. All the soldiers were encouraged to keep glancing down as they walked along. "Remember your first driving lessons, lads, and read the road ahead," was Guy's way of reminding them to share in the responsibility for the platoon's safety.

They appreciated their luck; no IEDs found, no shots were fired and they had already arrived at the first compound, Number 61. It was an exceptionally large featureless mud compound, the mud walls were over seven foot high, and it was essentially nothing more than a square enclosure originally built to protect crops or animals. At first glance it appeared to Gareth, who had climbed up the folding ladder that he had brought with him attached to the back of his Bergen, that there appeared to be no living quarters built into the sides, but he advised caution, informing them that there was evidence of recent occupation. There was a pile of innocuous rubbish stacked against a wall, it appeared fresh; there was no dusty covering blown over it, the way anything left out in the open in that part of the world easily collected, as an indicator of the time elapsed since it was dropped. Guy was grateful that the older man had an uncanny sense of the markers of a human presence; he reminded Guy of an Indian tracker, checking broken twigs, dropped faeces, bits of fibre hanging on branches. There was no doubt in Guy's mind that Gareth Hughes could be left to fend for himself in open country. But, as for the rest of his men, he was unconfident of any such success; too youthful and inexperienced was his assessment of most of them. They were boys who had to grow into men before they were to be returned home to a world that couldn't understand why they went to war in the first place. Yet, he himself was only twenty-four and responsible for them.

Gareth slowed their attempts to gain entrance via the rather expensive-looking locked metal gate; the possibility of a booby trap was uppermost in his mind.

Staff Sergeant Gareth Hughes then suggested they organised a blasting into the side of the compound; Guy accepted his advice, the explosive was laid, and through they all went. To the men it was just another mousehole used because they believed them safer than booby-trapped gates. The Staff Sergeant immediately nominated look outs and as the day was already getting hot, he suggested,   "Lieutenant, sir, they could all do with a cooling off period." One side of the compound offered some shade. Again Lt.

Williams accepted the people skills being shown by Hughes, and complied with the plan.

Meanwhile the Staff Sergeant went over to check out the discarded rubbish; his careful approach meant that he used an extending telescopic prod, until he was satisfied that it was safe to go nearer. After further careful examination of the cast-off food canisters, food wrappers and wasted food, he came to the conclusion that they were no more than a few hours old.

"The food has not even begun to dry out. They can't be far away."

Again Gareth made use of the folding ladder he always carried on the back of his Bergen. With masterly organisational skill, he succeeded in arranging a sequence of inspections, north, south, east and west of the compound. His height meant that he could easily see over the wall from just a rung up from the bottom of his ladder, and use his field glasses to scan the areas beyond the compound.

Guy and Gareth then sat together and discussed possible scenarios and the different options open to them. Their maps indicated that the next compound in a direct line west, was Compound 65. Two, three and four were more towards the south and there was no protective vegetation going via that route. They opted for 65 first, then to move in an arc from behind 65 down towards 64 and on towards the others. Gareth agreed with him and suggested that as it was now nearing noon, and very hot, the men could do with a further rest, and that they should all set off together when things were cooler. He even reminded Guy to make sure the men were drinking plenty of fluid.

"Mad dogs and Englishmen!" said Guy with a smile. Gareth Hughes smiled back. It was good to find some rapport with the younger man; Gareth could see that he was obviously nervous; he knew that Guy had only recently been promoted to full lieutenant. This was his first time of working with the 5th Platoon in the role of lieutenant, whereas Staff Sergeant Gareth Hughes was completely confident in his judgements when dealing with military strategy. It was to be several days before Guy came to realise just how experienced Gareth Hughes was of life in Afghanistan. If that eventual revelation was to be misinterpreted by the younger man, more is the pity; for Gareth Hughes had the best brain in the army for dealing with guerrilla warfare.

Chapter Ten
Camp Leatherneck, Meeting the General

It was my first morning in Helmand; I was dressed and the bed made by the time Holford returned to take me to breakfast, in what she pronounced as a 'Dee-Facks', and I suppose we Brits would call it a canteen or a mess, or the cookhouse. Leaving most of the paraphernalia of the journalist in my billet, I nevertheless had the Olympus recorder in my pocket and my camera hanging around my neck. I felt it might reinforce the concept of a journalist to those I was to meet, the idea that I really was one.

As we approached the vast dining space that was the D-FAC, I observed soldiers checking that their weapons were not primed, by pointing their rifles or handguns into one or other of the safety boxes placed either side of the entrance and pulling the trigger, to check they weren't loaded. Then I noticed that most of the men slung their weapon over their shoulders to sit across their backs. I soon realised why, when after being shown where to sign in and being given a pass, I saw the men had no trays and needed both hands free. Instructed that food was unrestricted and plentiful, we collected ours and ate heartily. I was hungry for freshly cooked food and indulged in a plateful of fried protein, as near as was possible to a 'full English'; the bacon was over-crispy, the sausage without any cereal bulking it up was not quite English enough for my taste, which ran to Lincolnshire's or Wall's for preference. But truthfully it was just bearable, and the eggs over easy just had to be endured. No dipping in of toast soldiers here!

This was followed with a ride in her jeep for a brief tour around the camp. She seemed friendlier this morning. Whether it was the heat, or the fact that I had missed my wife's morning loving, I admit here and now, Holford aroused me to the point that the only way I could deal with it was to look away, as if intensely interested in the monotonous structures called Camp Leatherneck, and occasionally take photo shots of things that looked remarkable, but probably weren't.

How do you describe the perfect looking woman? Combat fatigues could not hide the perfect shape of the woman driving that Humvee. Neither could the flat-topped cap called a head, destroy her appeal. Private First Class Holford was a picture and I had joined the ranks of the besotted. Her face was a sunflower, opened and turned to the sun, even as her eyes sparkled and her laugh enthralled.

There's no need to tell of the prefabricated units housing various offices, the medical centres, armouries and other necessary storage, repair shops and transport facilities, as well as the vast tent-like structures that were everywhere. I didn't really follow all Holford was saying; it seemed unnecessary, believing I was to be given the promised map of the area at some point soon. Anyway my brief did not concern the camps or FOBs, it was the usual Western panic; it is always money and politics, in this case the domestic issue was winning an election because the voter felt the PM not had done enough for the troops and foreign policy relations with Pakistan, who wanted their hands on Turkmenistan's gas! Need I say more?

"Feeling how awesome it all is ain't you?" she said as if trying to understand my silence. "It grows on you."

I just nodded my head and smiled a thanks as she drew up outside the main offices and escorted me into the General, whispering,

"He's my uncle, truly! But he's a sweetie, really, yer gonna like him, I promise."

General Michael Raven was introduced to me and on shaking hands without a salute. It seemed to me that he was acknowledging my non-combatant status. As Holford left the office, which like everything else in Leatherneck was hidden beneath the camouflage canopy, the General generously put me at my ease by saying,

"Mike, please!"

"Matthew, sir, pleased to meet you."

"So, they dragged you out of retirement! Never mind, you'll cope, I'm certain of that. Do you mind, Matthew, if we call you Matt? You'll fit in better."

"Sure that's fine by me," I said, laughing,

"So, Matt, I expect yer gonna be glad of any help we can give you. With luck it will be a two way street. Has Alice shown you the camp?"

At last I had her name. I liked it. I smiled and nodded my head.

"She has? Good, she a reliable one, that one. I'm effectively lending her to you; she's my assigned gofer and a good one. I've personally briefed her; you'll be safe with her."

Something told me that I doubted my own resistance where 'Alice' was concerned. This was as new to me as being here in this strange land. I remained standing and silent, as Mike Raven walked over to a tray obviously set up with mugs and a flask; presumably of coffee or tea.

"Please, do sit down, Matt, drink?

I was somewhat surprised, being uncertain: was it for coffee or tea? It was obvious that he sensed my hesitation.

"Please, no sugar!" I said, trying to look unbothered.

"Good man."

Next moment I had a cup of really good quality black unsweetened coffee in my hand, and watching Mike's obvious ability to swig his drink down his throat and refill his cup before I had taken my first sip; I immediately decided I would control any attempt at a drinking match. There was no need to worry. Looking across at my cup, Mike Raven just smiled with obvious satisfaction, that he believed I was a slow drinker and intended leaving him to empty the flask.

"So, Matt, having trouble with the old poppy sellers, are we?"

I began the rigmarole that was the official lie for all outside SIS, and hoped I sounded sincere.

"It isn't just a question of drug running; we all know how universal that problem is, and we are hardly surprised to find that several of the shipments we have tracked have come from Helmand. We've captured a couple of individuals with Afghan passports, who unsurprisingly stoically refuse to answer questions. It's proving difficult, because every known route out of Helmand appears completely in the control of one terrorist group or another, or should I say one tribal leader or other? It's as if there is some mysterious Khyber Pass still in existence, a route only the natives use, because they know they will be protected by other natives. I am pretty certain even the good guys collude with the traffic, with money in their pocket, why should they care about the disastrous end result in some faraway place called England? We realise that they are probably using camels, and going off road, while we are manically searching motors on tarmac roads. It seems strange to me being in such a vast and ancient country, which has been home to the British on at least separate occasions that there is no evidence of railways, no trains. Yet look at India, trains everywhere. Ah well, back to today. I am told that we British are fairly careful with our checks and so are your lot, but this country is vast and the PM can't get his head around the fact that we can't control the drug trade. This is the twenty-first Century and it is still all camels or cars! And because the natives know our dogs sniff out the poppy quick enough, all they have to do is keep their distance with their ships of the desert. At least the camels can cope without water for longer than the car or the driver can, in this heat."

I pointed towards the concrete structure dividing the Bastion camps from the Leatherneck Camp. "Somebody...probably over there, is orchestrating at least some of the trade and if this is true, it's my job to catch them; hence this deception! The PM wanted it done quietly, but could hardly ask his special friends over the pond to do the job for him!"

"Risky business; it could get you a knife in the nether regions, so watch your back! You should be OK here on Leatherneck; can't speak for Bastion."

"I realize that, still we must take a chance and believe we will find the ringleader."

"We? There are more of you here?"

At that point in time I did not realise how much Mike Raven knew of my cover story, but common sense told me that his rank would surely indicate that he had been briefed with some of the matter in hand.

"Yes, we have a young guy in Bastion. I'll be linking up with him as soon as possible. Do you know Guy Williams, a young lieutenant who gave us the information in the first place, about a certain group of bad apples? He was unable to identify the ringleader, so he let sleeping dogs lie and reported the matter to his commanding officer, who agreed that a watch and wait approach, was best, but then without telling Williams, he immediately got in touch with the section dealing with drug enforcement back in the UK. Since yesterday, he does now know that our superiors went one step further and have embedded me into Leatherneck."

I felt I had delivered my cover story reasonably well and General Raven seemed inclined to go along with my story, even if he knew differently.

We talked on and he added to my knowledge of the camp, of personnel and of the activities already set up with Afghans, both inside the camp and outside. I filled him in on my undercover work in Mexico and Columbia, all of it drugs-related. He seemed impressed and said,

"Well, Matt, drugs are not exactly my field of expertise, but if I can help, just let me know; Alice can liaise for you."

Motor transport was to be provided for my use; I breathed a sigh of heartfelt release, no bikes! But I was advised that Alice Holford was not to be my driver off base. I felt even more relief at that, for I already realized the dangers of going off base. I had been advised that helicopters would be arranged for me when necessary. This did slightly bother me, wasn't one of the reasons for my being in Camp Bastion the shortage of the birds?

After further advice about how far my freedom to move around the camps at will was legitimate, I accepted the suggestion that I always had Alice as official driver with me if venturing into the section named as Camp Shorahak, which housed Afghanistan personnel; and also to ask permission before venturing into a remote section of the camp which housed the special services personnel. And to be careful if hazarding a route around or anywhere near, the training ranges.

With some courtesy, I did however gratefully accept the promise of an American corporal as a driver, for when I needed to leave the camps; but I could never have imagined my reaction would be one of such surprise and delight, when I finally met the man. Six foot six and as thin as a rake, a military crew cut to the top of his blond hair and the sides clipped close to his head. So deep was his naturally acquired tan, that his hair looked white against it.

"Corporal Hudson Elliot the Third, sir! Call me HUD or Corporal; I answer either way, sir! Miss Alice will contact me if you need me at any time of the day or night, sir."

"Miss Alice?" I asked with a frown.

"Sorry, sir, I mean Private First Class Holford, sir."

Poor guy he was trying unbelievably hard to be correct in every aspect of his responses. So I smiled and said,

"Right, I see! Yes, Alice will do. So, you are from the south?"

He smiled back; the smile had an impish look, the voice that of a well-bred Southern man possibly from New Orleans, and I instantly knew that I was going to like him. The two stripes on his sleeve denoted his rank and yet they looked brand new. He saw me looking at them and grinned even more widely, as he proudly said,

"Yes Sir, just got promoted!"

"Well, congratulations, Corporal. Have you been out here long?"

"Six months, Sir."

I liked him, he had an affable and friendly approach to life and over the next couple of hours Corporal Hudson Elliott showed me around the camps. I viewed all the facilities for washing clothes and cleaning vehicles. I saw vast tents for ops rooms and training rooms for mission briefings. It was easy to pay attention to areas in Bastion set aside for men and women to phone home; at that time, each was allowed one call a month. At that time, such was the importance of that call, that it was jealously guarded, seen as important to the mental health of the soldiers.

Come on, MOD, I said to myself, *only one call, hardly going to help a frightened young squaddie to cope with the stress of being in a war zone.* The opportunity to Skype or work on the internet was dependent less upon the provision of electricity and more on available satellite availability. That things improved at a later date, was not due to my report, about that I was quite certain.

For a while I was bemused by the provision of vast tented rooms with satellite TV and film facilities. The British Forces Radio was to be piped over from Cyprus sometime soon, so I was informed by my new guardian angel. Then he drove me around to other places to spend money; I laughed at the British queuing up at American PX and vice versa the Americans wandering around the NAAFI. There was a post room and a quartermaster's vast storage based under canvas which was pulled over metal frameworks as big as an aircraft hangar.

But everywhere we went, I was initially shocked at the dreadful smell of sewerage, as we drove past Portaloo after Portaloo being cooked as they stood out in the heat with no protection. Then there was the noise level in all of the different areas of the camps. Although partly due to the planes and the sirens, the cars and the ambulances, the TV's and the radios, it was the ceaseless humming noise of the generators that I soon became conscious of as they worked to keep everyone supplied with power. It took me a while to get used to it; but I would gradually come to appreciate how valuable the provision of power and fresh water was to the forces. It produced enough power to keep a city the size of Reading lit up and working and with its own bottling plant, working to fill plastic bottles with fresh spring water. It was the water that brought the army to that particular spot in Helmand. The whole camp was positioned over a vast lake of a reservoir, far below ground, annually refilled with of fresh water collected from the melting snows of the mountains.

Why was I surprised at the size of the Camp Bastion area and its satellite camps? The area was as enormous as a town, had a perimeter roadway of over thirty miles that could host at least a one and a half-length marathon. Hudson informed me that in Leatherneck the American engineers wanted to build a swimming pool, but so far there was only one for the dogs. Special consideration was given to keeping the search dogs cool and healthy. They were important sniffing out explosives and IED! But when I was there I never saw a pool for the men. I don't know if they ever realised that dream, I never followed up on that one. I only know that the whole place was so vast you could be forgiven for closing your mind to what was going on in the rest of Afghanistan, it was surreal, like having Catterick Barracks' and the town of Aldershot housed under one enormous canvas, with Gatwick on the side and the M4 running through the middle.

We toured the perimeter first, travelling around beside the thirty foot high fence topped with triple concertina wire, and the inner concrete blast wall, also probably thirty foot high. It was a roadway often as wide as a dual carriage way. He showed me the British Education Centre and we stopped to speak with some young men gathered outside, having a break in their learning, all of them spoke of their countdown to going home and their hopes for jobs when they left the army. Each in turn explained why they had joined the Army or the TA; I was surprised that many spoke of the gaps in their education; limiting their choice of a civilian job, but praising the Army for the education they were getting.

Hudson did well, and time passed quickly. Later, I enjoyed an evening meal with him, after which we both joined a noisy gang watching a video of an American Football game, in an air-conditioned tented recreation facility. It was fun and there was a great deal of teasing and wolf whistling, yelling and jumping up when goals were scored.

But it relaxed me and cooled me off after the tremendous heat of the day. I can't claim that I slept well that night; the noise never seemed to stop and the billet seemed airless. If I unzipped the tent door, the dust swirled in from passing vehicles, and if I closed it, within an hour I was sweating more than I could have believed possible. I went for a shower at four in the morning and again at seven, before dressing and heading off to the D-FAC for breakfast. I knew that Guy Williams' Platoon would be out on the second day of their Patrol: I wondered how they might have got on sleeping out in the open in that heat.

Chapter Eleven
Second day of 48 hour patrol Helmand

The first day out had passed relatively quietly, there had been no sign of the Taliban, but the heat had been unbearable. The entire platoon was drinking water to counteract the thirst caused by the dusty heat; the possibility of being short of water was fast becoming a reality, Guy knew it would be as dangerous of a gun fight. He had seen other patrols brought back in before the end of their allocated time, because of the collapse of too many of the fighting men to make continuing viable. Hence the stop and drink orders he gave were maybe a touch excessive; but he was afraid of finding himself with a platoon suffering from dehydration and unable to cope with the real fight he was hoping they would have with the enemy. He wanted glory; he had a lady to impress, he had to prove to himself he was as good as his training said he should be; now he was in charge.

Sleeping out in Compound 63, which had proved as empty as 61, 65, and 64 he felt that the objective of 62 was going to prove decisive. The Taliban must have moved there.

If they had been watching Five Platoon taking the proposed tactical route; sneaking the long way round and finding the manoeuvre easy, with the compounds empty; surely the Taliban would be suspicious, and eventually think that the fusiliers would just get cocky and careless as they approached number 62.

Unfortunately for the Taliban, Staff Sergeant Gareth Hughes had also reasoned out that carelessness was not an option, and suggested to Guy that they tried a delaying tactic, to try and appear to be retreating back the way they had come, then to walk around towards the high ground behind Compound 62; that way they would be able to look down into it instead of blasting their way in as they had with the other compounds.

He thought about it; it seemed a good idea, until one of the youngest men came up to him complaining of dizziness. Calling up the medic, a T.A. guy called Chris; he was told that in his opinion young Brad was suffering from the early signs of dehydration. Gareth Hughes suggested a check of the available water; Guy decided there was insufficient water available to get all twenty four men through an extensive climb and on into a real fight. He felt the panic come up inside his throat, a deep breath, before he ordered everyone to rest, while he radioed for fresh supplies. Calmness returned, Hughes seemed to realise what had happened to Guy and stood by him until his breathing was steady again. He waited until Guy looked him in the eye and nodded his head. No word was said, but Guy knew that the older man had understood.

The helicopter came into the dead zone behind the compound and everything seemed alright. They had water; they could go ahead with the plan. But there was the strange incident of Hughes's little section.

Technically they could be charged with treason.

You might well ask why.

Lieutenant Williams had told Hughes and Norcross to go and meet the chopper; he had told everyone else to sit.

When Hughes and Norcross returned, there was Lewis and Johnstone following them. Was it Williams's fault that he hadn't noticed them leaving the line without permission?

With four men carrying as many as six packs of water bottles each, there was now sufficient water for the march and for the raid to go ahead, so Williams rallied the troops and kept his mouth shut; but his mind was churning around Queen's Regulations, trying desperately to remember the letter of the law.

They left the compound and headed towards the route discussed; everyone kept to single file and sensible spacing, when half an hour later the thing feared most was heard, the fourth man in the line, Bryn Jones, the young fusilier from Wales, was blasted by an IED. Even before the sound of the blast had died away, Gareth Hughes rushed past shouting, "Get on the radio," and he and Norcross, Lewis and Johnstone had the victim with both legs in tourniquets. Guy had just about got through to Camp Bastion, having registered how serious the injuries were for Bryn Jones. In fact, not even the medic was quick enough to help him, before the Hughes-Lewis-Johnstone-Norcross section had him strapped on to the ladder hastily uncoupled from off the back of Hughes's Bergen. Mercifully the medic managed to get some morphine into the lad and he then seemed to pass out. The four man section then raced back past the Lieutenant, carrying Bryn Jones to a suitable position in the dead zone, followed by the medic, who kept an eye on Bryn until handing him over to the MERT Team that had flown in on the chopper.

Guy froze; he looked as if he was going to collapse, until something inside of him forced a reaction. He gave the order; "We are carrying on when Bryn has been collected. Rest now; it might be the last chance we will get."

Then going to the head of the column he spoke quietly with the searcher; he tried to help the man accept that there was no blame on him for not finding the IED, after which Guy called up another soldier to replace him and his cover guard before sending the tired searchers to the rear of the column.

The bird coming to collect Bryn had managed to land safely in the dead zone, and looking up, Guy could see another bird, this time an Apache helicopter and it sent a missile into Compound 62 as offering protective cover to the Chinook. It was effective in that it reassured Five Platoon. It remained circling and occasionally firing off at the Compound 62.

Getting hold of the radio, Guy was told that there appeared to be about thirty Taliban moving about inside the compound. It was an enormous compound with ten foot high walls, and that there were several well-constructed rooms along the south side wall **of** the compound. As Gareth and the boys returned from the dead zone, a short conflab had all eager to set off up the pathway. The men seemed more relaxed and hearing the bird circling above, confidence came over all of them, within twenty minutes all were in position and ready for the fight.

Suddenly, from the Taliban positions there comes a series of white flashes, accompanied by the rat-tat-tat of the machine guns being fired up at the soldiers. Then more frequent fire was aimed back from the British positions down onto the Taliban, now trapped in the compound. With the bird flying high and keeping them informed as to the positions of the rebels, Guy handed the command to the Staff Sergeant while he doubled back to check with Stan, the medic, getting him to organize a medical centre in anticipation of casualties. He felt certain that someone could be wounded and he wanted to secure a field hospital site. Then with the help of the youngest member of the troop, for the next hour he kept up the re-supply of ammunition and water to the men firing into the compound. It was dangerous work as neither of them could avoid a couple of places where they were in direct line of fire to the Taliban down below. He soon realised the next disaster was the dangerous level of ammo left. He called in a re-supply and sent Johnstone and Norcross, as two of the fittest men, to meet the bird coming into the dead zone.

The rattling of machine gun fire was continuous, and then the firing from below seemed to slow down. He called a ceasefire and ordered his men to check ammo and take a quick drink; it was excessively hot and he was constantly aware of the danger with his men out in the direct sun. Gareth rushed to his side and they used their field glasses to assess the situation below them.

"What are you seeing, Staff?"

"They are trying to break out of the far wall, look, that barricade is useless except to conceal whatever they are up to. I think we will hear a blast soon, a hole and out. They've learnt that one from us, Lieutenant."

"Except we blast to get into the compounds and they blast to get out, nice one though! Shall we get some men round behind them?"

"Brilliant idea, boss! Let me go."

"Yeah, okay, take two men and try and get there without being seen."

Staff Sergeant Gareth Holmes crept past Craig Lewis and tapping him on the shoulder, they continued on down past some rocks until the two of them were up against the wall of the compound. Guy, watching through his field glasses, felt annoyed. Once again Hughes was doing his own thing, hadn't he said take two men? Wasn't he the platoon commander, not the older man?

He stayed where he was and with the glasses scanned both the activity inside of the compound and that on the outside, which came down to some masterful stealthy movements by Hughes and Lewis as they were creeping around to the rear, before moving up to be positioned facing the rear wall, with Lewis having his M249 balanced on a tripod and pointed directly at the wall of the compound, ready to attack any Taliban who might break through. Even Guy felt somewhat anxious for any escaping Taliban. Lewis would quite literally be cutting them down as soon as one appeared.

They did not have to wait long before a few wildly aimed sniper shots set the British boys firing back again, until without warning an almighty blast forced a hole in the far wall, just as Hughes had suggested it would happen.

As Taliban fighters started to exit the compound they were slaughtered in a hail of machine gun fire administered by Craig Lewis. Screaming, the Taliban turned back into the safety of the compound, several of them obviously badly injured. Meanwhile Johnstone and Norcross, having delivered a new supply of ammo, picked up several ammo boxes from the stack they had just collected, before heading off to join Hughes and Lewis.

Later that evening, the brigadier listened intently.

"Now, I became busy sorting and resupplying ammo, sir. I knew the guys just loved getting at the enemy, they call it 'getting stuck in', sir, my predecessor always let them get stuck in and get rid of some of the tension; I mean if we're not careful, sir, the men can get very bored out on patrol," Lieutenant Guy Williams told him.

"Did you see anything else amiss?"

"Not then, sir."

"I see, but you still feel unsure about that section? And you think Hughes is a law unto himself?"

"Maybe I'm being a bit sensitive about things, sir. They just don't wait to take an order, sir; they seem to know what I'm going to say before I've said it. I describe it as they remind me of predictive text, if you understand what I'm trying to say, sir."

"Doesn't that imply that you, Lieutenant, are slow in giving orders? Think about it. Anyway the upshot is I'm delighted with the results from this patrol and we can cross off Compounds 61 to 65 and let the natives back home. Well done!"

Lieutenant Guy Williams was somewhat relieved, no reprimand, even though he still worried about his authority within Five Platoon, the Lancashire Fusiliers.

He made his way over to the Camp Bastion Hospital to see if young Bryn Jones was awake yet. He wasn't, but he was already programmed for his return back to Britain.

The Surgeon Commander Peter Wallis stopped Guy as he was leaving the ward.

"May I have a word, Williams?"

"Sir."

"Please tell your men that their quick reaction with the tourniquets saved Private Jones's life."

"Sorry, sir, what did they do?"

"They used the new tourniquets, I didn't know they had arrived yet, but your men have proved that they work."

"Well, that's good, but I didn't know that they had them," Guy said quietly.

"With any luck there's a supply of several hundred arriving soon. I want every man to carry one; know how to use it and help change the ghastly statistics surrounding blast injuries."

After a few polite words of thanks for the lifesaving surgery carried out on young Bryn and the work of the hospital staff, Lieutenant Guy Williams walked out into the dusty world that lay between the hospital and his billet. He tried Alice's number; no reply. He sent a text; no reply. Tired and dispirited, he walked alone the mile and a half to his billet, before collapsing into a deep sleep on his camp bed.

Chapter Twelve
The day Bryn Jones was injured.

Breakfast was a jolly time **but** I still felt strangely disorientated in the dusty atmosphere, the sand or grit which seemed to get everywhere, in my eyes, in my throat and up my nostrils. There was even more discomfort in my eyes, whenever the air was stirred up by passing trucks, cars, jeeps and every size and shape of military hardware screaming past me. It was Alice Holford who said I was free to wander at will, but she suggested I was particularly cautious if I got as far as the airfield, which with all the perverseness of my curious nature; I promptly did just that; followed the directions for the airfield.

When walking, the vastness of the camps was somehow even more emphasised by their very flatness. It was like wandering over the seemingly endless Norfolk Broads; where you can quickly feel you are about to fall off the end of the world, because there are no defining features rising up, as if to mark a boundary. I found it somewhat depressing and turned back thinking I would walk the couple of miles back to Camp Leatherneck. I was cutting across what I would eventually came to call the short route, when suddenly I only just missed being thrown against the side of a cargo container as a MERT hurtled passed with sirens screaming. Landing heavily, I was winded and cut in several places on my left arm. My only excuse was that I must have become so acclimatized to the noises around me that I had failed to hear the siren. The fall was not serious; but other men who had jumped more efficiently than I, came to my rescue and insisted that I get the cut seen to immediately.

So that was how I ended up in the first aid area of the hospital labelled the MTF as in Medical Treatment Facility. Standing to one side I witnessed the speed with which they processed the injured man who was rushed through to the triage section of the hospital.

A TA nurse, nice woman, who told me she was out on her third stint at Bastion, cleaned and dressed my cut arm. I reassured her that I was fully covered for tetanus jabs, and then I kept her talking for the best part of ten minutes, while she gave me the lowdown of the scanners and the blood systems they used in the emergency rooms. If I looked squeamish, her very matter of fact tone chided me for being a wimp at the mention of blood.

She suggested with a cheeky grin, that as I was a non-combatant I went back to my quarters and avoided becoming a burden upon the camp's medical corps. But wandering out, this time thinking I might get the bus as it wound past on a perpetual circular route, I again found myself just standing and watching as I saw a Chinook coming into land in an open area almost in front of my eyes. Was it going to land in the roadway in front of the hospital? I needn't have worried; it came in across the other side of the road, in an area marked out by large blue crosses. A male nurse came and standing beside me explained, "We bring them in as close as possible to the hospital, we call the area Nightingale." With that he laughed and added, "I wonder why?"

I saw the helicopter coming in to land, and I was snapping away ten to the dozen. I could just about see the medics unloading the injured into the MERTS before I heard the screeching sirens of the MERTS and finally looking at my watch, I realised I had witnessed them racing from the landing site called Nightingale to the hospital entrance in less than ten minutes. It was phenomenal and I stayed to watch and, with my camera doing its best to get dramatic angles, I recorded several more such amazing transfers of the battle-scarred to the hospital.

Remembering that I had work to do, I eventually hopped onto the bus and half an hour later settled to spend the rest of the morning sitting on the edge of my bunk, using my laptop to check out the names Guy Williams had given to his Brigadier and which SIS had now emailed to me. If they were troublemakers, it didn't seem to be a reputation that had come up the ranks with them. They were all given total clearance; one hundred percent. I had been told not to spend too much time on the cover stories surrounding my mission. 'Red herrings' were only useful if they advanced the mission.

But it was an enlightening exercise and gave me much food for thought. I was still puzzling over some of the details I had gathered, when I headed off to the D-Fac; must remember to think and speak as an American, for a late lunch. Suddenly Alice deposited her plate of food down beside mine and climbed over the bench to sit next to me.

"Hello stranger!"

I laughed, whether at her choice of words or at the tone of her voice, I don't know; did it matter? No, I just felt happy to see her. The woman had something that every woman wants and I silently said to myself; *and so does every man.*

Alice was sexy and it showed. Alice was intelligent and it showed. Alice was the sweet girl next door and the untouchable vixen. But she made every man who had to work alongside her feel a little bit better, a little bit less afraid, and considerably more convinced that there were things worth fighting for in this life. Maybe that is a sexist comment, but I exonerate myself by adding that Wasima was also worth fighting for with or without her niqab, women are special and should be respected, it was still bugging me, what I had seen at Karvelk. Let go of it, I said to myself, it has nothing to do with gas pipe lines or helicopter shortages.

I relaxed and asked, "Got time to talk?"

"Crack on, mate!"

I laughed and told her she was sounding like a Cockney, at which she too burst out laughing. Men sitting on the opposite side of the table asked her what was so funny, and she had fun telling them,

"Gee, Commander Fleming thinks I sound like a Cockney!"

"Bleeding hell, what's a f**ing Cockney?" asked a burly soldier as he stuffed meatloaf and beans into his mouth, before my frown reminded him that he was swearing in front of a lady.

"Sorry, miss, didn't..."

"No bother, Chuck! A Cockney is a Londoner who uses funny language."

"No, I mean, I was swearing."

"Didn't notice, Chuck, how's your day been?"

I listened to his account of the IED that had nearly taken the legs off his friend from Idaho, and how he and another guy had tried to stop the bleeding.

"Yeah, he's lucky the IED must have been an old 'en, 'cause had it gone off properly he'd 'ave lost his legs and probably his gongs as well. Do yer know what I'm saying? He's lost a bit out of his left leg and his heel on his right foot; but we got him back here alive; he's over at the hospital now. He was here in less than an hour. And yer know there was another one; an English fellow brought in with same injury!"

Alice was brilliant; she offered to visit the injured man later and then reassured Chuck that his friend would be flown out to an American military hospital in Germany, as soon as possible.

"Wouldn't be surprised if he isn't there by this time tomorrow," she said in her warmest tones as she added, "and his family could visit him there."

I continued to munch on my king-sized burger and fries. The side salad was a bit limp in the heat and I ignored that, until I saw the tomato disappearing as Alice reached across to pinch it from my salad bowl; even as she chatted on to Chuck about his family. That was a cosy familiarity, reminiscent of my wife's behaviour, and I like it. My wife always scavenged off my plate, even before I'd finished my meal. It was something I came to expect; I think she put things on my plate she liked, such as tomato and radishes, which I rarely ate, preferring green vegetables and green salad foods.

Coffee and a stroll over towards the Karzi, sorry I mean the bathroom, no, I mean the head! Yes, it was a good block down from the D-FAC; that meant that I had her to myself for another twenty minutes. Fascinated by her eyes, I hardly listened to what she was saying. Such a missed opportunity; I chided myself as I later settled down to re-check the material that had been forwarded to me concerning the four men who worried Guy Williams.

They turned out to be Midlanders, but from four different towns. Private Craig Lewis was a Brummie; Staff Sergeant Gareth Hughes was from the Potteries, Private Tom Johnstone hailed from Nottingham, while Private Andy Norcross seemed to come from the carpet-making town of Kidderminster. All came from families where both parents worked: the Lewis family were all in the car making business. Royal Crown Derby was the pottery where Gareth Hughes family all worked. There was only a mother and two sisters in Tom Johnstone's family and as such they helped manufacture Nottingham lace. Laughing to myself, I said out loud,

"If that's the case, no doubt the Norcross tribe are weaving carpets, if they are still making carpets in Kidderminster!"

There was no evidence of even petty crime in the background of the four men. Equally obvious if the evidence of the information was true, it seemed to me, that they had formed their gang of four a long while ago, possibly during their basic training. Their whole history was of sticking together, avoiding trouble, no drunken brawls, no dope-laden parties, no going AWOL and always back well before any deadline for the end of R and R.

Four perfect individuals; so why did they bother Guy Williams so much? Was the problem with Guy?

I thought to myself; *it is all too perfect, these have to be artificial records; agents or terrorists came to mind*. I looked up my own records. What had they done to me? Yes, there I was, Matthew Fleming, nothing to worry any employer; everything was off pat: The real Commander Matthew Fleming who had worked on foreign assignments for the old MI6 for fifteen years, much of it concomitant with twenty years spent in command of his own frigate, had disappeared behind the cover story of Matthew Fleming a man who had worked in the field as war correspondent, having covered the Bosnia and Iraq wars. Then it hit me squarely between the eyes; the format was the same; everything screamed that there had to be a four man section embedded in deep undercover in Williams's unit. If Williams hadn't been told, then higher up the chain of command there must be someone suspicious of Lieutenant Guy Williams. There had to be a question mark over Williams.

I sat there thinking of the options, for a man of his age, rank and experiences, what could he possibly have done to make him a target for Intelligence? If it was a good thing maybe he might be under investigation for an approach from the modern day SIS, to work as an agent. He was just ripe for recruitment; young, fit and with a good university degree, an indication of some brains? Well, one would hope so, but was he an unnecessary worrier? There is no doubt that 'C' and his cronies had a system for assessing suitable new agents. I remembered how I was mentored when first working for the firm.

Other than that, if the guy was a traitor, it would be incumbent upon somebody like me to find out. I still had not met the guy; time for action. I needed to come face to face with him, but enquiries showed that he had been off base for twenty-four hours.

Getting in touch with Hudson and Alice, I discovered that a column was leaving the base the next morning. Williams's platoon was to be the tail end Charlie; dropping off at the village named as Karvelk. It was apparently a good will visit following on from work done several months previously, when it was cleared of Taliban. The villagers supposedly now lived in peace and held a Friday market. They liked the military to come along and help keep the armistice, with the Taliban. The ANA was not yet big enough to provide enough remote cover and they also welcomed the support given by the British.

Meanwhile Alice acquired a requisition form for extra uniform and Hudson became the organiser of that trip; body armour and helmet, knee pads, elbow pads and gloves, another pack of Wet Ones, a lunch pack of dehydrated food and several bottles of drinking water.

When I queried the knee pads, Hudson simply said,

"Hear gunshot, stop, then down on one knee, gun so; don't go for prone unless you are sure there are no IEDs around for you to land on! And of course if bullets are flying over your head, well, risk it!"

He demonstrated how to lie prone with his weapon ready to fire. I played along knowing full well that he was enjoying teaching a civilian, for that was what I was in his eyes. Telling him I was glad I could now see the reasons for the pads, elbows resting on stony ground and weighed down by a heavy weapon needed at least some protection, if they were to hold the position for more than a few minutes, I nodded in approval and thanked him for his advice.

I think I overdid the gratitude, but he was effusive in his appreciation of my quick learning, when it came to the rifle. Using his own weapon he went over the firing positions several times and I played the dim but willing student, until I was tired of the routine. It was several years since I had carried any weapon on a daily basis, and felt that maybe Hudson was right with his 'practice makes perfect' routines.

So, when I had taken what was to be my rifle from the corporal working in the stores, Hudson suddenly took it back off me and quickly dismantling it and reassembling with noisy movements, he nodded with a look of satisfaction, as he handed it to me.

"Is something wrong?" I asked.

"I worry about the M4; I wish we had the British SA50, or the L86, either will suit me. We've had several incidents recently," he said and I weighed it in my hand carefully before with a cheeky grin on my face, I repeated the dismantling and reassembling. Hudson looked surprised and I laughed out loud.

"Top of the class, when it came to firearms," I boasted.

Now it was Hudson who laughed, and apologised for forgetting I might have been a big game hunter or had a military career, in a previous life. He looked embarrassed and suggested that maybe I'd done National Service.

"No, Hudson, you are right, it was a long time ago and things change all the time."

I went quiet and handed the American M4 Carbine back to the man behind the counter, saying, "I think not. Well, not for tomorrow's outing, maybe later."

Hudson grinned and said, "Yer gonna be okay t'morrow, sir. I'll have my weapon, but I still think you should sign for it, I do think it best if you carry it."
I paused and said, "Okay, you win."
"Great, it's all good!"

"Well, shouldn't think I'd have to use it; it's not as if we were heading to Combat Outpost Margah," I said under my breath.

"So you've heard about Margah?" Hudson asked with a solemn face and a look that asked if I truly knew about that battle.

"You bet!" I said and nodded my head as an affirmative.

"Thank God!" said the young Hudson and I knew he was as much aware of the fighting that went on there as I was; it being extensively reported.

Chapter Thirteen
A Village in Helmand Province Friday 0800 hours

It was eight o'clock on the Friday when we left the base, as the tail end Charlie of a column of vehicles setting off for other areas or what I now acknowledge as FOB's. I was learning fast.

They were no more than twenty feet away from me and I could see everything, I could read them like the proverbial book, such was their body language. Williams was standing as erect as he could with the weight of his full body armour, and his webbing loaded with pouches of gear and bottles of drinking water two were even sticking out of a bag hanging from his webbing. His hands, holding a plastic file of documents, were not free to hold his rifle. This was slung over his shoulders, to sit in an ungainly manner across the top of his loaded backpack, the stock and the barrel sticking out either side of his head. His face was covered by dark glasses, as well as a piece of cloth to keep the swirling dust out of his mouth and nose, and with his helmet sitting low over his forehead, the chin strap hanging down, his personal PRR set over his right ear, causing the helmet to be at a jaunty angle, with the NVG turned up, there was no way I could see his face. But it was Guy Williams, alright. The total effect was one of height and power, when contrasted with the miniature frame that was Alice Holford.

I knew just by their face to face position, standing so close, the tilt of his covered head towards her pretty face, and hers lifted with a smile any man would be ready to die for, that here was a young couple in love. You didn't need to be an expert in body language to know what was going on; I almost envied him, she was so beautiful.

On that day, the one when I first saw Lieutenant Guy Williams, he was directing his platoon to muster and form up behind a long column of military vehicles, about to leave Camp Bastion. His section, the 'tail-end Charlie' group comprised five vehicles and Hudson; my American driver had placed us behind Williams's group of Lancashire Fusiliers. Suddenly a tall Staff Sergeant walked up to Williams and spoke with him, before they both turned to look at us sitting in our American 4x4 Cougar, at the end of the entire column. The Staff Sergeant headed for us; he being British obviously forgot that we were in a left hand drive vehicle, because he came and stood as if to speak with me. Looking carefully at me, he surprised me with his command.

"The Lieutenant would like you to move up two places," and then he looked across at Hudson and said,

"Move back and out and I'll get these two Jackals to let you in, OK, mate?"

Hudson, a Marine, answered with a sharp, "Oorah!" and started up the engine, and I watched as the Staff Sergeant moved away to organise the two British Jackal reconnaissance vehicles in front of us to reverse and give us space. The manoeuvre completed, I saw Williams mount the front 6x6 Cougar and with the staff Sergeant taking a standing position behind a 12.7 heavy machine gun, I felt fractionally safer. We were ready for the off and I watched with interest as Alice stood to one side and waved to Williams. If their forbidden love was so obvious to me, I was certain others would be aware of it; how long, I asked myself, before it would cause trouble for him and for his sweetheart, if they were so obvious about it, in front of his platoon?

"That guy who told his Staff Sergeant to tell us to move, well he's the f**ing famous Lieutenant Williams."

I countered with, "Oh, why famous?" as I tried to ignore the sudden introduction of the 'f' word.

"He rescued some poor mother f**ing bugger that would have died, if the f**ing Lieutenant hadn't gone in and f**ing carried him out. His men respect him, f**ing believe me they do."
I was getting used to the language of the boys on the frontline.

How long before I would begin to swear in unison with them seemed a pointless worry. Out here the colourful language of the squaddie was a safety valve for the boiling point of stress and fear that was their daily lives. In fact I had almost ceased to notice it, but every time we went off base, Hudson's use of colourful expletives made an appearance. I decided it was his security blanket when fear doesn't want to be acknowledged, but is being felt deep in the gut of the dutiful man.

So, I merely nodded in approval at the thought of the man's bravery and watched Hudson close up and secure our transport, before we walked off into the village, behind the Lieutenant's platoon.

The village we were visiting was a collection of mud-coloured single storey buildings created as compounds with a carpet of dull greenery surrounding the perimeter of each one. In the centre of the village a larger compound with a single entry point of cargo-sized double gates was obviously the chief residence for the senior man. But who was he? Everyone was identically dressed in neutral rather colourless clothing and wearing enormous turbans created from the winding of long lengths of fabric around the head, yes, that was what I noticed first. They all wanted to blend in; to avoid attracting the attention of snipers. If there were important people about, at that moment, I was uncertain as to how to distinguish one from another. If the size and shape of their head gear denoted rank, I was yet to discover.

We met up with different villagers and spent time walking through a modest sized bazaar with their market stalls, such as they were, often set up in doorways; rather than out in the open. I played the journalist and took snaps and made notes. Children ran up to me, seemingly wanting to have their photographs taken. Others peered at my notebook as if wanting to read what I had written.

Hudson was adamant, he told me to be careful of even the smallest children. They were fearless and would play happily with you, but many a soldier had been stabbed in the back by an older child, as he knelt to play with the toddlers.

"F**ing mean it, sir! Stay standing, sir!" was his advice. "If you must squat down, make sure you are against a wall and fuck me, don't let one of them get f**ing behind you. Mean it, sir, even the kids are good with f**ing knives."

For a moment Hudson looked embarrassed as more children ran up. Looking about at these grubby-faced smiling urchins, it seemed impossible to believe that they posed a threat, but they were all part and parcel of the cruelty that exists in a war zone. Born into this war, they lived with no idea of peace. My mind was almost hurting with the realization that no matter what I was to find here in Afghanistan, the children were to be forever impressed upon my mind. Their cheeky grins in grimy faces, their tears leaving muddy grooves down their cheeks, those with sullen looks, and those too young to know that hatred was already implanted in their eyes. Even as I looked about at the topography, smelt the dust and saw the weariness on the old men's faces and felt even more a personal deep seated hatred of war; I knew that the lack of proper schooling, the bomb-damaged housing, the difficulty of accessing medical care and the harshness of the climate all added to the awareness of how tough these children had to be to survive at all. Hudson still had an uncomfortable blush on his cheeks, as he said rather shame-faced,

"I shouldn't f**ing swear in front of the kids, should I, sir?"

"Don't worry, Hudson, do they speak English?"

"Very little, sir, except for some single words; like sweets or dollars. Some of the boys say the names of f**ing footballers."

"Then don't worry about it. It doesn't bother me."

"Thanks, sir! Yes, would you believe it, they know f**ing footballers."

Watching Guy Williams and his troops going about their business in a calm and respectful manner, it struck me that just as I found the American soldiers somewhat taller and seemingly overpowering, so too the Afghans must feel the same about the powerfully built British squaddies. It all added to my sense of unreality; then there was the problem in hand; how on earth was I ever to get to the information I needed?

I could not speak the language.

Apart from observing the strange ratio of men to women, looking around the village, there was the growing sense of familiarity, brought on by realising the comparison to village life, back home. The men sitting at the gates, the women working in the background: was it any different to that of Proverbs C 31? Life is timeless and needs are universal and once again I felt the truth, that the world is no more than a village, set against the vastness of time and the infinity of space. The old men seated along a wall, were they any different from the old guys sitting on the garden benches outside The Bells of Peover? Were their needs any different? Old men need food, drink, home comforts and friendship; young children need the same. But children the world over need education, there lies the difference between my world and theirs. Education! My mind queried the need to submit them to all our western principles, except that I felt for the invisible women of Afghanistan.

Hudson walked away towards a stall set up near the front of a compound, as I watched him I saw Norcross stride up to him and begin a heated conversation with a great deal of gesticulating that ended with Norcross grabbing at the front of Hudson's jacket. Even as I walked towards them, trying to look nonchalant, I witnessed Lewis, Hughes and Johnstone racing across to grab hold of Norcross. They pulled Norcross away from the area by the stall and were aggressively berating him about his behaviour, just as I came up to Hudson and demanded to know what was going on.

"Norcross believes that he alone has the right to her!"

"Who?" and even as I said it, I knew what his answer would be; there was only one woman in all of Helmand who could possibly get a man so riled up. And he said her name!

"Alice! Sorry, sir, but I love her. Nothing I can do, sir, nothing, it's the general order."

"The general what, who; what are you talking about?"

"General Order Number one, sir! Can't touch a girl, not even if you are married to her," Hudson chimed in on the conversation.

"You've got me, Hud, what are you talking about?"

"It's the number one rule. Courting is out while on the camp."

"Courting, you still call it courting, going after a girl. Bit old fashioned, isn't it?"

"Not where I come from, sir! If I was at home I would address her as Miss Alice. Not like this lot who call her Alice as if she's available to any old dick. We have very strict rules where I come from."

"I see, and are you suggesting Norcross has an advantage over you?"

"Yes, sir, he isn't an American for a start and maybe the rule doesn't apply to him."

Turning, I watched the three English soldiers still arguing with Norcross.

"I'm not so sure of that, Hudson. I image it applies to all armies in war zones."

Hudson and I stood listening to the angry voices. Interestingly I could not help noticing that their choicest swearing contained more 'bloody' and 'bleeding' vulgarities, as well as the damn, blasts and the occasional bollocks! It ended with Hudson and me standing only feet away from the British men, amazed at the sudden vulgarity from Gareth Hughes stating,

"Private First Class Alice Holford is bleeding well off bounds to you, Andy, you f**ing clump of an idiot. He can't have her, neither can you! It's no sex please; we are all bloody soldiers, Yanks or bleeding Brits, savvy! Put yer itchy bloody balls back in yer pants and leave that guy alone, he can't touch her any more than you bleeding well can."

Turning, Hughes saw me and as he took his helmet off to wipe his forehead, I could swear there was a faint blush of embarrassment; he smiled at me. I looked back into a genuinely pleasant face that had clear blue eyes and a smile that reached them. I like it when the smile reaches the eyes; it tells you something about the person and today I hoped I was right in my judgement of this soldier.

"I'll keep them apart, sir, no need to worry," Hughes said, and I nodded and turned away, putting a hand on Hudson and propelling him back to the market stalls. Hudson nodded in a rather defeated way; he knew it was more than his life was worth to cause a fight. He went back to his shopping while I walked to the very edge of the village, to where a younger man was crouching half hidden by a bush. He was cradling an enormous piece of hardware and without looking up at me, he spoke.

"I'm ready for them."

This threw me a bit, until I realised my clumsy footsteps upon the dusty shingles had given away my presence, long before I came up to stand behind him. Then I noticed my shadow lying on the ground alongside him, it clearly indicated the shape of the helmet I was wearing. He would know I was not an Afghan, hence the English.
But the English was perfect, the dress Afghan, but the weaponry British.

"Sorry I don't know any Afghan, but you speak English, so may I speak with you a moment?"

"Ten years living with yer, I get good! Since I was eight, I speak with Brits. I learn. My father is him, over there, I can translate, and he likes that. I tell him what yer say and even more when I think yer lying."

"Oh, I don't lie!"

"You speak excellent English for a Yank," he said to me as if he were some junior officer.

"You're not so bad yourself. Who taught you?"

"Only speak with English officers, don't like Yankee voices. Not understand other soldiers; like him, that tall one there, he's odd."

"Hudson is my driver. He's from New Orleans."

"Yeah, so he's an f**ing Yank then, just like I said."

Listening to the young man's voice I could hear so many layers of pronunciation that I was puzzled, so I plunged in, head first so to speak.

"People everywhere sound different, but you don't sound like an Afghan; actually you sound like an Englishman!"

I said this because he sounded like a cross between an English public school boy and everybody's idea of a Hollywood version of the boy from Jungle Book. I queried,

"Do I not sound OK to you?"

"Sure, you sound posh, I thought you were English, but looking at you, you're dressed as a Yank."

I looked at the young fighter; it was believable that he was no more than eighteen. He was so slight, that he looked as if a puff of wind could bowl him over, yet his face had a hardness that spoke of war.

"I'm looking to hire an interpreter; you interested?"

At that the eyes squinted up at me and the silence spoke louder than you could ever imagine. As his eyes opened to stare into mine, I knew I was being assessed, judged as never before. Young as he was, his scrutiny of me revealed how important his safety and the safety of his family, and his village, were to him.

"My name is..."

He paused and spinning his head around to look out into the territory surrounding the village, and simultaneously holding up his left hand to silence me, he swiftly locked his eyes on some bushes about two hundred metres away.

I saw nothing.

I heard the rapid fire he gave and dropping to the ground, I kept my eyes on that bush, as two men leapt up firing automatic machine weapons back at my young companion.

He killed both of them.

Satisfying himself that there were no further assailants nearby, he lowered his weapon before sitting up, and turning towards me, he spoke as if nothing had happened. No juvenile glib comment; just an adult voice in continuation of our disturbed conversation.

"What is your name, sir?" In the crispness of his question, he sounded like a senior commander, rather than a young village boy.

"How about you call me Matt, or Matthew if you prefer?"

"Fine, Matt, I'm Ramin."

"Ramin, good, I'll remember that."

I looked back at him as he nodded his head in approval before speaking; but I knew he was listening to the quiet noises that came in from the world outside his village. It was an amazing vigilance and yet I felt sad that this boy had to be without the joys of youth; he was a man before his time.

"This work, it is paid?"

"Yes, and it will only be for a few weeks, twelve at the most."

Ramin's face told me that he didn't need to think about it, it was a job and he could do it.

"Yer wear Yankee clothes, but definitely British then, I don't work for the Yanks?"

"Yes, I'm a journalist of sorts, not a soldier."

"Why that?"

He pointed to the USA motifs and the uniform, so obviously American rather than British in origin.

"Do you understand what I mean by undercover?"

"Sure, I'm also undercover."

"No, I don't mean hiding under bushes, I mean..."

"Wearing the enemy's uniform. I know!"

"Ah! So you do understand."

"Yeah, I go undercover when I leave the village. Sometime I dress as a fighter, sometime a farmer, one time I played madness. That was to a stupid Yank who was mouthing off at my dad; but it got us through the checkpoint on the border. I played up so much they never checked the baggage on our camel."

I looked at him and heard the teenager in his voice, even as he stood up, trying to stand as tall as myself. No chance; he was no taller than five foot five and so thin he looked half starved.

"Come, I show yer my father."

"Thanks," I said with a solemn voice, knowing he was trying to be older than his years.

We walked back into the village, and at the large gates to one of the mud-encrusted compounds, we found Ramin's father speaking with Lieutenant Williams, in a somewhat heated three way exchange, with the Afghan interpreter helping. Ramin stood respectfully and listened into the conversation, while I became fascinated by the lush green grass and the activity I could see in the centre of the compound. There was a domesticity that was so universally akin to life in Peover, my village back home, that I nearly choked. There was washing drying, there were children playing and there was a veiled granny sitting minding the baby, while a mother swept the floor. When Mohammed turned to look at me, his eyes shone with pride and his smile told me he had registered my acceptance of his home and family. Nodding his head in approval, he gestured Ramin to come forward and I think he was asking Ramin to interpret for us. Thus I found myself in a conversation with Mohammed as I progressed to a modest understanding of the economics of Afghan life; I could see his problems, but I knew he would never be able to understand mine.

To me the poppy is dangerous; to him it was the means of feeding his family, which extended like blood in the human body, to every extremity of the organization that was his village. All who lived within its boundary were his responsibility. Looking around at the dry dusty world his village was housed in, who could blame him when growing the poppy was less stressful as it used less water and made more profit? There was a saying, 'Half the water for twenty times the profit!'

I asked myself, if my children were hungry what would I choose?

Then I saw his eyes looking over to where Lieutenant Guy Williams was now talking with a young woman who had removed her veil, and her face was clearly visible. She was gesticulating anxiously before handing Williams a piece of paper. Suddenly an elderly man dressed all in black except for a white turban reached out and grabbed the paper from Williams. The girl rapidly covered her face with her hijab as she tried to run away. Too late the man with the white turban had her arm in a vicelike grip, as with his right hand still holding her note, the man hit the girl violently across her back as he led her away. The noise of his heavy hand upon the frailty of the girl, who looked no more than fourteen, was there for all to hear. Her cries were pitiful.

I heard Ramin cry out, "Wasima!"

heard her cry out, "Ramin!"

I turned to look at Mohammed; he was almost smiling as he nodded his approval. I felt my heart turn to stone as I watched the girl being dragged into the compound behind him, the beating she took would have floored a grown man. Her cries were heard by all the people around yet none of us moved to help her. Then I saw her pushed behind a door, which was then barricaded with an iron bar. Suddenly, I felt a cold hand grip my heart and the illusion of universality was shattered; this was not like any village in Cheshire.

Maybe I should have felt a twinge of understanding and sympathy for his burden; presumably he was anxious about the girl's purity, but it seemed a bit excessive to lock her up. My head questioned how all of us had just remained silent: why did we not stop the beating of a girl no more than fourteen? All the girl was doing was taking to the Lieutenant, what was wrong with that?

I turned to speak to Ramin, thinking we could arrange to meet up soon, when I was silenced by his blazing eyes, so full of anger and hatred, his whole body tense with the violence of the emotion he was feeling. Turning his head, Mohammed saw the anger and shouted at Ramin.

Not even an Olympic runner could have fled the scene as fast as Ramin ran out of that village. He was still running when Hudson drove us past him, I had seen enough and wanted to get back and write up what I had witnessed. Hudson drove on in silence until he suddenly spoke and I realised he was giving voice to my own feelings.

"They treat girls and women worse that they do their dogs, and we just have to stand there and say nothing."

Her name, Wasima, was burning a guilty mark into my conscience, I would not have stood by if that had happened back home.

I silently said, "Forgive me, Wasima."

Chapter Fourteen
Later the same day

For a couple of hours, I lay on my bunk bed and marvelled at the very feeling of anger that was pounding at my mind. I knew it had nothing to do with the task in hand; rather it was that feeling of being removed from the normality of my home life. I don't care what you call the condition; I call it frustration and anger. On the one hand I had witnessed the most violent treatment of a girl so small and fragile; on the other the sight of the most beautiful girl in Camp Leatherneck exposing herself to the threat of military discipline, because she was in love.

What was wrong with me? There was a laughing Alice Holford not helping; I realised that I had succumbed as badly as the rest of them. In the midst of so much dull dusty life, she stood out like a flame burning, warming and lighting up the darkness all around her. Just watching other men looking at her, you could not fail to interpret their longing for her very softness to be focussed upon them. Shit, it hurt! For the first time in my life I was truly missing my wife and longed for all she embodied as my lover and confidant at the end of each day. Middle age was hard; no wonder so many fail to get through it without succumbing to drink, drugs, or other women.

Later, the evening meal was an extraordinary experience. I arrived at the D-FAC, showed my ID pass and signed in. Grateful that I did not need any cash, waiting my turn at the busy queue, I took the opportunity to really look about for the first time. Three days and at last I was beginning to feel familiar with the place and the routines surrounding it. Once inside the facility, you were confronted by the entire visible cooking section, all gleaming stainless steel and full of cooks and the wondrous warm comforting smells of hot steaming food. The whole structure seemed more solidly built than the rest of the camp; only Bastion Hospital was more rigidly structured. Here it was all a sign of the apparent importance of the kitchen; obviously an army likes to march on its stomach. The food heaped up as in any works cafeteria was basic and plentiful. The smells, the clattering of trays full of food being added to the hotplates, the silence that seemed to come from the men queuing, all added to the unreality that had been bearing down upon me, ever since we had arrived back from the village. I must begin to feel at home here or I would not survive.

Hudson had disappeared and as I reached out to pick up a plate, I felt Alice's hand collide with mine. The physical shock was ridiculously real; that sense of pleasure that flared up in my brain had lasted only a moment, then it had disappeared again. Was I to hope for her companionship, as I ate my meal?

"Had a good day, Matt?"

Her voice had sounded flat, almost unemotional. Had she had a bad day? How to lift her spirits? I tried keeping my voice light and comforting.

"Hopefully as good if not better than yours; I now have an Afghan interpreter, so I'm feeling positive."

I reached for a helping of bread and butter just as a civilian catering assistant piled meat and two veg onto my polystyrene plate.

Looking down at the end result, I felt all sense of a possible cosy rapprochement fade away. It was all so mundane; there is no glamour in disposable plates and plastic cutlery, I assure you. What was it about war, that contrary to Hollywood's take on the sex life of soldiers in a war zone, I was fast becoming aware that the men all around me were more akin to 'A Band of Brothers' than any portrayed in the jollity of a sex-starved Hollywood South Pacific musical? Maybe only the navy had time for the pursuit of the female, the joke being there actually was a dame in a skirt in every port!

I waited a moment for Alice to collect her cold drink before we moved off together, to sit away from other people, people who might talk and spoil my chance to chat with Alice; because Alice had chosen the spot, I believed there was a modicum of a hope that she would enjoy a conversation with me, as we relaxed over our meal.

But no!

She ate, she sighed, and she was silent.

I ate; I cleared my plate of every last crumb in my frustration and then I sat back watching her. Eventually, Alice put down her cutlery and said with a beatific smile,

"God knows I needed that. Sorry, I missed lunch and tea and was starving."

"I gathered that much."

If I sounded sarcastic, I was immediately sorry.

"What was so bad, your boss, the weather, bad news?"

I knew I had ruined it for myself, not because I was hoping to flirtatiously pursue her like some groin-aching teenager; no, I had convinced myself that I liked female company and was seriously missing my wife. Our evening meal was always a time of pleasant conversation, even when we were discussing some of the distressing news that invaded the peace of our home, we managed to enjoy and appreciate each other's opinions. Was I deluding myself?

Still not looking at me, Alice suddenly shook herself, as if coming out of a private space. She said,

"Thanks, OK, I suppose. Well, what was your day like? How exciting, an interpreter?" So she had heard and noted my statement in the queue at the servery counter. I chided myself, as I realized she had been too distressed by a gnawing hunger to be sociable.

Be kind now, was uppermost in my thoughts as I said,

"Yes, a young man called Ramin. Do you know him?"

"We all know Ramin; a devious bastard, even though we've supposedly met his father. Don't look at me like that, he's wild and a crack shot and claims half the old men in Afghanistan as his father. I kind of think of him as the 'Artful Dodger' or whatever."

"Talk about bursting my bubble. Thanks very much, Alice! I've just worked out an hourly rate for the hiring of this evil character. What do I do now?"

"Oh, don't worry, he'll do you proud, so long as he is paid well and you boost his ego every now and then. Not too much, mind, just once a day will do."

"Hoo-rah, mon captaine, Alice!" I said teasingly, as she asked,

"Coming for a walk?" My spirits lifted at her invitation, and I eagerly helped clear our dirty things to the dumb waiter by the door.

We left, and strolled out towards the perimeter wall. It was dark and there was suddenly a surprising coolness in the air, as we walked in silence, until she spoke quietly, as if afraid of eavesdroppers.

"I've arranged for Guy to join us. Thought you two could make use of the distance from Bastion One; it would be less public here. Don't look so surprised, there is more than one Bastion, they were marked on the map you were given. It just happened as they were developed several years apart, and the place is

so vast it makes it easier, like having different boroughs, like Queens and Manhattan!"
She looked worried as she added,

"He said he'd be here by now."

I looked about as if querying her; I hadn't been seriously listening, not to her, but to the growing noise all around us. I regarded at her with puzzlement, what had she arranged, and who were we to meet?

Her face caught in the arc lights was still and thoughtful as we watched the flashing beams swirling down from yet another helicopter. Swooping low over our heads, coming into land, its blades making that defining *whoop, whoop, whoop* noise, as if cutting through solid slices of air. The noise was ear-splitting, the downdraft creating a painful dust storm, and both of us tried to cover our eyes and ears with our hands. I felt the grit hit the side of my face and it stung enough to make me wince in pain. It must have hurt Alice even though she had pulled her jacket over her head; her bare hands were exposed.

We stayed silent and just waited, I wasn't certain why, was she running out of conversation or just listening out for the arrival of Guy Williams? Four helicopters later we heard MERT ambulances in the distance followed by a silence that had an eerie atmosphere. Then Alice took the two way radio she had hanging from her webbing; I heard the voice announce that 'Op Minimiser' was in place, I heard nothing more of her conversation; I felt sick at the news.

She turned to me, as she said,

"It's two of yours, I think."

Now I really did feel ghastly. Three days at Camp Bastion and already three young soldiers from back home were dead and soon to be repatriated. I could not speak, memories of Bert sitting beside me on that RAF C130 came crashing back; the vision of young soldiers carrying coffins draped in the Union Flag seemed unbearable. This was where it all began, but it wasn't where it ended; I thought of families weeping at endless funerals and trying to put on brave and dignified faces, while their hearts bled with pain. That wasn't all, no, my heart, my mind thought of all those lost to the evil growing in the fields beyond this wall. They too have parents, children, siblings and friends who grieve when loved ones die, because of the wrong use of the opium poppy. I knew why I had years ago opted for the Drug Squad, at last I had a chance to do something about the anger I felt about the malevolence it spread throughout society.

"Did you get my message about the weekend?" Alice suddenly asked.

"Thanks, yes, I think it's a great idea, it'll be very helpful, and I need to see the southern end of Helmand." I said, realising that she had organised the weekend off for herself and needed to know I had something to occupy me. If I felt my heart groan, my mind accepted that the idea of a visit to that particular FOB was going to be interesting, it took me into the heart of the country for photos vis-à-vis pipelines and drug running. *Good one, Alice,* my mind said, realising that she probably wouldn't be coming with me.

Whatever was going on with Alice, I realised something was troubling her. She had been odd throughout the evening, and now she looked troubled and nothing like the sunny woman who had met me on Tuesday. Alice stood silently at my side, I let myself believe she felt the sadness consuming me and I was glad; it was impossible to speak when there was so much going on inside my head.

Eventually I asked, "You say Ramin can't be trusted?"

"No, he cannot, so be careful, pay him well, but he is little more than a thief, and he's known to have killed people on both sides of the Afghan fence. He probably killed his famous father, as well as there being a strong possibility of his killing at least one of ours and several of yours."

"Does he trust any of us?"

"No, he does not trust anyone, only himself and your Brigadier Clitheroe."

"I take it Clitheroe's been out here several times and is responsible for Ramin's excellent English pronunciation," I said quietly.

"Yes, I'm told it started the first time Clitheroe was here, he was young, very much as Guy is now, he seemed marvellous with the unruly boy, apparently Ramin wasn't even ten years old, but he could shoot to kill. At the time he so admired the then Lieutenant Clitheroe, that he was mimicking his voice and was persuaded by him to go to school."

"So, that's how he can now read?" I speculated.

"And write some English. He's quite brainy if the truth be told; it is just a question of what does he do with knowledge that is so foreign to those who live with him. What we call education some would call an evil proselytizing of the mind and heart."

I thought about the variety of education that was denied to the children in many Afghan schools. Then Alice continued with,

"There are other incidents of soldiers befriending children that have proved useful; but where Ramin is concerned, well, he remains a threat because he is brainy enough to be duplicitous at the best of times. Only Brigadier Clitheroe knows him well enough to know when the truth is being twisted to suit Ramin. Use him, but know what he is, savvy?"

"Savvy! Is Clitheroe around these days?

"Unfortunately not at the moment, he's not due back for several months. He's tied up with closing some of the Brits' German bases. You will have to make do with Williams for now."

At that moment Guy Williams drove round the corner still dressed in his full combat gear and even in the gloom of the night you could see his weariness.

Hudson and I had driven back hours earlier; Lieutenant Williams had just returned. I marvelled at his stamina, he had been off base for thirteen hours.

Alice seemed to fade into the night, as Guy literally jumped down from his jeep, and walked up to me holding out a hand in greeting. I shook it and tried to smile, but I could see his exhaustion, even with the caked dirt all over his face and much of his dusty uniform. He still had his helmet on his head, with the NVD tipped up away from his eyes and the chin strap hung down in front of him. His weapon was slung across his back, he looked like a soldier and yet he seemed to suddenly sag, as he came to a stop in front of me.

"Lieutenant, you should be hitting the sack. Have you only now got back? What happened?"

"Fine, I'll be fine, a couple of hours kip and I'll be fine, sir. That was one of ours. Landmine wrote off a vehicle. I had to stay with them, duty of care! Two are dead, ISAF men. Three injured, one's an alpha injury, sir."

"ISAF men, which ...?"

He seemed unable to speak for some moments; his stillness seemed to exaggerate his sadness, in a manner I had never seen before, in so active a young man.

"Dutch soldiers, they were in front of us, took the full blast, we were tipped over, only one seriously injured, I think it's spinal."

Looking at him in the half-light coming from the floodlights behind the wall of containers, I placed him as possibly no more than twenty-four; but you couldn't tell when a face was that tired it looked almost bloodless, beneath the dirt of battle. Suddenly he turned and walked away from me. He climbed into the driving seat of his jeep and indicated I should join him. He drove us back to the D-FAC. Jumping down he headed for the entrance, checking his weapon into the safety box, before slinging it over his shoulder and letting it settle muzzle downwards across his back. I followed in silence, listening to the noise beneath our feet as our boots continued to scrunch their way back into the Leatherneck D-FAC. By the time we were settled with coffee and he had an enormous Dagwood sandwich in front of him, his face had regained some of its liveliness and his eyes seemed less fixed in that look of quiet despair that is a characteristic of over-fatigue. This was our first face to face meeting, I knew more about him, but what did he know or understand about my mission?

"My name is Matt Fleming and I'm here as a military journalist. I'm actually from Cheshire."

The look he gave back to me over the top of the paper mug of hot sweet coffee that he was devouring with such pleasure, made me laugh. He put the mug down and took a mouthful of his sandwich, and then even as he chewed his food he suddenly said,

"Yeah, I know what you really are; let's not pretend! You're the investigator from Intelligence services and you are here to help find the traitor in our midst! Is complaining about a situation now a capital offence? Sounds like a mediaeval plot to overthrow the Commander-in-Chief, if you ask me. All I wanted, all I asked my boss for, was some advice as to what I should do with a group of men I was unsure of! Oh, and I just happened to mention that we seemed to be short of rescue helos; had to wait nearly an hour when I had a man down, and we were only a fifteen minute flight time from Bastion! It is turning into a can of worms. It was the same just now, heading home, roadside bomb, no helo for fifty five minutes, no way would a man survive, the golden hour is like an imperative. What next?"

His voice and attitude changed when, after spending a few moments deep breathing and sighing loudly, as if trying to find the strength to be nice to me, he said,

"I got the communique about you yesterday and made contact with Alice. I recognised you this morning from your photo, by the way. Alice's our go-between if you are stuck over anything."

Guy seemed puzzled about something and I elected to keep quiet.

But suddenly he said,

"I thought they would have sent a younger person."

"Thanks for nothing; I haven't come here to fight!"

"Yeah, yeah, sorry, a bit rude of me; I've no idea what it is you intend doing, but I gather you've managed to get young Ramin on board. Good work, sir." He shrugged his shoulders, I asked,

"Is it? I hear he is a thief and a killer."

"We're all killers one way or another. The trick is to only kill your enemy. Our trouble begins with, who is my enemy? The Taliban are the most devious fighters, they blend in and we just can't see them."

"It's their religion, surely?" I replied.

"Matt, if I may call you Matt? Sorry, I'm not always so rude."

I shook my head as if brushing aside any feeling of annoyance at him; I realized how tired he must be after his long day outside the security of Bastion. I smiled when he said,

"What a funny sort of religion, I mean they don't educate themselves or their women, whom they beat violently at the drop of a hat. Wasima, did you see what happened today? She had no chance to explain, they don't give justice a chance where women are concerned. What makes then believe that twenty-seven virgins are available when you die, provided you've killed somebody on the way up to heaven! Ple-e-e-ease! It's not just the women who are uneducated; I think the men need teaching."

"But at the end of a gun?" I almost whispered, but he came back at me quite loudly, as if he was annoyed at my comment.

"That's all they understand! Shoot first or be killed. Most of the Taliban have never been in a classroom, have little idea of military discipline, treat women worse than you'd treat a cow and kill even their own kids if they get in the way. What else can we do?"

I kept calm and eventually said,

"True, so we educate them."

"How do we do that?"

He looked at me as he took another mouthful of sandwich and then swigged the remaining half his coffee in one go, before letting out a long drawn out sigh that signified a feeling of normality was slowly returning, after the stress of the day. If his spine sagged a little more, who could blame him? I lowered my voice and looking about me, realising that we were fairly isolated inside that enormous American cookhouse tent, I asked,

"Are we okay meeting here? I mean..."

"It's fine, you're supposedly a Yank in sheep's clothing and I'm your guest, you signed me in, so nobody will query my being here."

"So who do you suspect is helping the drug runners?"

"As I said in the report I sent in, there are four possible suspects, all from the Midlands area back home. One from Birmingham, one from Stafford, one from somewhere near Nottingham and the fourth is from Kidderminster. All nice guys, friendly enough with everyone, but no one breaks into their inner sanctum, if you get my meaning? I know... I know they came as a section and I left them set up as a section. Is it my own fault? I had no idea what they would turn out to be, and truthfully one of them is a staff sergeant and is older than me and seems different to everybody in the platoon. He's been useful as a staff and there have been times when I've been grateful for his treatment of some of the younger men. He has a wonderful calmness about him, it makes them feel secure."

"And you don't?"

"Pardon?"

"He is calm; are you the opposite, fussy, noisy, fearful or just unsure of yourself and it shows?"

"No, no, I think I do a reasonable job. But it's that all the other men mix in with others in the troop and somehow they all share off-duty time together, but not these four. Somehow they are obviously a closed shop in terms of who they are and what they are doing. You have to accept them as a foursome, not as individuals. Other men have tried to invite one or other of them to join in a run or a footie kick about, but they don't budge from their foursome. I twice got some resistance when I tried to split them up, when we were on a patrol just in the past few days, and it makes me suspicious of them. Somehow they don't seem to work well as individuals, I've never succeeded in driving a wedge between them. Oh, I don't quite mean that. I don't mean that!"

He shook his head as if trying to clear his thoughts.

"You have to keep section loyalty safe, but I just mean if I asked one of them to help me, he always looks round for one of the others. It seems a bit childish, I suppose? Perhaps I'm the one being childish. They're never rude to me, just excuses that seem farfetched and a bit ridiculous, but never obviously disloyal to Queen and Country. Front line every time, so long as they are together. What to make of them? It bothers me."

"Did they join up at the same time, same age, are they gay?" I asked, continuing the deception expected of my undercover role.

"None of the above, Gareth is older than me. The other three are about my age, twenty four. Gareth seems to be the ringleader; he's the one from Birmingham. He's a nice guy; I can't understand why he didn't go for officer training. I know he had a grammar school education. Yes, he seems to me to be more than a kid from the backstreets of Birmingham."

"Birmingham is a large place. People say Birmingham as if it is a generic name. He's white, she's black, so what! They do the same with the likes of London or Manchester. Where are you from?"

"London."

"But, where in London?"

"Boston Manor."

"Never heard of it."

"It's west London, on the way into Heathrow."

"See what I mean. We can't say Birmingham where this Gareth is concerned. People say Birmingham when they mean Solihull. Chalk and cheese, Birmingham and Solihull! Perhaps Alice could help us."

Why I said that, I'll never know. He flashed his eyes up to look hard into mine, as he slowly said, "Alice is a very busy person, Matt. You do realise that she is the female equivalent of the old fashioned army batman." Then he seemed to relax as he said,

"I laugh at her and call her Batwoman."

"That's a cool code for us to use. Her boss described her as his gofer, but he's lent her to me for the duration of my stay."

"Is that what he said? That means that she has to fit you in; because he'll still have her running here, there and everywhere, morning, noon and night! He's an old so-and-so and McNaughton's worse."

"McNaughton?"

"Captain Gwen McNaughton, in charge of females deployed to Leatherneck. Alice's terrified of her; probably with good cause!"

"And there was my driver's set-to today with the one he calls Norcross?"

"Yes, that and a few thousand others!"

"But not you?"

"Not me…" His voice faded away, until he said,

"I think what happened to Wasima is more important. They beat her, you know."

In his tiredness, it was obvious that Guy was repeating himself. His mind was still distressed by events witnessed that day, so I played along.

"You mean the girl who tried to give you a note, the girl the man hit and dragged into the compound?"

"Ramin's love, he wants to marry her, she was promised to him when she was six, but Mohammed has gone and married her."

"What?" I almost screamed out in horror.

"I thought the older woman inside, the one hanging out washing, was Mohammed's wife."

"You'll learn!"

"I'm shocked; he must be sixty if he's a day."

"And probably more, welcome to Afghanistan. Ramin is heartbroken about what happened today, he says Wasima has been beaten and her father sent for, and he could be worse, he's a brute if ever there was one. I'm told he beheaded his wife and beat up his younger daughter. He sold Wasima to pay for a debt. They do that to girls. It is as if the girls are no more than sex slaves, obeying or be murdered."

"Nice people!" I said with a cutting edge to my voice. He noticed that and felt obliged to add,

"They are tribal leaders, not necessarily Taliban, and some of them are worse than Taliban and others are simply the loveliest people you could wish to meet. You'll see them here at the market."

I nodded and smiled as if to say I understood he was trying to be fair minded about the locals. Looking at his tired face and feeling my own aching bones and horrified mind, I made a move to stand and clear our things to the dumb waiter by the kitchen doors. Guy followed me and soon we made our way towards my billet.

As he drove, I had to ask, "How's the young man who got blown up the other day?"

"He'll be flown home sometime tonight."

"That's quick," I said, for want of something to say,

"They don't hang about, but Jones was lucky we didn't have to hang about waiting for a bird; one was with us in no time."

"Everything seems to come down to speed; at least from what I understand."

"Speed equals available helicopters, as far as I understand," he said with bitterness in his tone.

"And doctors and nurses, surely?"

"Yes, but you have to get to the doctors and nurses. That takes birds, and even the birds have to be protected! The Taliban love it when a soldier is blown up; they sit tight, you think they aren't there, wrong! Helicopters make better targets, they are big, so then they start firing on the helicopter they can't miss. It's big enough for them to do at least some damage, enough to keep it out of service for a while. Solution, you can't send out a solo bird, the big bird needs watching up above; like having an eagle watching your back, ready to swoop and kill."

My next comment, "Two helicopters to save a life is an expensive exercise," seemed to change Guy's mood yet again.

"And the public moan about the cost of the war, when the heaviest cost is a man's life."

I felt his anger, and frustration. As we stopped outside my billet I tried to sound sympathetic. "Is war worth any man's life?"

"Not when the Taliban have the cheapest weapon since the crossbow." he countered before pulling a grimacing face and shrugging his shoulders.

"You've lost me," I said, not immediately understanding him.

"Think about it, an IED probably costs less than two pounds; it's even cheaper than a landmine and is just as effective at taking a highly skilled soldier out of our army. Some equations are not in the balance, sir, what price a cappuccino these days?"

We had arrived outside my billet, but I stayed where I was in the front passenger seat, as turning I asked this weary young man,

"Why did you join the army, Guy? What makes you stay in the Army?"

He looked at me long and hard before whispering his heart out to as we sat focussed in the light of an arc light. There was something incredibly sincere in his attitude and in the lowered tones of his well-bred officer accents.

"I was sixteen, the Towers, the 9:11 towers."
There was a long pause as his eyes looked away and seemed to be remembering that horrifying time.

"We lived in Burscough then, do you know it? No? Well it's a village in West Lancashire, my school was Merchant Taylors and I was in the school Cadet Corp. We were all riled up by what had happened, particularly me, all sixteen and ready to go and fight, when the next morning my mother came in with the papers, full of pictures and speculation about the wickedness in the world. She said, *'Son, the wickedness starts with bad education, they have no respect for human rights.'* Well, from then on Human Rights became a topic in our home, Mum and Dad both had set ideas about what was right and what was wrong, and it was Dad who said, *'If you want to fight evil as it exists today, then either become a politician or a soldier.'* I decide on the second option and now looking at what happened to Wasima, maybe I'm pleased that I did make that choice. But, at this moment I feel incredibly angry with myself; I just stood there doing nothing. We all just stood there doing nothing. Am I a coward or was I behaving as the army and the politicians expect of me? There are hundreds of others just like Wasima; in this Province we call Helmand that looks like a Scotland without the beauty of the heather!"

His passion showed through, but I felt he needed to reconsider his role in life and counselled,

"Stop blaming yourself for what's happened today."

"Thanks, but I should have said something, and now Ramin has disappeared again."

"He was angry." I said as I moved to get out of the jeep.

"He loves her. Goodnight, Sir."

I watched him drive towards Bastion until he disappeared through the dividing wall. What I didn't see, was his route which took him behind the British NAAFI and into the arms of the waiting Alice.

Parked in a deep shadow, but with a perfect view of the young lovers, was a darken Humvee with Captain Gwen McNaughton watching and taking photos of them, and muttering, 'I'll get you, Holford!'

In another shadow, Norcross stood, his face screwed up in anger.

Chapter Fifteen
Saturday Morning to FOB Bartkowski

Hudson was hung-over and grey looking, when at five in the morning, I met up with him in the D-FAC. We both opted for a big breakfast, knowing we were unlikely to see any part of Bastion for two days, and unsure what the catering was to be, we ate well. As instructed, we had packed clothes for a forty eight hour mission. Naturally I packed my camera with all its accessories and a notebook; I was mindful of the real reason for my mission.

Looking round at the men silently devouring plates full of cooked food American style; eggs over easy, crispy bacon, sausages, pancakes and maple syrup on the side plates and vast quantities of freshly squeezed orange juice, I sensed that they were the bulk of the team we were to travel with, on this the first Saturday of my stay here in Helmand Province.

Our target was to get supplies to various outposts, ending with a stopover at an FOB, as far south of Camp Bastion as was possible, which had a clear view of the plain leading to the foothills of the mountains that I was most interested in, as a possible route into Pakistan. I had not forgotten the real reasons behind my mission. I had my camera with me, as well as ordinance survey maps collected from American satellites. Our transport was to be a Chinook, and one of the Americans sitting nearby suddenly stood up and said, in a voice loud enough for all to hear,

"Right, you guys, let's rock and roll."

Suddenly, I knew we were off to resupply Camp Bartkowski and other observation posts scattered along the way. It was to be my first flight in a Chinook, and my theory was they were big birds flying low enough to be targeted by hand-held rocket launchers. My stomach was already in my boots. This battle zone was unlike any other I had been in because of the invisibility of the enemy. Do we blame the topography of Afghanistan for that? Or is the enemy cannier than we are prepared to acknowledge?

My heart changed its beat, it wasn't up to panic level, but it certainly was a level of fear of the unknown intruding into the very centre of my consciousness. Watching the soldiers striding out of the D-FAC in a silent formation which was almost balletic in nature, I marvelled at their obvious commitment to each other, as they each in turn quietly stood back respectfully, to let the more senior men pass in front of them, before almost subconsciously lining up in rank order, ready to hike to a waiting bus which had been ordered by the logistics officer. Hudson and I were the last to board and once we were seated the bus set off for the Camp Bastion airfield over two miles away from where we had been picked up at the Camp Leatherneck D-FAC. Even as we travelled on the bus, I was snapping away at the visuals of early morning activity. I had long since realised that the camps never sleep. Perhaps that was why the men travelled in silence, catching up on sleep!

Equally obvious was the evidence that soldiers have an amazing capacity to respect each other's need to focus on the task in hand. I was very impressed by this, until I realised I too needed that silence. Maybe if I remember correctly, I thought about my wife, yes, I'm certain I did, and looking about me at the young faces still and tight-lipped beneath the helmets, I saw men who knew that whatever they were, they were soldiers for a reason; they were men of character and conviction. These were no mercenaries they were fighting for their America's honour. Once at the airport we were split into three groups and I found myself separated from Hudson.

I turned to look for Hudson; he was being lined up behind a group about to board another Chinook, and surprise, surprise he was surrounded by some British squaddies. I could not see who, but I believed one of them was Gareth Hughes, one of the four on my list of possible smugglers, or was he an agent like myself?

Hughes was unusual for a British fusilier; taller than most, he reminded me of Peter Crouch the footballer. Yes, it had to be him, but was he here with or without the other three? Had I imagined it; there was a great deal of dust being stirred up by passing vehicles and an early morning gust of dusty wind, I couldn't see clearly and I just had to hope Hudson was OK, perhaps I was in the wrong queue?

Three Chinooks fully loaded with the supplies were waiting for us, and I made good use of the time to get some amazing pictures of life around the helicopters preparing for take-off. Again looking about for Hudson, I couldn't see him and I was told, "Get on here, mate, or go back to bed, yer holding everybody up!" The blades were whirring; I swear all I could hear was my own heartbeat. We were to sit along the side walls and once in, that was it, nowhere to move to; the Chinook was fully loaded and I wondered how on earth it would lift off without an accident. My crazy thoughts must have shown on my face. Suddenly the soldier sitting next to me patted my arm. I turned to look straight into his eyes; they were smiling as he mouthed,

'We'll be OK, mate, relax!'

I grinned back and let out a long silent breath as I let my shoulders sag and my head nod in thanks to him for his kindness. I was never to know him, but I was to remember him for the rest of my life, for in that moment I understood the brotherhood that is the bond that holds the military together. Was that all Guy had to worry about, four men who had a close bond? I had always sensed it when out at sea, the ship's crew has to bond or jump overboard, it appeared to me that the army was the same, 'All for one and one for all!'

Blades whirling, whoop, whoop, whoop, whoop, the noise was extraordinary in its force, and the wind it produced caused the ground dust to rise up and cover the Chinooks as they lifted away from the safety of the airfield. Within moments we were away from Bastion and heading south. My companion lifted his thumb presumably as a sign to reassure me that take-off had been successful. It felt strange, this silent bonding that was slowly developing a sense of belonging, inside my hyperactive brain. Once again I nodded back at him and settled down for the journey towards the area of the Baba Mountain Range.

It was Alice Holford who had suggested I had a look around that area and try and realise the extent of the problem facing any law enforcement authority; she had said that even the ANA, the Afghan National Army were no better placed than international forces, to control the drug industry of Afghanistan. For me, today's work was to be more educational for myself, than anything else. It was also the day I was to realise that the map in my pocket bore no resemblance to the terrain below, hopefully my pictures would allow me to explain things to the PM. As we journeyed on I mused on the fact that like many Englishmen, I had only a slight ability to mentally picture the various topographical relationships that exist between the vast distances, such as those unfolding below us; whereas it was probably true to believe that those who knew the American prairies or the Australian outback had a better chance of planning the policing of this vast area, than a man from a small country, one that size-wise would always be labelled a small island.

Again I was amazed at the distances and the time it all took. Uncertain if this was a problem for all people who came from country villages, such as my own, I again looked at my companion and this time I wondered where he had hailed from; should I try and speak over the noise of the Chinook? Too late, we were descending into the centre of a FOB, one completely surrounded by concrete barriers with an inner ring of cargo carriers as well as divider protection between the living quarters made up of metre and a half wide Hesco blocks; an indication that we were landing in an area that was not safe from snipers or even larger missiles. I sat still until told to disembark, as squaddies begun unloading the supplies we had brought for the camp.

Chapter Sixteen
FOB Bartkowski on Saturday

I was still uncertain of our geographical position. But it didn't matter for within ten minutes of walking down the ramp onto terra firma, I was able to climb up the side of a cargo carrier and look out at the terrain slopping away from the site, and stare with incredulity at the Baba Mountain range stretched out less than twenty kilometres away. A dozen or so further camera shots later, I thought I could get better shots with my wide angle lens. I realised that if I turned the camera on its side I might just get the entire height of the Baba into one shot. It was my first experience of trying to photograph such an enormity.

Attached as it is to the western end of the Himalayas, the Baba Mountain range was a surprise to me; my only previous experience of mountain ranges was confined to the Alps and the Rockies. Baba dwarfed them to an awesome unimportance in my mind. Looking at the overwhelming sight before me, I felt insignificant and almost useless. I, who had once chased Columbian drug barons and Mexican villains; had been skiing in both the French and Swiss Alps, and who had once hiked up a fair bit of the Blue Mountains during a holiday in the States; was now left speechless in awe. You realise how small man is, when you confront a mountain range as high as the Baba, that is sixteen thousand, eight hundred and seventy feet above sea level, and yet it is still nowhere near the highest mountain in the region. Its value to the Afghan poppy grower is its remote passageway for climbers, carrying the harvested drugs on their backs, to get through to Pakistan.

I climbed down, found my gear and changed the lens, before getting back on the container. You snap away with your camera and you feel the exhilaration that comes when you know that this is a once in a lifetime experience. I didn't even mind that the oxygen level felt as if it was restricted, we were high up and I knew from experience, it all comes right in the end; just take your time. I sat down with my legs dangling over the side of the cargo container and began collecting pictorials of the troops off loading and other visuals, as the other birds arrived, throwing up enough dirt and dust to completely obliterate the helicopters for several minutes. Remembering my brief about the pipeline, I decided that I was going to play tourist for a while. This was different. How did anyone get over or under this range of giants? They were all part of the mountain ranges that gradually build up to the highest mountain in the world; this was one of the little sisters that get higher and higher, as they reach out to Everest, further east in the Himalayas.

Then I turned round and took careful pictures of the plain that spread out away from the mountains. Again I stood, and realised that I had an uninterrupted view of at least twenty or thirty miles, maybe more! A British squaddie below called up at me, as I stood there, occasionally looking through my powerful military eyeglasses at the snow-clad mountains spread out for mile upon mile, and rising so steeply out of the flat plain of south Helmand Province..

"Yer okay up there, mate?"

"Well, it sure beats Snowdon!" I said hoping it was seen as a joke.

"Beats a lot of them mate. That f**ing beauty is over seventeen thousand feet; bigger than the f**ing American Rockies!"

I smiled down at him; he obviously thought I was a Yank! Turning away I continued to focus on the world outside the base. Northwards, the grandeur was even more impressive. I knew that further north there were a couple of higher ranges and that one safe route through them was the renowned Khyber Pass. It had more than a passable road, when open, when not harassed by tribesmen and when the state police on both sides of the border were in control. Forget about the road tunnel near Kabul, that was unlikely to be a drug route, it did not cross any border; or so Mike Raven had said. But open roads were a different matter when controlling from the air, he had explained,

"You can easily pinpoint a camel or car when it's on that road. The sun helps by casting the shadows of the camel and its load. You'll see cars or Lorries send up dust clouds visible for miles."

I got down from the cargo carrier and walked towards the newly arrived Chinooks. Hudson had been on the last of them and I questioned the lateness of their arrival.

"What's the matter, did you break down?"

"Delivered supplies all over the place, Matt; they just open the tail end and push the stuff out. Bingo, we never had to land anywhere, just kept flying. Zigzagging all over the place, it felt like this bird really knew his stuff."

I was puzzled; and said so. Querying what might happen if supplies fell wide of the mark, it was the base commander, who overhearing us turned and said,

"The packages have AGA's attached. We call them screamers, but they are part of the usable development from guidance missile systems technology. You've gotta be impressed; they are being used for carrying supplies and not warheads. It's ingenious, we even deliver fully loaded ISO containers using nothing more than a standard round parachute and an AGAS that delivers the package to within centimetres of a specific site."

I looked at him incredulously.

"I hope to God that never gets into the hands of the drug barons of this world!"

He put his hand out towards me and as I shook it, he added,

"Too true, and you've gotta be the man I'm looking for? Matt Fleming, I believe? Don't worry, Commander Fleming, General Mike Raven spoke with me and asked me to help if I can, without giving the game away. My name is Tim Colbert, please call me Tim. I like a few hours off to forget I'm a general, so please, just Tim!"

The two of us walked slowly towards the D-FAC and although it was not yet noon, we decided to eat first and then he promised to show me what he believed was happening in his local area.

Surprisingly, I felt hungry enough; it was several hours since breakfast. That was it, the first real comment between me and the relaxed and friendly Tim Colbert was about something that puzzled me about 'time' here in Afghanistan.

"Tell me, Tim, am I imagining this: that you lose all sense of time out here? I can't believe that we flew out of Bastion thinking this would be an hour's flight, and yet it took forever. Why?"

"It is several things. We can't always fly in a straight line because of the terrain or the known enemy positions. Then the distance disorientates everyone. It's a little bit like driving on Route 66, unless you get distinctive markers to divide up the distance, you can't mentally relate to it, nor can you divide up the time. It throws most of us one way or another, it's my belief that it can make a man stir crazy, if he is off camp for too long. Anyway, I know what Mike said about you, but, what is it you want to find out here at Camp Bartkowski? It hardly seems an important base, named after a dead Pole shot by a sniper and as with all camps that is what gives the camp some meaning; one of ours was killed here. But it's stuck right at the bottom of the Garmser District and next door to Pakistan and a little bit of Iran, surrounded by desert and mountains, what can you make of that?"

"Precisely," I said, "mountains that must seem to be very enticing to the drug lords of Afghanistan. Tucked down at the bottom of the country, away from central government, just this modest FOB making a stand against the deviousness of the natives determined to sell their cocaine and heroin to the highest bidder! Simple! So I'm asking you, how do they move the stuff over the Baba Mountains?"

"Well, not with an AGA, that's for certain."

"We don't know that," I replied with a laugh.

Looking back on the next couple of hours, I recall feeling that Tim Colbert was not seriously committed to helping me solve any problem dealing with drugs and the Afghans. The sense of disappointment was, looking back, quite profound. At the time I really did not know how to deal with it. I wrote copious notes and occasionally laughed at his comments, but when I left him I was weighed down by a feeling of disappointment and weariness.

Settling into my berth for a late afternoon shut-eye, I was disturbed by a footstep outside the tent. It seemingly was too close for my liking, so I shot up and was standing just inside the entrance as Gareth Hughes entered without any hesitation. He did not seem to be surprised, rather the opposite:

"Ah, good, well done, sir; glad you are awake. The guys and I need to speak with you privately and we don't trust the tents, if walls have ears, so do tents! Would you mind joining us for a coffee break in the open air, so we can be more private, as we speak?"

Well, for a start I was completely thrown by his manner and his tone and choice of words. He sounded more like a senior officer than a sergeant. Looking him in the eye, I knew by the unflinching look in his, that I was probably right.

Pocketing my recorder, I followed him out to an area near the perimeter wall, which had various plastic tables and chairs set out almost as if it were a picnic area, set for sunbathing and R and R, where we found the other three men were sitting with large mugs, a flask of coffee and bottles of water. There was even one for me, which surprised me. Had they been that certain I would join them?

Lewis, Johnstone and Norcross stood up as I approached and shook hands, each in turn giving his name before mentioning his rank. Then Hughes added;

"And I am Staff Sergeant Gareth Hughes, sir, the Foreign Office decided to use you to assist us, but it is extremely sensitive, I can't roam around Leatherneck dressed as a British agent."

"I might have guessed. So you really are SIS."

"The truth is we were put here for a reason, initially to uncover the suspected traitor in our camp, and yet we could not reveal ourselves to any of the men. We are the reason you are here."

I remained silent.

"Initially we believed Williams was the traitor; he always seemed to be in the wrong place at the wrong time, or absent when he was needed. Generals, brigadiers would come looking for him and he was nowhere to be seen, sometimes for hours on end and late into the night. We'd split up and check all the R and R places; he was never playing darts or dominoes, watching a video or playing one of the many PlayStations that are everywhere in all the camps. It lasted days until Norcross parked himself in a jeep ready to follow Williams one night. That's when we realised he was going into Leatherneck and Norcross discovered there was a lady involved."

Norcross looked pleased with himself, but Hughes continued their story.

Once C told us about the anxiety felt by the Lieutenant, we reasoned that he isn't the real problem. Where it lies we don't know, in the meantime we are looking for the leak and have begun to suspect it is across in Leatherneck; there are as many civilian workers there as there are military personnel and we are uncertain of the whole shebang! We needed a man in Leatherhead, you!"

I looked back at him with a frown and before I could get a question out, Hughes said,

"For now all you need to know is that Williams is a posh kid out of his depth when it comes to giving orders; he's too nice all of the time. We told Williams we wanted to visit here to look for trading opportunities for after the war, start our own business type of thing. Big lie, we wanted you on your own. He swallowed that one, no questions, just an 'Off you go lads!' and so here we are following you around and hoping to talk away from Williams's eyes and ears. We need you working for us in Leatherneck!"

They all laughed, until they realised I was not joining in their merriment. So, C had marketed me as a retired policeman posing as a correspondent, to these men I was believed to be SIS. Fine! Seemed like a good cover story. But, I asked myself, how many more versions of who or what I was in a former life existed here in Helmand? Although I had worked for Intelligence over many years, I was a loner who seldom had any contact with fellow operatives and so I acknowledged to myself, I could not immediately feel comfortable with this group; something bothered me.

I wanted more proof of their legality and status. Was I being set up as a sucker by the SIS authorities? Were Customs and Excise or the police authorities using me for some unknown and nefarious ends? In spite of my own web search I knew it was possible for the whole thing to be an internet scam. If it was, then were they just four clever crooks, mercenaries, traitors or what, another example of a clever internet sting?

Think! They don't know what I know, play along, but be wary.

"Is there any chance of proving that you are who you say you are?"

I thought I sounded rather tame by asking such a weak question.

I need not have worried. Had they produced any document as proof, I would have been even more suspicious. Of one thing I was certain, SIS members would not carry any such papers. Tom Johnstone laughed and said,

"Would you show us yours, first?"

"Touché." I said, feeling a slight sense of relief, adding, "So what is going on?" I made myself comfortable and poured myself a drink.

Gareth started to explain and I quickly realised he was the senior member of the group. He made no apology for what had happened and seemed content to put me squarely in the picture. By the time he had finished I was left with an incredible picture of undercover work in Helmand Province. They gave me maps of all the drug running routes, the main tribal leaders who grew the poppy in bulk, and the names of various ANA leaders who were untrustworthy.

"So, if the authorities have all of this, what else is there that could satisfy the Prime Minister?" I asked.

"No much truthfully. It's difficult for those who've never visited here to understand the complexity of the native Afghan. The tribal leaders are not necessarily warlords, but some with Taliban leanings are, and some Taliban are remarkably peaceful so long as they are in charge. It must be their religion and politics if you want peace. And then the very size of the place makes centralized government impossible, but, truthfully some of the 46 provinces are quite peaceful and some very nice people are happy with their local leaders, until the Taliban arrive on their doorstep!"

"Sounds a bit like Europe, if you think about," Tom Johnstone said with a smile that added to his meaning. I laughed and we were all silent for a moment.

"And Lieutenant Williams?" I queried, "Where does he fit in?"

"The man's a bastard! He's top of my list," was the answer given with such vehemence by Andy Norcross that I almost jumped out of my chair. "The man is a genius and a crafty one to boot." He added with a sudden anger kicking the words out as if spitting, before standing and walking away towards a block labelled 'Portaloo'.

I looked around in astonishment. It was Craig Lewis who came to my rescue.

"Andy believes that Williams..."

"Andy knows, Craig, tell the truth. Andy knows it was Williams!" countered Lewis as he slammed his fist down on the cheap and rickety garden table.

"Hold on, I take it there is bad blood between the lieutenant and Norcross." I held my peace, preferring that they did not realise that I was aware of Norcross's temper over Alice and that I had suspected last night, that Alice was fond of the British lieutenant; why else was she so circumspect in his presence, why fade away when he drove up? For a long moment I felt the weariness of an old man, watching teenagers playing games with their emotions and messing their lives up to boot.

I sat waiting for them to tell me what was going on and why. It usually comes down to a discipline question between squaddies and officers; I already knew Guy Williams found these guys difficult to control, now I had to ascertain how close to the mark he was, or face the unpleasant truth they were the ones holding the veracity on the situation. I kept quiet and looked from one to the other, just as Norcross returned. He resumed his seat and took a drink from his bottle of water.

Staring back at me he said, "Well?"

"You have a problem with Williams?" I asked, and Norcross lowered his eyes and kept silent.

Then with venom in his tone of voice, Norcross almost spat out his theory that Williams was breaking the rules with Alice and if he was caught, that delectable creature would be sent home. Again there was a long silence, the other men avoiding my eyes, Norcross glowering at me, as if he could fight me for her hand, and me trying to look as if I didn't understand.

I waited, and then Gareth got to his feet and with just a slight change in the disposition of his head, indicated that he wanted me to follow him. I nodded back; we moved to another table, quite some distance away from the other three men.

"Best we talk alone for a bit. Now, why they sent a retired man out to do a young man's job, I'll never know. I've been told by my boss to help you find drug runners or the routes or whatever it is you are after. But this is Afghanistan, not sweet well-ordered Chester. I grant you there is a difficulty existing here that maybe has relevance, both here in Afghanistan, and back home in England. Drugs are a universal problem, whether you grow them, sell them or use them!"

He looked weary for a moment; Norcross walked across as if to listen to what we were saying, Gareth shooed him away.

"I'm senior to the others, being out here one way or other these ten years. In fact, Matt, I have been here every year in one guise or another and probably know more about the place than any officer in the field. What they know is probably from the intelligence I gave them in the first place, and from the contacts I have made over the years with local leaders; with some of the Taliban even, so listen to me now." He looked intently at me as he said,

"I am here to help you and so are my boys. We will help you find the routes you want to know about; in fact we've given you all bare one of them so you know most of them already. Before you go back we will hopefully get that sewn up too. I only work with professionals, understand?"

I nodded in silence at the young man and understanding the depth of his concern, I accepted his authority at that moment, my mind saying to itself, that until I knew otherwise I accepted his control of the situation. I looked at him with a reasonable expression on my face and asked,

"I can help police Leatherneck, but why suspect Guy Williams?"

"Because he is a lying, two timing bastard, who doesn't give a dam about his men, because he believes he's in love. His platoon has lost more men than any other and all because of him; he can't put his bleeding dick away. He doesn't train up new lads properly. We were initially put into his platoon to try and find out why his boys were so unlucky!"

"And have you?" I asked calmly.

"Only insofar as he seems unaware of how important the first ten minutes after a blast injury is to saving a man's life. We call it the Platinum Ten minutes, the first ten minutes in the Golden hour. It's been around for a couple of years now!"

I kept quiet; I also was unaware of what that meant. I didn't know what to say. I was almost glad when we were all overwhelmed by the sudden 'Op Minimiser' announcement, coming over the tannoy.

Gareth pulled out a pager, it had one word on it; *Brit.*

Chapter Seventeen
Towards the Baba Mountains, Sunday Morning

Andy Norcross puzzled me; his demeanour could fluctuate from happy to serious and all stations in between. I had watched him over the next hours, as we spent some time discussing the region we were in and what they could show me the next day, with regards to different routes over the Baba range. It was agreed we would set off at first light; Tim Colbert had suggested he gave us just two vehicles for our intended exploration of the most suspicious route. It suited me to go along with them; routes for drugs over or through a mountain range could easily carry oil, gas or contraband! My mind was at rest at the thought of the co-operation being offered.

We would carry enough supplies for forty eight hours, the standard practice for any patrol going away from base, for such an exercise. Again Tim came to our rescue and provided a sharpshooter to travel with Hudson, an Aussie who was large, tanned and silent. I was glad; knowing Hudson was important to my future position at Leatherneck, I did not fancy losing him. That would definitely cause me to lose Alice's approval. Of one thing I was certain if there had been dreams in that young lady's head regardless of the 'No sex you are a soldier' rules that exist in combat zone camps, it would be superseded by Alice's soft-hearted regard for all. Hudson was a fellow American soldier;

his death would affect Alice, and she would probably blame me for it.

Early as it was, it was already hot and dusty when we eventually drove out of the camp. As we left I noticed a chopper taking off and heading in the same direction as ourselves.

"Where's he off to?" I stupidly asked.

"I asked for a high level recce," was the answer from Gareth, who was driving, with me sitting in the front beside him. I'd been deliberately placed there on his instructions; he said to allow me a clearer view of the terrain for photographic reconnaissance, his words not mine. I believed it was to keep me away from Norcross, who was obviously continuing to show signs of a really nasty temper. I had felt it at breakfast, when he challenged me with a supreme example of bad language.

"I don't f**ing well see why you're f**ing well coming along. We have f**ing given you as much f**ing info as we have, and now you're f**ing well going to f**ing well put all of us f**ing idiots in f**ing danger, f**ing civilian!"

"Cut it, Andy," said Gareth, giving the younger man a hard stare and then turning to me, and smiled. I grinned back and shrugged my shoulders. Yes, I had counted at least six 'f**ing' in that mini tirade; but I knew that was a minor score, compared to some of the language dished out by troopers from all the different armies. *Stress needs a safety valve*, I said to myself, as a way of excusing the young man. Truthfully, he was possibly right, he could easily regard me as a civilian and as such he could not foresee my possible reactions, if threatened by the enemy. Age made me a liability to these younger men and Norcross knew that made me a threat to his own safety.

We sped ahead towards the mountain range in front of us. Then as the ground changed from dirt to rock, the noise changed and the smoothness of the ride could be felt beneath the wheels, Gareth suddenly turned left and we travelled on for several miles, probably about thirty or forty miles, if the truth were known. I could not tell, being overwhelmed by the vastness of nothingness that is the effect upon one when nature reduces you and your humanity to a mere biblical grain of sand, when confronted by its majesty. Some would call it the creation, some the hand of God, whatever another's belief, I was feeling small and insignificant. The thought occurred to me that we could crash, fall down the side of the mountain and be lost forever. A shiver went through me and Gareth seemed to realise, for he said, "Overwhelming, isn't it?"

Then we came upon a rocky crag balanced on a mini plateau that had once upon a time had a dwelling on it.

"What is it, an old Taliban outpost, perhaps?" I asked,

"Nah, a checkpoint, abandoned for some time, pretty much a useless spot." Gareth said as he drew up besides the derelict single-storey building. This close, it appeared not only abandoned, but almost roofless and silent, when suddenly two heads appeared through some of the mouse-holes in the shell-damaged walls.

I couldn't believe my eyes; were we in an outpost manned by British fusiliers? Their kit included heavy machine guns, as well as all the usual hand-held rocket launchers. Suddenly I felt as if I was on the front line, at last. There were no Hesco blocks or cargo containers for protection. If I shivered it was only momentarily because I also realised the wind had come up and the mountains were shielding us from any warmth from the sun.

Watching Gareth and Hudson park the vehicles behind the battered property, I notice another armoured vehicle parked close alongside the building.

It was Hudson who added his ten pence worth of enlightenment with the information that we had arrived at a now disused checkpoint, previously named CP Kernark, named after an American killed in action, on that site some years previously. I was getting used to the different ways the Americans had for honouring their heroes. Originally built to shelter between twelve and twenty men, it was now a battered ruin, but it still had the advantage of height over the world in front of it, and any lookout could see for twenty miles in front; and about a half mile behind, where trees had been cleared away, either for security reasons or for fuel, I didn't know and at that moment I felt it was not important. I followed Craig and Tom inside to find the two young squaddies who had been the lookouts, checking out our arrival. Plus, imagine my surprise when in the centre of the ruin, and sitting on the dirt floor, there was not only Ramin, but also Lieutenant Guy Williams,

"Good morning, Lieutenant, sir, nice surprise!" Gareth said, with an edge of sarcasm to his voice.

"Hope so, Hughes! Ah, Matt, you OK? Good, we have work to do, all of us! It was a good job you guys had left camp when you did, sorry about your expedition, but time enough later. I'll see what I can do for you next weekend in the way of R and R. Right, everybody ready, get your notebooks out these are instructions from ISAF, sorry to spoil your fun, but you might manage to gain some time back, if this goes down quickly."

I was mesmerized by the change in the young lieutenant, who now gave detailed instructions in a very confident voice. Nobody argued with him; firstly we were to booby trap the already ruined shelter, while we did that, Hudson and Norcross were to remove the two vehicles and hide them back along the route we had just come from. After that when all was ready we were to proceed up the mountain to an area which seemed to offer the chance of some cover, because it had several trees, and useable bushes. It was about another hundred metres straight up, above this deserted building, but would give us a clear view of it and the tracks approaching from both the east and west. Then we had to rest, but keep watch and wait; what for, he never said. The four Intelligence men went out to unload and move the vehicles.

My mind was in turmoil; Williams had reacted to our arrival as if he was expecting us. Had he been in contact with Gareth, or Tim Colbert? Then I witnessed him turning to Ramin and quietly speaking in a voice that was almost a whisper, but I heard him clearly.

"Get them bedded down; then get some sleep yourself, it could be hours before they show up. You understand? Good, watch Norcross; no showing off!"

"I understand, Lieutenant," answered Ramin.

"Have you any news of Wasima?" Guy asked in a whisper at least two decibels lower than his earlier whisper.

"They cut her nose off and her ears; they say she has escaped, but I think they killed her."

My heart and mind froze with a sense of helplessness. What next could they possibly inflict on that tiny creature?
What was Guy Williams playing at; I got no clue from the other men. In front of Williams and Ramin they acted as if they were just troopers who accepted and understood the task in hand. In silence we did as instructed, the cars having been moved and

camouflaged, the traps set, we set off, leaving Ramin hidden behind some bushes, looking very much as he had done the first time I had seen him in his village. There was no time to turn around and try and see where Lieutenant Williams and the two young soldiers had hidden themselves. By the time I reached the tree line there was no sign of them.

Had they disappeared into some undergrowth? Had he high-tailed it away from the scene to betray us to the enemy? Norcross and the others made no comment about Williams's disappearance; they seemed to accept it as perfectly normal for the officer in charge to evaporate from the scene.

Taking several deep breaths, I tried to change my worries to something I could deal with; Ramin was he still there behind those bushes? My initial thoughts on this occasion were centred on the problem of whether or not to trust Ramin. In my head I could still hear the voice of Private First Class Alice Holford warning me of Ramin's history of betrayal, of duplicity. If the lieutenant was the traitor, then pairing up with Ramin to set a trap, which could eliminate an undercover team from British Intelligence, seemed more than a possibility. My mind said an undercover team - plus one! Wipe out five agents in one go. The Taliban would be ballistic with joy.

Was I staring straight into a trap, which could also bring about my own death? Never in my life had I felt so vulnerable, so completely at the mercy of a traitor's cunning. All I could hear in my head was the memory of Norcross, sounding off in rage at the very mention of Williams's name; yet here were Norcross and the others seemingly obeying without question the man they suspected. I turned to Hudson and whispered,

"We need to separate ourselves from the Brits, just in case this is a booby trap."

Hudson looked at me in disbelief, whispering.

"Who don't you trust, Matt?"

"All of them."

Hudson gave me a long and puzzled stare and I nodded my head as if confirming his need to be suspicious and to trust no one. After a moment Hudson bowed his head just once, as if he was confirming his understanding of what I was implying, and we began to crawl like crabs on all four limbs, inch by inch, as we moved further away from them.

The wind was rustling the branches around us, but it aided our slow, but surreptitious movements away from the rest of the group. It was then that I was glad of the knee and elbow pads, but my back felt every ounce of the weight of my loaded ILBE. I was sweating and hurting and questioning my own wisdom in trying to escape.

Escape from what? Heaven only knew how dreadful I felt, the thought of being lost out in this wilderness was petrifying. We must have covered nearly twenty feet off to the right, when Gareth suddenly called out,

"Matt, where are you? Stick together, man."
I thought for a moment. *Do I reveal our whereabouts or do I keep silent?* Silence would make him more suspicious. *Answer him, yes, say something innocuous.*

"Having an f**ing dump, mate; Hudson's keeping watch!"

If he was still suspicious he said nothing, but I realised I could have exposed my real intention, to separate Hudson and myself from the main group.

In the silence that followed, Hudson and I slowly edged further and further away, until Hudson whispered,

"Boss, there's a spot up there."

I turned my head and saw a ledge jutting out beneath an overhang of a thickly wooded group of bushes and half dead trees. Thumbs up in silent agreement, and we set off in a crawl, up the side of the mountain until we were firmly secure on that ledge. It transpired that the view it gave to all that was below us was quite phenomenal; we could see as far back to where the other five men were lying beneath in thick undergrowth and also further down the mountain. But of Ramin, there was no sign. Initially I did not panic, knowing his ability to blend into the background that the natural environment afforded him. I could well believe that he had moved to a more suitable position.

Settling down, I said to Hudson,
"Hour about?"
Sure, boss, you go first, I'll keep watch."
The next four hours passed quickly as we rested and watched in turn. By some miracle I managed to sleep that first hour and when Hudson shook me awake, I realised how necessary that time had been to my over-stretched nerves. I felt almost brave as I rolled onto my stomach and took up position to survey the world spreading out beneath our vantage point. All was as it had been before I had slept; was this how a false sense of security develops? The second time around and munching on MRE dehydrated rations of Irish stew and apricot compote, which sounds lovely, but tastes appalling, I began to realise how demanding such prolonged surveillance could be on the soldier, in comparison to sitting in cars and vans with a thermos flask of hot coffee and sandwiches made by my wife. *Given the choice, I'd take the coffee,* I said to myself.

Every nerve in my body froze; there was movement below and I could not see who or what was there. Putting a hand gently over Hudson's mouth I whispered in his ear, Company!"

For such a big man he managed to silently roll onto his stomach and within seconds had his weapon aiming out towards the bushes below us. My heart was thumping, I was certain that any terrorist could have heard it from a mile away. *Dear God, a sign that I'm getting too old for this game,* I said to myself.

Hudson suddenly rose onto his knees and lowered his weapon.

What the heck was he doing? I didn't move.

"Okay you f**ing Brits get up here before I take your f**ing ruddy useless balls off."

Out of the bushes rose first Norcross, then the rest of the group. All were silently laughing as they clambered onto the ledge, and Gareth explained that he had got worried when we hadn't returned to the group and a quick recce had shown up our passage through the long grass.

"So what took you so long?" I asked with a modicum of sarcasm.

"We thought we would frighten you into thinking we had done a bunk and see if you'd come back down. Were you frightened up here on your own?" Norcross chanted as if trying to scare little children.

They were all laughing at us in that almost silent way that a soldier does when the tension of a stake-out is momentarily relieved. It is as if once again the internal elastic is allowed to retreat to its original length. The gut repositions itself and the sense of tension dissipates for just a moment; then it comes back as the next challenge throws itself into the ring.

Years later I, Matthew Fleming was to ask myself, who'd choose this life? For now I settled down to wait for the enemy.

Was it the PM's fault? Was it my own, a stupid need to be of some importance for one last time in my life? Had I been so flattered by the invitation from 'C' and surprised by his comment that the request was directly from the PM, which made me think I could still be useful? A much needed feeling of 'there's life in the old dog yet!'

Maybe it was the pretty eyes of a Miss Moneypenny lookalike which had created the illusion that had me feeling like 007, when she said, 'C will see you now, sir'. Whatever the reason, I admitted to myself that having wound down from full time work to picking and choosing projects that interested me, I, Matthew Fleming was not enjoying the transition towards full time retirement. My mind hated all that was expected of me, as men I had watched grow from rookies barely arrived in the Foreign Office as desk clerks, challenged to take up my position in the service, and who were treating me like an extra from 'Old Tricks' or a relic from what they teasingly call the Real Fleming's day! I did not feel old, but lying in full combat gear on the hard earth of Afghanistan, waiting to die by a sniper's bullet, I admitted to myself that I felt old in every bone in my body. Not for the first time I asked myself, "What the bloody hell am I doing here?" as I thought of the comfort of my own home and the love of my wife.

Lying flat on my back and pretending to sleep, I came back to reality when I felt a hand come down on my chest, and looking up I saw Hudson, who had been on point, with his hand preventing me from moving. Slowly turning my head, I witnessed all the others positioned as if about to attack an unseen enemy. Quietly Hudson picked up my helmet and gave it to me, followed by my weapon. In complete silence I prepared for battle. As always the cerebral part of me intruded upon the physical, now, I understood; you knew that by the very fact of being a soldier you had to use your weapon to live, because you know that you have to kill or be killed. That is why you are trained to fight, to save the lives of your brothers and yourself. Your weapon is a defensive weapon first and foremost.

Know when to use it!' Now was the time to use it, I argued with myself as I turned to find the SIS men had disappeared, so silently that I was momentarily shocked. Looking down on the world below I saw that there was no visible difference, no movement of undergrowth to indicate a foreign presence. The sun had disappeared, but it was not yet completely dark. Hudson and the Aussie driver had taken up positions to the left of me, while the four SIS men were nowhere to be seen in the landscape below. I put out an arm and pulled at Hudson's sleeve. I mouthed, 'Where are they?' and he pointed down the mountain before adding silently, 'The Taliban!'

The silence was a blessing and a curse; knowing how silently the Taliban could move through the undergrowth with all the cunning of a snake, I knew that until a shot was fired we had no idea of their position. Is hope a prayer? If it is then I was praying at that moment, that we would all come out of this alive. Did that hope include the Taliban? Maybe not; I could not at that moment in time see them as human beings. The more I heard about them, the more I hated them and their concepts of life, particularly their treatment of women and the rejection of education. What was I thinking about, I was facing the possibility of death and thinking about Taliban ignorance? I lay still and hoped the silence outside of me would last and last; I could cope with the storm in my mind if it did, but I was uncertain what would happen if the bullets would begin to fly, if the noise took the upper hand and my brain was silenced, maybe forever.

Again the voice in my head filled the silence, my instructor from way back when, who kept saying,

"You ne'er 'ear the bullet that'll kill yer, lad!"

He was my first firearms trainer from the time I was training with the Marines ready for a trip to Columbia to arrest a drugs baron from Liverpool, who had gone on the run and hopped over the Pond to escape arrest in England. This was different; the terrorist believed they were invincible and would fight to the death for their dream of twenty-seven virgins. Drug barons would endeavour to stay alive in the hope of escaping the clutches of the law and enjoying their twenty-seven virgins in this life! On that one, I'm with the drug barons, please!

I shook with fear as the first shots were fired. It was all happening down below and the three of us lay peering through the leaves at the now invisible SIS men shooting rapid automatic flashes of gunfire at the invisible enemy.

"Keep yer bloody head down yer bloody Pom," came from the Aussie, the driver General Tim Colbert had given us and whose name I had never picked up, nor realised he was an Aussie until hearing him speak. What he was doing there at that time seemed more than mysterious. Equally, I was aware that my presence probably seemed annoying to him. It was only later that I discovered he was one of ISAF's most trusted undercover operatives, an Aussie special services man, code named Simon. He was tough mentally and physically, and before the day was out I was to be glad of his presence and his firepower.

The gunfire continued for nearly an hour and we were pinned down awaiting instructions from Gareth. When it came, no one was more surprised than I was as we crept back down to the CP, and on the way passing several injured and dead Afghans, until finally reaching Norcross who was standing over Guy Williams, with his automatic rifle aimed at Williams's head. There was no sign of Gareth Hughes, Tom Johnstone, Craig Lewis or Ramin. The radio was there beside Williams, but who had summoned us down; Williams? It was Hughes's radio!

There was a look of triumph on Andy Norcross's face that somehow said 'I told you so!' But his eyes never left Williams's face. It was a stare out, which dictated the belief that Norcross was saying, 'One move, you're dead!'

As we drew level with Norcross, he demanded that one of us tie up his prisoner's arms behind his back and bind his feet, so that Williams couldn't take off, although I suspected the Lieutenant was injured and unable to make a run for it. Once that job was done, Hudson and I settled against a tree and waited. Eventually Simon and Andy Norcross came over to us and suggested we headed back to Camp Bartkowski with the prisoner. No reference was made concerning the missing men, so I decided that I was within my rights to ask.

"What do I tell the General?" was my opening gambit.

"Anything and everything," Andy Norcross replied with an almost disrespectful shrug of his shoulders. I felt, I tasted the ire in my throat.

"Come off it, you bastard," I demanded, "All we know is that the other three men are missing and you've tied up a British lieutenant after shooting him in the legs. Am I right, you did that?" I pointed at Williams's bleeding leg wound and waited.

"Get the bastard out of my sight before I put one through his f**ing head, and if I do that, I might just finish you off as well. Bloody geriatric! Get out of here and take that rubbish with you: tell Clitheroe that's his traitor."

By now my heart was racing fit to burst.

"Tell Clitheroe? Why did he say that, what was it that Clitheroe needed to know?" I asked myself.

My mind was trying desperately to disbelieve the story being set against Guy Williams.

In spite of his injured leg, Guy Williams began the walk back to the cars; as soon as possible Hudson got us into the first vehicle, leaving the one with the supplies for the men, in the hope that they were still alive. Setting Guy on the rear seat, Hudson drove at speed back to Camp Bartkowski. If he was reckless, who cared, all I wanted was to put as much distance between us and Andy Norcross. Was Andy Norcross the real traitor everyone was looking for or was it Guy Williams?

Your guess was as good as mine, at that moment in time.

General Tim Colbert was waiting for us, and immediately had the Lieutenant taken to the medical tent, where his leg was dressed before he was brought back to the admin tent, and sat down in front of Colbert and myself. Other officers joined us as the General, with a modest degree of civility, asked Williams to give an explanation of the day's events.

I was still in the dark and had begun to believe I might be the one being set up as the fall guy, with the so-called SIS men making an escape from right under my nose.

Chapter Eighteen
Camp Bartkowski Monday Morning

I was tired even though I had slept a dreamless sleep for the best part of eight hours. Waking with stiffness in every joint of my body, I had hurriedly showered, dressed and breakfasted within a half hour of waking. Looking about the camp for signs of life, it was obvious that activity was centred upon the heliport area. Chopper after chopper was landing and taking off in quick succession, as dozen of heavily armoured troops were being brought into the base. The worst thing was the dust storms caused by the rotors, which spread higher than the helicopters, masking them from our sight, and causing the Marines hurrying down the ramps to be unsure of the direction in which to head, so all moved straight ahead and gathered near the technicians waiting to re-fuel the bird. I now knew enough of camp life to know that Camp Bartkowski was preparing for a major offensive and after the unresolved situation from yesterday, I hoped it was a search and rescue operation to retrieve the missing men.

"Just two more loads and they'll be off," said a voice from behind me. It was General Colbert; with the chopper noise filling the airwaves I had failed to hear his approach.

"Did you sleep well?" he politely enquired and for once I felt he meant it. His voice had lost the flippancy I had heard before; even his stance was more disciplined. I smiled back at him and managed to avoid some swirling dust by turning my back on the view of the heliport. Facing Colbert, I asked,

"Is Williams guilty?"

"It does look as if he might have to face a court martial, but until we have witness corroboration of any guilt, it remains doubtful. What did you make of his statement?"

"It's difficult! I was there insofar as I was in the area, but I saw nothing more than what I have already told you.   The waiting was tedious; I slept for an hour, then watched, then had another half hour before Hudson woke me. Lewis, Hughes and Johnstone were very much alive when they arrived with Norcross. When I woke, well, that was the last time I saw the three of them. I cannot say where they are or where they were even planning to go. It was very barren immediately beyond the area and I saw nothing to indicate they were hiding. The only bodies were Taliban; I'm certain of that, well, as certain as I can be. Only Williams was there, I'll swear to that. Shot by Norcross, as far as I can be certain."

"There's no news so far this morning, we sent a recce party in late last night to join up with Norcross and Langly…"

"Langly?"

"The Australian, good man and loyal, wouldn't want to lose him. Mind you, he's a tough one, survived the Aussie special services training, do yer know what I mean? Kind of like your SAS."

"I thought he was all brawn and no brains; never spoke and seldom looked at anyone; then when we got back down he seemed somehow alive. Weird!"

"Weird, yes, and now this morning there is no sign of him. Norcross has also disappeared. The radio was sitting on the floor of the OP and the only bodies were of Taliban laid out on the ground outside. Who collected them and arranged them so, we don't know."

"Do you believe they have been taken as hostages?"

"The Taliban don't take hostages."

We talked on as we walked back towards his office area, a hut set inside a large camouflage canopy. A gofer was sent to fetch plenty of coffee and we settled down to await developments, when suddenly General Mike Raven's voice came over the radio.

"Hi, Tim, I'm on my way in. Be with you in ten!"

And he was!

Mike Raven marched into the office followed by PFC Alice Holford and two other American officers. He was in full combat dress and seemed completely at home in Colbert's territory, until I realised he was probably Colbert's superior. That much I gathered, as I watched the deferential side of Colbert's character emerge at speed, as he stood to attention until Mike Raven had seated himself in the only comfortable chair available. Alice, looking as if she had been crying, stood dutifully behind her uncle until she noticed the table with refreshments and without asking simply played hostess to the men, providing both generals with hot coffee and a bottle of water each. They took no notice of her and did not even nod their heads in thanks. The next moment a polystyrene cup filled with steaming hot coffee was placed in my hand. I had the good manners to say, "Thank you," and was rewarded with a smile, but I saw something behind those beautiful eyes which told me Alice was worried. If she wasn't careful her heart would move onto her sleeve and complicate her military life.

Alice left and suddenly two British captains entered, both armed with radios and paperwork, which included better ordinance maps for the area to be covered.

"Right, Ted, you take this area with your men. One Chinook should do and the code will be Southway, head east into the Kandahar region and, Bruce, you head off over here, there are plenty of caves and pathways for your men to check and we will give your group Homeway as your code. Got your medics sorted? Good. Do a four hour sweep and report back when and as needed. If no sight of them by then, we will regroup and rethink our options."

Not even a 'good luck' from General Mike Raven. The two officers were dismissed. Soon I heard the Chinooks lifting off and I waited until the noise died down, before chiming in with my own question.

"What if they have been moved west, away from the mountain and back on to the plain?"

That struck me as an intelligent enough question; the Taliban had trucks and cars and could by now be hundreds of miles west, truthfully they could have crossed the entire width of Helmand into Regional Command West and once in Farah we'd never find them, at least not without further help from ISAF.

"You may be right," *was* all Mike Raven said, when I had finished, but I had a feeling they knew differently and had not mentioned all their available intelligence.

I left them talking over the removal of Lieutenant Williams to Camp Bastion and into the hands of the Military Police; I walked over to the D-FAC where I found a lonely Alice sitting looking forlorn and stirring the bottom out of an empty cup of coffee.

"Chin up, chicken!" I said, in as cheerful a voice as I could muster.

"What has he done?" she pleaded, with eyes very near to tears.

"We don't know."

"You mean you don't know or they don't know?"

"Well, I certainly don't know."

"I don't trust Gareth Hughes."

"I can't say one way or another, but he has been out here a long time and certainly knows his way around."

"Yes, but the rumour is that he's now dead, thanks to Guy. They are going to blame Guy."

There was that little girl again, scared and wishing her love was there with her to comfort her and take the fear away. I was no substitute, no matter how hard I tried to comfort her.

"You said it, sweetie; the rumour! Nobody knows if Gareth is alive or dead. My theory is that he and the missing guys have gone off after some amazing and mysterious lead. They are probably half way up the mountain and heading for the foothills of Everest by now."

"Now you're laughing at me."

"Am I? Well it made you stop crying."

"I want to cry, I'm fed up with the dust and the stupid repetitive jobs I have to do. I don't even feel like a soldier any more. Most of us feel like that; I mean how war is just boring. If only people knew they'd realise how futile it all is. The Taliban will win."

"You are down, what's brought this on?"

"I like him, I mean, I don't want him court martialled."

I waited a moment and putting an arm across her shoulders, I whispered,

"More than like, I think, sweetie. You believe you are in love, and maybe I also recognise the signs in you. Yes, love hurts, especially for a soldier living under Directive One!"

I got up and replenished our coffee cups. Picked up a couple of enormous doughnuts filled with raspberry jam, simply because they were there and I felt a momentary freedom from my wife's vigilance over my waistline. I sat down again, this time opposite the wee creature hunched with elbows on the table, still white-faced and moist-eyed. Her hands were playing with a wet tissue, now twisted into a long tubular item she could tie into a knot, several times. It all looked childlike and unhappy, and I longed to hug her better, but I dared not give way to such an impulse.

We had our doughnuts, yes, I had made her try and eat one, and once started Alice gave way to the sweet doughy comfort of the food and the sweetened coffee, even as she explained between mouthfuls that she didn't eat sweet cakes nor did she take sugar in her coffee. I nevertheless smiled and carried on eating mine with great relish as I enjoyed her innocent explanations. With almost the last mouthful, a tannoyed message came, ordering all returning to Camp Bastion to report to the duty sergeant's office at once. I felt delighted, in an almost paternal way, I had got the child to eat and believed it would be helpful to her. She was so tiny and white-faced; I could forgive myself if I had overstepped a mark.

In the circumstances I believed I had helped her towards a semblance of recovery. I had soon finished my coffee and with some surprise, eaten the whole of the outsize doughnut, when Hudson caught up with us.

"I've got your gear, boss, we take off in fifteen."

The Chinook was revving up as we approached its tail end. We hurried aboard and headed back to Leatherneck. Lieutenant Guy Williams, General Mike Raven and Private First Class Alice Holford were all on board; seated to the front of the Chinook, I was unable to speak to any of them; somewhat relieved I fell asleep, and I can tell you nothing about that journey beyond the fact that during it I moved from Camp Bartkowski to Leatherneck. How long it took, how many refuelling stops or what the weather was like, I could not tell you.

Chapter Nineteen
Camp Leatherneck: The Prisoner

I walked the length of Leatherneck simply because I wanted the exercise. It had rained overnight; the din was like hammer blows over my head and yes, it did bother me, as it had added to the noise from the flapping of the protective camouflage canopy tied down over the ISOs and the huts to supposedly protect them from the weather and to partially disguise them from the air. All the camps have that beige covering which is fine when you can sleep, but last night was not one of those, it was horrendous. You don't concentrate, and you suddenly wish for your bed back home.

Now in spite of the pathways, boots were still picking up mud and mine were no different. By the time I reached the end of the central roadway I had had enough, and was glad to jump on the regular bus that was just passing. It felt like a strange trip around the centre of Chester or some other town. I began relaxing into a false sense of security, that with the oddness of a bus stopping and starting as it slowly moved around the camp picking up passengers, I felt like a naughty schoolboy going unwillingly to school and plotting how to avoid the next task confronting me.

I stayed on it until it reached the Bastion One headquarters, where I made the effort to visit the prisoner. It wasn't easy to collect a pass to officially make a duty call on Lieutenant Williams. The Military Police, who had charge of him, were quite reluctant to give me a pass, until a call through to General Raven settled the matter. Overnight Guy had sent me a request to visit him, saying he would be happy whenever it was convenient to me, as he had nowhere to go, and stating that he had things to discuss. He was being held in a detention block just a hundred yards from the HQ. Realising that he was being kept well away from any Afghan detainees, I hoped he was housed with sufficient comfort to make him amiable to my presence; I did not want an angry scene, I did not know if he blamed me for the occurrences out at the OP.

He was waiting for me and stood to attention, saluting me as I entered the room. There was a table and a selection of chairs stacked against the side wall, except for the two at the table, set opposite each other, obviously set for a face to face interview.

Initially I said nothing beyond a, "Good morning, Lieutenant, I hope your leg is healing well." If it sounded formal, that decision was made when I saw his ramrod stance. Then I seated myself with my back to the door and waited to see what Guy would do; I was determined to give him the option to stand or sit. He chose to sit opposite me; I took a notepad out of my pocket and fiddled with more pockets searching for a biro, but secretly I was switching on my recorder. Then I sat back and waited.

As I waited I let my eyes note every detail of his appearance.

His eyes were lowered as if asleep, his hands, clasped together as if clutching at something precious, were resting on the table. But with his erect posture speaking of military control being countered by the whiteness of his face, it was as if his usual tanned fit look had been airbrushed out; then add in the tensing of his jaw and the puckering of his lips, and he appeared a caricature of the man I had observed in the last few days.

I waited, he had asked to see me; let him speak. After what seemed like an hour, it was only five minutes, if the truth were told and my recorder measured, Guy Williams sighed and drew in his breath, before speaking in a calm and un-self-pitying voice.

"Matt, I am not guilty of the charge."

I played for time.

"Well, I'm glad to hear it, but it would help if I knew precisely what it is you are charged with, murder, magic or mayhem?"

"Treason."

"Treason? Why would you be charged with treason? Are you plotting to kill Harry Wales?"

"No, that would just be murder."

"His grandmother might not think so."

"You're laughing at me!"

"What else can I do, Guy? I'm in Afghanistan because of you and your plea for help over Hughes and co.; now they have disappeared, so why wouldn't the Brigadier and I wonder if you have got rid of them? If you are not the cause of their disappearance, tell me who is?"

It took some time for him to make the decision to speak; I made no attempt to hurry him. I did try looking relaxed, sitting back with my legs crossed and my hands casually clasped in front of me. It achieved my objective because seeing that I was not taking written notes, he opened up at last. Do I feel bad about secretly recording him, no, not in the slightest?

"It started some time ago; I cannot remember off the top of my head what it was that first made me turn and double check Hughes. It certainly goes back to a day when we were out near the Greenbelt and patrolling along a line of trees and hedges. We were under orders to clear a Taliban post that was still a mile ahead of us. The heat and the dust was just horrible that day and we were all low on water, so I stopped and radioed in for a resupply, because I reckoned a chopper could land quite near, there was a good dead zone to the east of us that was big enough for a jumbo jet, never mind a helo bird. In fact I was given to understand that drones had shown that we had a reasonable dead zone all around us. I had reasoned if the bird comes in low, it should land safe enough and I could send two guys back to pick up the delivery. Now don't laugh, I know the whole world thinks we're so strong, that we can dehydrate with impunity, but we can't. We needed a resupply before we got into the face to face battle; my men were tired and had slept the previous night in the open, in an abandoned courtyard. I needed my men on their feet and fit to go and the fight was only twenty minutes ahead of us, if we kept up our walking pace. Twenty minutes to a full scale battle and men dropping from dehydration, it wasn't on. I had to do something! It was about nothing worse; just that I knew most of them could soon collapse with dehydration. The decision seemed reasonable. So I passed the message along the line to stop, ordered a short rest, told them to rest and eat. I know it had to be cold MRE packs, we couldn't heat them, but it kept them seated, and resting while I sent Hughes and Norcross back to bring in the water. I gave them the marker for the chopper, I had a piece of bright red material, always do when on patrol. That is handy because you could wave it or put it down with some rocks, but getting the chopper near to the men was important. Thinking on it, I remember I also called up some artillery fire onto the Taliban co-ordinates, just as cover, while we took delivery of the water. We all rested, at first I didn't notice that when Hughes and Norcross reappeared half an hour later with packs of water, Johnstone and Lewis were with them. They had left the line without permission, that's an offence, that's more than just an AWOL thingy, it's possible to call it treason, but I let it go, we had the water. That was the first time and now weeks later they are still doing just that. Ignoring my commands and setting a bad example to the younger men."

His distress showed up in his voice and he suddenly seemed to slump into the back of the chair, as he continued in a repetitive manner.

"I know that I could have lost some good fighting men. If they are dehydrating you have to leave them behind, and you are legs, arms and fighting power short, all because of bloody drinking water!"

Again a pause, he shifted before standing up and leaning both hands on the back of his chair, his brow now creased with the effort of trying to remember what had taken place. He appeared older and distressed, as if trying to remember something significant.

"Anyway, why was that day important? Yes, it was the first time I noticed Lewis ... and Johnstone! They had run after the other two, and in fact with four pairs of hands to help, they had brought back a massively good supply of water. We went on to win a really decisive battle that day, and when it came to the debriefing, I failed to report the issue of Lewis and Johnstone's leaving the line without permission."

In his fatigue he started repeating himself saying,

"It was a treasonable offence in most circumstances. At the very least, I could charge them with going AWOL. It was Gareth Hughes who had said that the battle was successful because of the resupplying of the water. I let it all go; grateful that we had won something at last. The Brigadier praised me for a successful patrol. I was relieved I was OK in his eyes. I breathed again and felt I should forget about it, but it kept happening, and now this business."

He sat down again, paused as if it was something he was wishing he could forget about; as if he didn't like the success of the action being attributable to the men and not to him. Then he shook himself and started repeating himself. I didn't interrupt him; I knew it was a nervous reaction.

"It was more than a month before that I noticed that the quartet had a cunning way of overriding my orders. It kept happening. It was never done noisily, never very much said, but if I asked two of them, for example, to help stretcher a wounded man, somehow or other the four of them stretchered him; and ... everybody let them! All the rest of the platoon just let them. Why?"

By now he was sweating and his voice felt as if he would choke with tension. I took a packet of barley sugar out of my pocket, I even unwrapped the sweet before handing it sitting in the centre of the golden wrapper to him, by sliding it across the table.

"There, how about that, suck on it, it's untouched by human hands?"

He took the sweet with a look that pleased me, he was grateful and his smile said it all. So I helped him out, this time by reminding him where he was up to in his account, even though the outcome was as muddled as ever.

"Do you think the platoon is lazy?" I asked.

"No, no, no, I'll tell you why; because Hughes and co. seemed so eager to help and they were brilliant runners, no matter how heavy the injured man. It took me a couple of weeks to realize that I was suddenly having more injured than dead, and it felt brilliant! You try feeling good about yourself when one of your men is shot and fighting for his life. I didn't know what to make of them."

"And why are you in here now?"

"They've disappeared."

"And Ramin?"

"Him too."

"So do you believe they always went for the stretcher-bearing job to avoid front line combat?"

"How can I say that? But, yes! It could be that the younger men preferred the action. They would get restless if they had nothing to shoot at. 'I'm bored' was quite common between sorties, especially when out at an isolated outpost, no NAAFI, no showers, no Americans to josh and tease, and worse of all, with the very young, nowhere to kick a ball about."

"Really, I thought that was discouraged, at least off base."

"Well, you know what I mean, any stone or rolled up piece of webbing would do. Most of the young ones in my troop are from Merseyside. They live breathe and sleep Reds against Blues! And the rest are Manchester United against Manchester City."

"So you had a very young platoon?"

"At first very young; two were still only seventeen. They were the first to be killed. I did my best, but I lost six quite quickly. That's how Hughes and co. came in together."

He was rambling again, I handed over another sweet.

"At first I was grateful; I felt that at last I had some experienced men. Yes, I know, I was still getting injured men, but somehow they weren't dying. They weren't dying, can you imagine what that felt like? I could not believe my luck."

"No, I imagine not, but was your platoon held back to easier sites? I mean it's a known fact that some places are attacked more frequently than others."

"Not to my knowledge, no, we were all getting rotated, fair shares as you might say. Where do you think Ramin and the others have got to?"

"Probably half way to Pakistan by now for all I know."

"Poor Ramin, poor Wasima." I looked at Guy as he said that; his tone so completely sad, that I just knew there was a story behind that emotion.

"Why do you say that?"

Guy sat there and I swear there were tears in his eyes as he spoke.

"Ramin was, is in love. Wasima, he loves, loved her, Oh God it is horrible how that girl was murdered."

"The girl with the letter?" I knew I was being devious acting as if I had forgotten about Wasima, but it kept Guy talking.

"Yes, Wasima was asking for my help; she was promised to Ramin when she was six. There's no real news of her. Ramin's in love with her, that much is obvious."

Sitting in silence I thought through all the images of that day at the village.

"But how did the Taliban know we were in that obsolete observation post?" I asked, "How did you know?"

"It was only meant to be a practice, all I had been asked to do was give the two new men a taster of the terrain and talk fight strategy with them. I was told to take Ramin, in case I needed an interpreter if any stray Afghans came by. We were dropped in, car and all, by a Ch49 about an hour before you arrived. It all seemed plausible, Ramin was pleased, he always says yes to cash."

"Yes, I can see all that, but who sent you? Where did the order come from?"

"The Brigadier, I think!"

"Here in Bastion?"

"Yes. Em, well, hold on: I don't exactly know. It sounded like; yes it was our logistics man, Bunny Enright. Yes, that's right, it was Bunny who came through with details of the chopper to be used and he just read out the job details over the radio. I never saw the order."

"Nor the officer's name?"

I looked at the young man and realised that he was at that moment feeling stupid. He should have, at the very least, have asked Enright to deliver the instructions. Silence sat uncomfortably between us for several minutes, until I tried to push him about the order.

"Tell me, Guy, what are the specific details as you remember them, now?" I pushed an unopened barley sugar at him and opened one for myself. As I popped it into my mouth I thanked my wife for being once again the source of comfort. As we both sucked at the sweets, Guy carried on explaining the events of that weekend.

"There was a preamble about my platoon being rather reduced with two in the hospital and several members on R and R, meaning the men having downtime, and also it mentioned that a further four men were off site at Camp Bartkowski, making the

215

weekend a good time to train up the two new ones. I thought the rest of the platoon could enjoy a rest day. The suggestion was given to airlift a jeep and use the old observation post and it ended with a 'be back by Monday'; yes, that about covers it."

"And that didn't strike you as odd?"

"No, I understood what was implied by the order. I wonder if Enright still has it. It would help if he has it, wouldn't it?"

I nodded in agreement and offered to go and find this oddly named Bunny Enright. Guy's face relaxed.

"Thank you, sir, I would appreciate it, I don't know what else to do." He stood up at that, and then stood to attention, just as if I were the most senior man at Bastion.

"Relax, Guy, I'll try and find out what happened. Do they feed you here?"

"Yes, sir, I have everything I need, thank you."

"Tell me Guy; is this your first tour as lieutenant?"

"I was here as a second lieutenant, sir. I was in Germany before that."

"What were you doing there?"

Training on the tanks, apparently I'm good at getting things across, sir. I know, I'm now with the Fusiliers but I think the idea was to help me appreciate the heavy weaponry side of things."

I smiled to myself; his youthfulness was re-emerging at the thought of his previous posting. I held my hand out as I said,

"Bye for now, Guy. Keep calm and don't drive yourself crazy in here. Got anything to read?"

He shook his head and with a glimmer of a smile he clasped my hand before saying,

"Thank you, sir."

It crossed my mind that even his handshake had sincerity about it. I had to believe he was speaking the truth as I headed off for the Bastion cookhouse and had a meal, a second cup of coffee and then indulged myself by a trip to the NAAFI for a wicked bag of Haribos; didn't want to go through all my barley sugars too quickly, they were my memory of home.

Strolling about in the noisy pathways between the NAAFI and the gap in the wall that led to Leatherneck, it suddenly occurred to me to seek out a medic and ask about the statistics concerning the original battlefield deaths in Guy Williams's platoon. The war had been waging one way or another, since 2001 and in the last year many changes had come into place. But, in late 2007, Guy Williams was second in command of a platoon that had shown signs of being out of luck; the log book indicated six dead in as many weeks. Then so far in 2009, he had lost none, even though seven of his men had been badly injured. Extraordinary! To find out why, I turned and headed for the hospital.

Chapter Twenty
Camp Bastion the Hospital

I stood back mesmerized as with MERT ambulance after MERT ambulance, each of their sirens screeching out in agony on behalf of the wounded within, the reality of injury on the battlefield was played out before me. It was as if within the space of an hour the hospital faced the consequences of a major plane or train crash. I thought of the bombing of the London Underground known as the 7/7 bombings of 2005. This hospital faced such trauma every day and truthfully, sometimes every night. The war raged on without any regard for the convenience to the protagonists or for those who had to put them back together again.

Out of respect for all of those facing the urgency that surrounds the efforts needed to save lives, I just stood back and watched for the best part of an hour. The noise in the access area was deafening, the sirens did not stop until the ambulances came to an emergency stop that was terrifyingly fast. Not a second was to be wasted to save a soldier's life. The medics were lined up in silent groups, ready to receive the gurney and continue the fast pace to the triage area. Silence was broken again as the next ambulance arrived in similar haste to be greeted by the next group of medics. After a while, a man I would come to know as Surgeon Commander Peter Wallis walked past me dressed in green scrubs.

Suddenly he turned, and seeing me writing notes, he asked,

"Correspondent?"

"Yes, sir, American."

He smiled at that, as looking at my name tag he laughed and said almost teasingly,

"I've heard about you, Fleming. Why don't you follow me? Just keep to the outer edges of the theatre, so as not to interfere with my work, but you're welcome to watch. So remind me, which part of England are you from?"

"Cheshire, sir, does everyone know?"

"No, only those of us who needed to know. I was asked by General Raven to give my opinion should you approach me with any questions on the matter; I certainly have my own opinions. Never mind the kit, your English accent gives you away. Don't worry, I won't tell on you." He laughed before saying, "I'll make time for you later."

We were moving the short distance to the emergency triage area with its six stretchers lined up, three of them occupied and three ready for the next patients. I felt almost bewildered, the room was not locked down against the outside world's germs and bacteria; people came and went with amazing speed, though the door-less entry. As each wounded was brought in, they were also accompanied by the MERT members who had treated them on the Chinooks. These MERT medics were almost shouting out descriptions of the injuries, the vital life signs, and the amount of blood already transfused. At first I thought no one was listening, until I realised all the staff were silently responding like some well-oiled machine to what was before them. Within ten minutes most of the injured were passed on to be scanned or operated upon and the next were being carried in. There was a moment when a nurse almost crashed into another coming in with a box full of blood. It was dizzying to watch and these medics were volunteers from the NHS and the TA. Later I discovered Peter Wallis was from Hull, in the North West, and that this was not his first time at Bastion.

For over an hour I watched; sometimes I nearly choked with grief at the sight of young men mutilated by IED blast injuries. Part of me rebelled against the charge being levelled at the young Lieutenant Guy Williams. If a soldier is that injured, why is it the platoon leader's fault? Then I realised that there were as many ANA injured and even children being brought in for life-saving surgery. Peter Wallis had long since disappeared into the actual operating theatre and I continued to watch until, unable to bear seeing yet another little child blasted by an IED being carried in and followed by her dazed and bewildered father, a gracious bearded man, who was probably younger than he appeared. It was unbearable watching him frozen in agony as he saw the child's injuries. I went and stood outside.

Sometime later I wandered back into the hospital and ended where I had begun, in triage, just as Surgeon Commander Peter Wallis re-entered that space. We all realised that if we were lucky there was time for a few moments of rest and for a revitalising drink. Lifting his head up as if listening for a MERT, he smiled at his team and said,
"Keep your ears open, they won't give us too long; but I'd love a coffee." He turned and looked at me, "How about you, Fleming?"

Even as he spoke we were moving to a bay with drinks available and as he poured me a hot sweet coffee and we leaned against the wall drinking with relief and enjoying the pause in the ceaseless activity that had confronted the team, it was now that we were afforded that sudden moment, when the internal emotional elastic is once again allowed to relax. Was this how they survived? I know I felt wrung out, heaven alone knew what it did to these amazing men and women.

"It's all in the blood," the surgeon commander suddenly said. "The first five to ten minutes a man can lose all his blood."

I looked at him with a frown clouding my eyes; he saw it and recognised the ignorance of the civilian, the layman, in medical matters.

"Any bullet is bad, if the entry point is clean, if the bullet lodges there, then there is usually some hope of stemming the blood loss. But blast injuries from an IED can kill within minutes, because the heart goes on pumping and there is nothing to stop the loss. Femoral arteries need to be blocked within seconds and that's where we are experimenting with the new tourniquets. Every soldier is to be trained to use them, that and the question of speed in removing the injured from the scene. My colleagues and I are also experimenting with controlling the clotting of blood."

"I see, so are you saying that young Williams was not necessarily responsible for the heavy losses from last year?"

"Yes, I think that is a harsh non-medical view of the situation; ignorance of each other's responsibilities is not necessarily culpable, but nowadays we have made every soldier aware not only of the golden hour, but also of that precious ten minutes, to stop that blood loss. Added to that I'm now asking for the MERTs to carry blood, then transfusions can begin to go in within half an hour; while the injured are being flown here. It is precious time that makes a hell of a difference. It's all very difficult, especially if a man is still conscious and tries to pull off the tourniquet."

"Why on earth would they do that?" I asked with a frown on my face and a feeling that the wounded had no right to be difficult. Wasn't life as a medic difficult enough without the patient fighting you?

"If used properly, they have to be tight, I mean really tight and it's painful. So we make sure they are carefully watched, until they are in the chopper and the MERTs take over."

"Stopping the IEDs would be best!"

"Couldn't agree with you more, but what can we do? It's not up to us! The Taliban plant about seventeen thousand a year; they don't seem to care if their IEDs kill Afghans, just so long as they also kill our people as well."

He shrugged his shoulders and put his paper cup in the bin, just as the noise of a MERT was heard overheard.

"We'll talk later, Fleming!" and he walked back into the triage room. Smiling to myself, I realised he knew my name and why I was there. Had he been the one to ask for my involvement with this case and not young Williams? Was Williams's platoon secretly being used by the authorities to experiment with medical rescue strategies? If so, why didn't the army see fit to tell the lad, instead of subjecting him to worrying about the SIS men? There again, were they really after another investigation altogether and just pulling the wool over my eyes about investigating Williams and the pipeline?

Whatever it was, I could not see Guy Williams as a traitor. Leaving the hospital I collided into Alice

Holford. Pale-faced and frowning, she stopped as her peaked cap hit my chest; she still did not look up, as I steadied her with my right hand on her upper arm and quietly said,

"Alice, what's up, kiddo?"

Tears started, and I pulled her back into the hospital and found a corner where I could stand her up and let her cry. She smelt of rose water and soap. I felt devastatingly like a teenager holding his first girlfriend and feeling his manhood fighting for control.

Dear God, I missed my wife!

Chapter Twenty-One
Camp Bastion Wednesday Morning 0600 hours

I was up early, breakfasted and waiting outside General Mike Raven's office before seven a.m. In my notebook I had made a series of questions to put to him, concerning the charges facing Lieutenant Guy Williams. Simplistic they might be, but to me they got to the essence of the problem. The general agreed to see me and as usual he offered me coffee; I said nothing, just smiled my thanks and settled down in front of him, until I realised that I was meant to start the conversation.

"Is Lieutenant Williams still in the brig?" I asked.

"Sure, sure, for his own safety, yes."

"Who is after him? You've lost me."

"The Taliban, who else?"

"You are saying a deliberate threat has been made against young Williams by specific Taliban? Why?"

"They say he had sex with one of the natives."

"Oh, come on, pull the other one. Anyway I'm convinced he's besotted by Alice Holford. That's it, isn't it? You are locking him up to keep him away from her."

"No! Local girls can and do come onto this camp and others. Look at our market stalls. Once inside the camp, the females often remove their face veils and I'm a man who thinks many of them are beautiful; big brown eyes in dusky faces. They don't wear well, they live a hard life and some of the older women are anything but beautiful to me. Beauty is in the eye of the beholder, so we're led to believe."

It seemed as if he was trying to be flippant, but I remembered Tim Colbert and assumed it was a front used by American generals to avoid speaking the truth.

"Yes, but he's in love with Alice," I remarked as casually as I could, hopefully without sounding as if it were Alice's fault.

"Hum! The Taliban don't know that; no, the fact is he was seen chatting up a young woman during a visit to a village, the one where Ramin lives. End of story, whatever the circumstances, he's toast!"

"There were no Taliban in Ramin's village. I watched him shooting two who were creeping through the green belt, towards that village."

"Matt, the Taliban are everywhere. Their one talent is their invisibility; they infiltrate every level of life here. There is every possibility that there is at least one embedded in each of our camps and FOB's. We're trying to create an Afghan army. What a joke, would you want to join the ANA or even just work alongside them with the possibility of being side by side with the Taliban?"

"What do you mean, joke?"

General Raven looked at me before sighing heavily and saying,

"Most of the suicide bombers turn out to be Afghans working for us, in one capacity or another."

I sat sipping at my coffee until he said,

"Top up?"

I nodded and held out my cup. He topped it up and added milk and sugar without asking. It was a bit too much for my liking, but I said nothing and cradled the mug, watching the swirling bubbles left by his rigorous stirring. As for General Mike Raven, he sat looking at me as if challenging me to a silent duel. I felt pressured.

"Exactly who asked for me to come out here and be the patsy between the two sides?"

"What makes you think that?"

"Oh, come on, Mike! I'm not completely brain dead. The PM said there was a traitor in Camp Bastion, 'blah blah blah blah blah!' stirring up trouble by complaining about MERTs arriving late and causing deaths as a result. So I am required to go undercover and find the bastard. Fine, I'm eminently suited for that task. There's a young man locked up because he asked for help with four older men who had a habit of disobeying him. I suspect that this quartet will turn out to be carrying out medical experiments for the hospital; waffle, waffle, blood and waffle and the magic of something ordered to be used in the first ten minutes, the so called platinum ten minutes! Now these four men have disappeared along with my so-called interpreter, while you and the British hang

227

young Williams out to dry. Truthfully, how do you know there's a price on his head?"

The silence was deafening and I had no intention of being the one to break it. Neither was I going to leave without an explanation of events and an answer as to the whereabouts of my so-called interpreter. At least five minutes went by while Mike Raven sat without so much as glancing at me.

"It is nothing to do with the poppy fields, then? What are you Brits up to?"

"Too many issues to explain in one word, General, but yes, the poppies are out as far as I'm concerned; try the Pakistani request for a gas pipe route from Turkmenistan, through the middle of Afghanistan and what, take it over or under the Baba range, I think not! A minefield of issues, not least that, yes, it would go straight through the dammed poppy fields! Then there is the issue of young women mutilated and murdered, trying to use the same routes to escape forced marriages to old men! Does that concern any of us? And, I suppose there are other human rights problems? Some want to escape simply because they want an education, or women who are just running away from being beaten because they aren't wearing the hijab or the chadri, or the burka, or because they were showing their ankles."

I stopped for breath and a sip of coffee before deciding that if I was to go home with my tail between my legs I might as well say it all. I put my cup down and spoke the words I wanted to say.

"If you can't be arsed over the women, there is still the political issue of Pakistan wanting a gas pipe! It is still a tribal land. To me it is a land of enforced ignorance; of massive brutality towards women and a crime against even Islamic law, which doesn't demand this treatment of women, but the PM wants to know about bloody gas pipes!"   My voice changed to even a deeper level of sarcasm. "Should he listen to the Pakistani request for financial support for this gas line, if I say I wouldn't recommend it, is my head for the chop from Pakistan? If I say go ahead, the tribal leaders will find me super-fast. Would I even get out of this godforsaken land alive, when even the military don't own me and might put me up as a scapegoat to share young Williams's day in court, if we ever get to a real courtroom? And his only acknowledged crime is that he had been seen talking to a young unveiled girl and as such, he is now marked as a criminal. Doubly marked, dear God! There was no chaperone, not even an interpreter. Oh dear, she had handed him a note, written for her by her aunt! For goodness sakes, what is going on in this country?"

The general was by now twirling a biro and suddenly he stopped and pointed it at me saying,

"But you don't understand, the girl was helping her aunt."

"So? What was Auntie doing?"

"She was running an underground school, for about twenty young women who wanted to learn to read and write. The note simply said, 'Help us to escape'. Williams was reading it just before an elder walked up and snatched it from his hands. Too late, the girl was bundled away, who knows where, she's probably dead by now. All we do know for certain is that according to Ramin, she was beaten."

"As in whipped to death, no doubt?" Even as I spoke I could feel the dryness in my mouth, at the sadness such evil triggered in me, and then I felt doubly foolish for asking such a question in the first place. Of course the girl was going to be whipped!

The general added sadly,

"Ramin never saw her again, there's nothing we can do against such ignorance. As for Williams, we are protecting him for the moment. My suggestion as put to the British brigadier, and currently being discussed by him and his superiors, is that they send Williams home. The Taliban can get a man on this site quick as anything, they'd find him and slit his throat; and yes, they would believe they are protecting their women by doing so, we are all evil sex maniacs according to the Taliban."

"Maybe you're right. I have never quite got my head around Norcross's attitude to the lad."
Again I was lying; I knew exactly why, Norcross wanted Alice.

"Why don't you go and ask him?" the general said with a shrug.

We talked on a while longer, and then I left to do as the General suggested. On the way over I called into the NAAFI and got the lad some Haribos bags, a packet of biscuits, a paperback book and a tub of Wet Ones. *Why not,* I had said to myself? I had been glad of the Wet Ones given to me all those days ago at the Chester Barracks. Was it really only eight days ago? Anyway, they had proved very useful, when the heat became oppressive or when you've no loo roll.

Then I headed off to something akin to a garage where after several attempts I met up with Bunny Enright. He had the work chit and assured me he had taken the order over the phone from Andy Norcross. Repeatedly checking, he never faulted; it was definitely Norcross.

It took a while to get a pass to visit Williams, I think the Military Police were still suspicious of me, but it was obvious that Guy was pleased to see me. Within a few minutes the bag of sweets was opened and he laughingly invited me to help myself. As I hoped, a sugar-induced placid well-being came over both of us as we munched our way through the jelly sweets.

"Alice is worried about you," I said slowly and quietly.

Chapter Twenty-Two
Camp Leatherneck Wednesday Evening

A gathering sand storm seemed to be drowning the atmosphere of Leatherneck: I found it hard to breathe, and my face felt dirty with the grit blowing onto me as I walked towards the D-FAC for dinner and hopefully a chance to talk with Alice.

Surely, I owed her some of the information gathered during my conversation with Guy. It felt like a duty, I said to myself, desperately trying to shut out any acknowledgement that I fancied the woman myself. There was no need to pretend; they were seconds, mere seconds, of doubt that flashed through my mind as to my feelings for her. I was not inhuman; I was in a situation that was stressful. I believed I was no different from the rest of the men who came into contact with her. There was a sexiness that was reminiscent of Marilyn Monroe about her, and I was a sucker for Marilyn! If men think of sex as often as the press would have us believe, I believed myself to be slow in comparison with my fellow men, maybe the Taliban were right. Men cannot control themselves and all are sex maniacs! But I would have hated it, if this lovely girl was shrouded away from the sun. I preferred the idea of men being able to control themselves in the presence of women.

I helped myself to a steak dinner and delayed collecting a pudding. Sorry to say, but even the native-born Yanks preferred the English puddings and I resolved to head off there after enjoying the pound weight of medium rare steak. Yes, the USA Army catering was a better provider of steak. The whole thing evened itself out, if you just planned your dietary needs with some care.

Half way through my massive piece of beef steak and just at that point where the meat begins to lose its heat, I felt her slip her leg over the bench and cosy up beside me. Dear God, my heart missed a beat and I almost cried out in my happiness at the very scent of her. I couldn't speak, but then neither did she, as without so much as a hello, Alice begun hoovering up her food, like a starving child. I let her eat, I finished my now cold steak and watched her as colour came back into her cheeks and the munching gradually became less desperate.

"Missed lunch and tea again?" I asked with a teasing smile and she nodded back with the cheekiest grin I have ever seen.

"If I were a man, I swear I would have been cursing all day long. I know he's a general, and did you know he's my uncle, probably not? But he is such a needy man, and he's my relative, but he's useless when it comes to doing things. He needs an army of secretaries and assistants."

Alice had turned to face me and yet she seemed to still be touching me, so close was she to my side. I kept my arms resting on the table, it seemed important not to look as if I had my hands or arms anywhere near her; she seemed to press closer as others pushed to get onto the other end of the bench, upon which we were seated. Glancing round I realised the D-FAC was filling up to bursting point, obviously the bad weather had brought more people than usual back to base. Time to move, but would she leave me if I suggested we went for a walk?

"I saw Guy today. Can't tell you here," I whispered, "Shall we walk a bit?"

The joy on her face was magic, but I knew it was all for him. *Take what crumbs you can get,* I said to myself, as I stacked our plates and deposited them on the dumb waiter.

We walked towards a tent that was set up as a recreational facility with Sky TV installed. It mostly roared out sports programmes and nearly always had young soldiers joshing each other over the winners and losers. The noise covered any conversation and seemed a good enough excuse to suggest we stopped and talked in the tent.

"I'm tired, Alice, well at least my feet are, I walked too much today, let's sit in here." She nodded and smiled and we settled again on one of those picnic type tables with attached benches. Again she sat close and I could smell her scent over the sweetness of her natural body sweat. It was like a balm and again I felt the inner tensions easing away.

"How is he?"

"He looked OK. You are worried about him, aren't you? Do you know something I don't know?"

"I've heard two things." She lowered her voice. Against the noise of the TV, I had to move nearer as she lifted her head up, so as to whisper.

"There is some talk of a Taliban contract out on him and there was something to do with the numbers in his unit being killed."

"You're telling me they are saying there's a 'you'll get paid if you kill him' contract out on our young Guy? Sounds more like the Italian Mafia to me." I tried to sound flippant rather than serious. Why frighten her more than she was already? She continued anxiously,

"But he was seen talking to this girl and she had no niqab on and then he took some note from her. She's been killed or kidnapped; nobody can find her, and now they are going to kill Guy."

The older I get the more I realise that every account of any incident in life, no matter how innocent, is always distorted by the informants' emotional motives, desires and perceptions of the event, as it applies to their personal needs. Gossip becomes Chinese whispers so quickly and even though I tried to convince Alice not to believe them, why should Alice be any different? So it was that she stressed the idea of Guy Williams being targeted because of overhearing the word 'contract' and, being a staunch follower of CSI and Murder She Wrote, to her mind the outcome was inevitable. She believed the Taliban would invade Camp Bastion, find the holding block and kill Guy. They were Taliban, and that's what they did; they killed people!

While scenario after scenario escaped her pretty lips, I unashamedly enjoyed the nearness of her lithe little body, with all the disgusting perverseness of the dirty-minded uncle in 'A View from the Bridge.' Thanks, Arthur Miller, I'm no different from other men! Thanks for reminding me how the artificial life of a soldier, when out in a war zone can play havoc with your hormones. Thanks for making me realise how important family becomes to lonely frightened soldiers!

Then it happened; MERT after MERT was heard WHOOP, WHOOP, WHOOPING their way across the skies and then ambulances screeching their way to the hospital, until reality took all sense of comfort out of our naughty half hour alone in a crowded tent.

I walked Alice back to her billet, and looking deep into her tearful eyes I graciously informed her,

"I'll protect him from the Taliban."

How daft can you get; a promise I could no more keep than I could fly to the moon, but I realised that I have a soft spot for childlike pretty girls. My wife often calls it my sugar-daddy, dirty old man mind! I call it my knightly spirit, but I don't think this occasion came under the umbrella of Arthurian legend. I just didn't know what else to say.

"Good night, Alice. Don't worry too much. If you can't sleep, why not write Guy a letter and I could take it to him tomorrow morning."

The smile Alice gave me reassured me that she would be alright, at least for the present. By now my feelings had demoted themselves to something akin to some protective uncle, as I left her smiling.

The night sky was dark, yet full of minute stars that seemed higher than usual, a deceptive picture with no appearance of the moon. It was 2009 and I had no idea what to look for in the sky over Afghanistan, possibly the bright star was Sirius, but I couldn't be certain, I only knew my own patch of the northern night sky, one well learnt walking home from The Bells of Peover after a pleasant evening drinking with my friends, Maurice and Evelyn. I hoped they were thinking on me, even as I was missing them at that moment.

Chapter Twenty Three
Camp Leatherneck, Thursday Morning

I had breakfasted early and wandered over to see General Mike Raven's offices, checking for news of the missing Ramin and the British soldiers. I was told that they were still missing and several chopper searches had proved abortive. I took the opportunity to contact C and report via a Skype link.

Alice joined me about half an hour later, just as I left the main office, and gave me a fat envelope addressed to Guy Williams. I took it without allowing her to see the smile I suppressed. Young love and fear had obviously kept her awake for most of the night. Dark circles under her eyes confirmed my suspicions were right.

"No news, yet, I'm afraid," I said, answering her enquiry about Ramin and the missing men.

Alice looked almost close to tears; shaking her head she said,

"I can't believe Guy would betray them to the Taliban. He hates the Taliban. He despises their treatment of women. I just don't understand how the Taliban expect us to be responsible for the weakness of men. I don't think I'm an object of temptation, do you?"

"Sweetie, nearly every religion likes to believe women are the sinful temptation, it allows men to exonerate themselves of sin. You know, the old, 'It was her fault, God!' The old Adam and Eve syndrome; Adam had no willpower against the charm of Eve's invitation to disobedience, that, I am afraid to say, means that today it is you as the prettiest thing around, in this horrible dusty place. You are the temptation."

She looked up at me with eyes like saucers and I watched her gradually hug herself as if trying to shut the world out of her own environment, out of the space she could regard as her own. I waved her letter at her and said with complete solemnity,

"I'll try and get an answer for you."

Leaving her, I made my way to the main road to jump aboard a bus. Fortunately I didn't have to wait too long, but the journey took nearly half an hour; the bus had to stop twice to allow for important vehicles to pass. I sat looking out at the business of Leatherneck then the various areas of Bastion, as the bus wound its way through four miles of roadways. Looking around I was amazed at the extent and variety of equipment and skills visible to me, it was staggering. A town in a desert bearing no relationship to the old fashioned tented cities of the past. It felt more solid, admirable, yes, but mind-boggling, when one tried to not think about the cost of war.

Stopping just one corner from the holding block, I was at the desk within minutes, asking for a pass. I found Guy was dressed more casually and seemed in better spirits. Saying nothing, I just handed him Alice's letter before sitting down and waiting while he read it. At first he hesitated but I gave him a nod and just sat back in a relaxed position examining my hands and occasionally glancing up at his pale face. He seemed to have lost some of his tan, he was so tense.

Watching, I felt positive I saw a tear in his eye. Not knowing what she had written, I could only surmise that she had declared her love for him and her belief in his innocence. He folded the pages and replaced them in the envelope, before putting it in his pocket. The feeling I got from his expression was that he was happy with her letter, but wanted to keep its contents to himself. I took my lead from him and said nothing, just sat in silence waiting for him to speak.

"Have they found the men?" he asked.

"No, nothing to indicate what has happened to them."

"Maybe nothing has 'happened' to them."

"What do you mean?" I asked him.

"Well, if they are just off on a jaunt of their own devising, why should we worry about them? They had asked for the chance to go looking for trade ideas for after the war. Do you see what I mean, as a section they just did whatever suited them, without much explanation to me? It made me look weak, when I should have been in control. Well, I was in control; I knew what I was doing and what the guys should be doing, except for those four. I found myself always having to check they were in line. Well, they were in line, but they weren't, if you know what I mean."

Listening to his verbal stumbling around I decided to push him further. I pulled a face, the sort where your mouth pulls down like a coat hanger.

"Not really," I said as I crossed my legs and sat back with my arms cosy across my belly, fingers linked and wishing I had a generous after dinner type of cigar to complete the picture of a comfortable middle-aged man, who had all the time in the world to listen and counsel his young friend. I was convinced that there was information to cull from his weary brain, if I could only get him to realise that it had to have been buried somewhere inside of himself. It must have worked, for he took a deep breath and kicked off with a stream of consciousness that required no prompting. Off he went repeating himself; he was more like an old man than I was, at that moment.

"They were always a step ahead of a command. It was like living with predictive text; they knew what I was going to say before I had finished saying it and they were off, whoosh!"

My head said to me, be patient, remember what he had said before, listen for any changes in the story. He went on the words were familiar.

"It was as if they were leading the team, because the younger men just followed them as they walked on always about ten or twenty paces apart. I mean I never had to remind anyone not to bunch up, I never had to say, watch where you are putting your feet. They just walked on behind the group on point duty, and I would watch from my position further back. I'd see them just pointing to suspicious-looking disturbed ground and then they'd signal to the following guys. Next moment I'd see everybody just move one step to the left or to the right. It looked like a snake swishing through the undergrowth or what? A 'follow my leader kids' game around the playground. Only it was no playground. Of course they couldn't do anything against sniper fire, but if a guy was hit and it was 'man down' well, then they'd race towards the man and were suddenly in charge, giving orders to the younger men. They always took control and the men let them. Hughes always said, 'Well done', to me, as he rushed past with the other guys carrying the injured man to the place where the chopper would land, in a dead zone. I never had to tell them. But the odd thing is he always made it sound as if I had personally saved the soldier's life, but I hadn't done a thing except radio in for a bird, a MERT, which I did as I felt it was something to do. I mean, I felt brushed aside by their efficiency and I couldn't swallow the fact that they were so polite to me, I couldn't challenge them."

"Guy, you are afraid, tired and locked up. Naturally a little paranoia is going to take some control of you. Look at me."

He lifted his eyes and obeyed my request.

"Sorry," he said as he shook his head and looked at me.

"You care about your men and at this moment in time, you are in a nasty bubble in your life. No officer likes to lose his men, whether by bullet or them just going AWOL. It is called responsibility! What's more, I'm quite certain your superior officers are not planning to lynch you. Until you know more, think of this as protective custody. Don't keep going over the rights and wrongs of this, just read your letter again."

I stood up to leave, but before I got to the door, he asked,

"Any answer from Bunny?"

"Oh yes, sorry, I forgot! Must be getting old! Yes, Bunny is quite certain that Norcross phoned in the order. Sorry, I'll have to get you the chit, left it in my case."

His lips compressed with a tension that seemed excessive and I suspected it was due to an unreasonable 'Alice and Norcross' thought.

I nodded and left with a reminder that I could carry a reply to Alice later that day. He smiled and said, "Please!" with an almost childlike happiness suddenly taking possession of him.
It confirmed the contents of Alice's letter for me.

But more importantly, Guy Williams, for all his repetitive rabbiting on about his grievances over the four man section, and their so called lack of discipline, never wavered from his story. I believed him now.

Chapter Twenty- Four
Camp Bastion Lunch Break 1230 hours

Lunch with the Brits felt wonderfully familiar. It was my second Wednesday in Afghanistan and almost a relief to eat English food. I indulged in a beer-battered piece of fish and real chunky British chips; well I call them British! I was dining, in the Brits' cookhouse, with Brigadier Henry Fulton; he was a good looking man of about fifty and currently in charge of Bastion. It seemed evident to me that he had not recently been out on patrol; his combat uniform smelt clean, an unusual occurrence even for the most fastidious soldier in Afghanistan, and it also looked as if it had been washed and pressed, as if it had just come from a high class laundry. Even my wife would have been impressed with the standard of care. I couldn't resist asking if he had a batman to attend to his uniform. He laughed so much, and I blushed at his noisy response, heard by most of the other diners.

"Good grief, Matt, this isn't the dark ages and I'm just a brigadier. Secret, when these are dry, but not bone dry, mind you, I put them between two boards I keep under my mattress. I got the idea from thinking about my trouser press at home. You know the sort you see in hotels. You should try it, it is quicker than ironing. And it's good for my back, sleeping on boards."

He was roaring with laughter and so were several others, as I just carried on calmly eating my fish. Chit chat followed, accompanied by a mug of real Yorkshire tea, strong and sweetened, and a pudding to die for, not seen since school days; jam roly-poly and custard. As the Brigadier said in one of his loud-voiced asides, "The Americans can't beat our puddings!"

Afterwards we walked out of the cookhouse towards the airport. The air was more settled now and everything felt fresh again. It amused me to think that we in Britain think we have the monopoly on rapidly changing unpredictable weather, when it's the same the world over.

By now Henry, as he reminded me he was called, was treating me to a description of the plans developing for the British troops at Camp Bastion in 2010.

"Things will change, you'll see."

I waited patiently, there seemed no point in stopping his stream of information; he appeared as a man who liked the sound of his own voice, I thought of it as verbal diarrhoea, painful to listen to and just wishing it would stop. However, my ears picked up as he progressed to the next bit of information.

"We're expecting a few thousand more troops and I propose we develop more FOBs to accommodate them. The hospital is to be expanded with a ward for ANA injured. Most importantly I have to assist the surgeon general with a teaching programme."

Now I was interested, I waited, hoping to learn something new; it came in the form of a black gadget he produced from a pocket. Handing it to me he asked,

"Do you know what this is, Matt?"

"Afraid not," I responded as I turned the black band round and round. I hadn't a clue and yet I hesitated to give it back to him. It was clear that he believed it was important, obviously it was neat and easy to carry by a soldier in combat gear, but what it was, I could not immediately guess, until he uttered the word, "Tourniquet!" Now I could see a purpose in it. Handing it back, I asked,

"How does it work?"

"Second question, how long does it take a man to bleed out?"

Here I was on safer ground, as I answered, "Four minutes."

At this Henry Fulton smiled and said, "Who've you been talking to?" before he explained that every soldier was to be issued with one of these tourniquets and the minute a soldier hears 'man down' the nearest man would run and block off the main artery affected, and the joy of it was that it could even be applied with one hand, if a wounded soldier had to apply it to himself.

"Only problem is to save a man's life you have to be ruthless and keep the tourniquet tight until the MERTs arrive even though it hurts like hell. Some have loosened it and bled out, orders nowadays are that you don't take your eyes off an injured man no matter how much he screams. It's tough on all the men, but the alternative is a box home."

He was like an excited kid showing off the greatest invention since sliced bread. Suddenly, he looked at my expression and realised that I didn't seem convinced; he changed as he said, 'I'll show you."

Fortunately for me, at that moment Peter Wallis come towards us and chided the brigadier with his tardiness.

"Henry, we'll miss the delivery."

Henry Fulton started off after Peter Wallis and shouted, "Come on, Fleming!"

I followed the two excited men and had to almost run to keep up with them. They were heading straight for the airfield and following various MERT personnel all running, and all excited.

Part of me wondered if the Queen was arriving, but no, it was a C130 taxiing to a space on the parking apron. We gathered and waited until the soldiers unloading suddenly deposited large crates with the obvious Red Cross mark and the word Hospital clearly visible on the side. I looked across and saw Bert coming down the ramp.

"Excuse me," I said to Wallis and Fulton as I detached myself from the group to make my way over to Bert, now coming towards me with a massive grin on his face.

"Hi, mate, how's it going? Been shot at yet?"

"Come on, Bert, want to get rid of me in case I stow away home on your rickety old bird? Looking at her now, I'm surprised she still flies!"

Bert roared with laughter and we shook hands like two civilised old men. He filled me in with what the last ten days had thrown at him and we commiserated with each other over the recent repatriations.

"So, how yer doing? Finding it difficult? Bet the food's terrible."

"That's about all that is OK. Just had fish and chips all fresh cooked, and jam roly-poly with real custard, and a cup of Yorkshire tea in which you could stand your spoon up. It was the colour of mud and tasted delicious, know what I mean?"

We both laughed at the image and were nearly ready to get onto the next bit of chatter when Hudson screeched to an emergency stop right beside us. I could see my ILBE and helmet on the back seat, together with Hudson's things and two M4 rifles.

"I've packed yer things kind of hoping I ain't forgotten anything, sir, but we are gonna ship out in five."

"Good God, Hud, what's up? Have they found Ramin and the others? Are they OK?"

Before Hudson could reply, Bert laughed and said, "Pity, I thought you were to come back with me." I laughed and slapped Bert on the back as I said, "Soon, I hope, Bert, it was good to see you. Have a safe journey home."

With that I was in the jeep and being driven to the far end of the Chinook apron, where to my surprise I found myself confronted by a team of twelve Australian Marines, already seated down the sides of the open Chinook. Hudson abandoned the jeep to airport staff and our luggage was taken from us, we boarded in silence as the tail ramp closed and the blades began their whoop, whoop, and endless whoop! Any hope of seeing an aerial view of Bastion as we rose up was blighted by the dust covering the Chinook completely as it rose off the ground, and the unknown emergency was highlighted for me by the direct route away from the camp. There was no circuit inspection of the site, which was often the method used to confuse watching Taliban.

The speed of the lift suddenly kicked my stomach into touch and thanks to the jam roly-poly I burped the discomfort out, without any embarrassment. Soldiers seldom notice such apparently anti-social bodily reactions, but I had felt a moment of shame as I remembered my lack of dyspepsia medication.

We flew to Camp Bartkowski and landed in a dust storm caused by the Chinook hovering over the landing site. Unable to see in the dusty cloud, I felt Hudson guiding me and our kit down the ramp, where we had to jump a good two feet to alight from the machine. Immediately it was up and away before we reached the edge of the open space that constituted the heliport.

Was that an indication of trouble at Camp Bartkowski? The afternoon passed quickly, with briefings and other meetings. I was forcing myself to keep up with these sharp-witted young men, I felt old and past it. Hudson helped me by keeping me on track, as we moved between weapons checks and explanations about the maps, about possible timings, followed by visits to the stores for a change of footwear to proper mountain climbing boots and woollen clothing, including long johns, vests, gloves and scarves, ready for the cold. That was when I began to fear that I really should stay back at the camp. No such luck, Tim Colbert was adamant, "You'll be fine, man, and stop fretting!"

We were all bedded down by nine to be woken at three the next morning.

Chapter Twenty-Five
FOB Bartkowski and the Baba Mountains

Woken by the tremendous din from a Chinook arriving with an ISO can hanging beneath it, I leapt out of bed and grabbing my jacket I ran out to see what was going on. It seemed as if everyone was up and dressed, except myself. Sneaking back inside, I quickly threw on the rest of my clothes and the new boots. I completed the outfit with the vest and webbing, loaded the bags with the MRE food rations, drinking water and extra Haribos. Tucking the knee and elbow pads into various pockets, I then checked my rifle and helmet and was outside lining up with the rest of the men, as we were corralled aboard the waiting Chinook, now minus its original cargo and being topped up with fuel.

As we took off, so another Chinook was seen heading towards the camp to pick up more Marines.
What I didn't see was who had been aboard, on its journey inward; but many moons later, Alice told me that she had watched us fly away towards Baba with a sinking feeling. Yes, Alice had flown in with General Raven, much to Captain McNaughton's chagrin; she would normally have been the accompanying secretary.

General Raven and Brigadier Fulton had come to spend the day with Tim Colbert and other ISAF senior men, to plan their next combat moves in the region.

But Alice later spoke of her uncle as if she believed he was getting paranoid about her and afraid to let her out of his sight. "It was as if I was glued to his side," and she explained that she had spent that day wearing a groove into the dusty ground, as she went backwards and forwards to the D-FAC with fresh coffee and cookies. But, as I was to find out, she still found time to write a love letter to Guy. What she wrote to him was to have far-reaching results for both of them.

Having no idea what was going on either in Camps Bastion, Leatherneck, nor Bartkowski, I settled down to the problem of where was Corporal Hudson Elliott? I couldn't see him in amongst the men sitting along the sides of the Chinook. There were four people sitting up front in the middle of the chopper, but I knew by their size and shapes they were not Hudson. For a moment, I chided myself with the hastiness of my reaction to the arrival of the bird; was I meant to have been on the second one? Would Hudson realise what I had done? What I did notice was the pile of climbing ropes and other equipment, all of which shouted loud and clear; mountains! I quaked a little with a fear that climbing was a young man's game. It seemed as if every ten minutes or so I needed to keep reminding myself that I was not immortal, I was racing through life, and the only hope I had of surviving to my next birthday was to tread carefully.

We flew for less than twenty minutes, the contrast to the same journey by car was very marked, and it felt safe in the bird. We were deposited just below the abandoned checkpoint at Kernark. Memories of the previous visit felt very powerful, and I made myself gear up a notch, to face potential danger. Surprisingly the sun came up to a warmer April day than was usual in this part of the Baba mountain range. I was grateful to find the patrol had settled down to brewing up some strong sweet coffee, and with two look-outs posted, the rest of the men settled down to sleep. I looked up at the guy standing with his weapon just poised on the edge of the broken window ledge and my frown must have spoken volumes for he smiled and informed me in a whisper, "Reinforcements due any moment!"

After that I shut my eyes and wished for Hudson to appear with the reinforcements. I wasn't being childish, there it was once again inside my head, and the bell was ringing. 'For whom the bell tolls' I silently screamed, 'not for me, please, not for me'.

If I shook it was because I clearly remembered that none of this was in the job description given me at Vauxhall Cross. No mention of dawn raids and no mention of having to carry a gun into combat. My first trip to Camp Bartkowski had been at Alice's suggestion. A bit of sight-seeing that had gone wrong, thanks to Norcross. Was Norcross no more than another star-crossed, love-sick idiot dreaming of the prettiest girl in Afghanistan, or was he a cunning traitor?

I suddenly wanted to know what the military were up to in their search for the missing men, and what did any of this have to do with the number one item on my list of assignments; the writing of a report about the possibility of running a pipeline from Turkmenistan to Pakistan across the centre of Afghanistan?

My cover was research about drug trafficking, the truth was also about the helicopters and the funding of cheap gas pipes for Pakistan!

Investment in such a scheme being secretly targeted by the Pakistan government at the major international players, who might be interested in supporting Pakistan's desperate need for cheap energy, was not something the PM was prepared to publicly consider without an impartial secret opinion. I was his chosen impartial opinion. What a responsibility. I seriously doubted my ability to assess the situation properly without spelling out loud and clear those contemptuous words – OIL and GAS! Yes, the East can always accuse the West that it is all about oil or gas. Where was the West when Russia invaded Afghanistan? Nowhere to be seen, and now Turkmenistan's available gas was changing all that. The complexity of history with its ever repeated political mistakes was not something I wanted to look at, yet the PM seemed determined that I should, without giving his game away.

I heard the incoming bird and with some relief closed down the arguments fermenting in my brain. If I was laughing inside myself, it was because I'd had been so placed in Camp Leatherneck with cover stories galore, that it was a wonder anybody believed any of them.

To the PM I was the man who was meant to save the Labour Party's face, just before a general election.

To young Williams, I was the genius who would restore his authority in his platoon.

To General Mark Raven, I was trying to prevent the illegal export of drugs to Britain.

To Surgeon Commander Peter Wallis, I was the man who would preach the success of his tourniquet.

To Brigadier Henry Fulton, I was the man to uncover any traitors in Camp Bastion and beyond.

To Gareth Hughes, I was a fellow SIS operative sent to help him find the unknown traitor in Camp Leatherneck.

To Hudson, I was just a bloke who got him a cushy number for the last few weeks of his deployment.

To Alice, I was the man sent to save her beloved's neck!

Was it any wonder that I felt confused, when all I believed myself to be was an observer for the viability of laying an oil or gas pipe line, through a 'post war-torn' country!

The PM had said, "We need to look to the future, we know there is gas in the Turkmenistan region, but just how possible is it going to be to extract it to the nearest port? And which port? Is Pakistan barking up the wrong tree, trying to get it via the land route? All I hear about is tribal leaders who would never allow such a pipeline over their land. Just give me an honest opinion, Fleming, that's all I ask."

Honest opinion, my eye! Fucking oil or gas, there's nothing honest in fucking oil or gas! was my angry thought at that moment, as I sat staring into space, my mind remembering the scene at Number 10, and the PM looking rather hangdog and tired as he shook hands with me, before he turned away to his election campaign manager, standing nervously in the wings.

Life came back to me as I watched Hudson crouching down to enter via a mouse- hole in the wall. There were several and he seemed to have chosen the smallest; I laughed out loud and woke everyone up.

That was the last occasion for a laugh I would have for quite some time. Within the hour we had set off up into the Baba Mountains, single file and spaced out so as to present a limited target to any snipers. There was little chance of an IED on this route. It was too precious to the drug traffickers making their way to Pakistan. I reasoned that this was my one chance to travel along a 'drug route' and so I made certain my camera was fit to shoot the evidence.

We must have climbed four thousand feet before we stopped and gathered beneath a massive overhang of rock. For a moment I thought they were going to ask us to climb the almost smoothed rock with its buttress ends, which somehow hid us from view, even if someone was above us. But how does one climb such an overhang? And the buttresses were smooth as glass to my inexperienced eye. It all reminded me of pictures I had seen of the famous La Dura in Spain; none but the experts would tackle such a threateningly impossible climb. I was no expert and I couldn't believe that most of the Marines sitting around about me, leaning against their two hundred pound loaded backpacks, would manage the climb. Watching them in total relaxation, as they took refreshment and rest before the next order was given, I marvelled at their ability to unwind at a moment's notice and to spring into action within a second of a command or threat.

The lead scout, an Aussie Marine called Bruce by his mates, was nowhere to be seen and the staff sergeant, also a big Aussie Marine, having finished his rations and drink, stood up and signalled us to gather round. There was sufficient space for all of us to get near enough to him without giving away our position to anyone further up the mountain. He waved his radio at us as he spoke.

"Okay, all you guys, Bruce has found us a less stressful climb, so, Matt, you can stop looking worried."

So it showed, I tried a watery smile of humiliation as he continued,

"We're going off to the left and we are going to be roped for a while. Just don't try and rush, we are only going as fast as the slowest. Which, Matt, will probably be you. Sorry mate no disrespect to a Pom, and you're not exactly a young'un either, but yer, well, how shall I put this? You're the Pom who could get totally whacked, sorry to say so."

"It's okay," I said with a shrug.

"Right, so hopefully yer looking like yer could keep going a while longer, but truthfully, yer no spring chicken, mate! I've never been up this high with an elder before, so shout id it gets too much for yer, OK?"

The guys all smiled and made murmuring comments like, 'Good luck cobber', or 'yer doing fine for a Pom' and I felt even older and more of a burden than I ever had in my entire life. But roped with Hudson taking up the end position as the absolute tail end, I felt safe. Hudson was strong enough to hold on to me, of that I was certain. But I knew if I had to hold him, should he slip, we would both be gone for good. So I smiled and accepted all the care around me; Hudson behind and a burly Marine in front. The rope around my waist felt fine and an hour later when it was removed I almost regretted the loss. We were very exposed on a narrow ledge for quite some time. I couldn't help noticing that it seemed well worn, a sign that it was frequently used. Then all of a sudden the world seemed to level out and we walked on until we disappeared into a rocky fissure.

For the next couple of hundred metres or more, we quietly walked along a tunnel-like crevasse. The gradient was more comfortable and we sensed we were nearing the end of the climb, when all of a sudden we walked out onto a fairly barren flat mountain shelf that had a complete drop on one side and a craggy wall of rocks on the other, which gave the bare minimum of shelter from the wind. Quick as a flash the Marines seemed to have assembled a camp-like base. Each seemed to know what was expected of him and against the rocky wall they somehow erected a shelter. It all seemed miraculous, yet I remembered my own training and was encouraged by their efficiency. Feeling cocooned by their preparations, I settled against the wall with the shelter over me, as the staff sergeant organised his men for the next stage of the mission.

Six of the Marines remained behind with Hudson and me. They were a friendly batch, two of them New Zealanders and four Aussies, but as they explained they were all SAS and had been called in for this particular mission because if we were found by the Pakistani Army, they were more amenable to the

Antipodeans, than they were to the Brits. We managed to get some rest. I dozed on and off and between the fitful dreams that kept jerking me awake, I found after four hours that I felt quite rested. Somehow a hot tea appeared in my hands alongside a bag Haribos, which does something to the brain, I'm certain of that; I was suddenly day dreaming of home and my bed. And my wife! Twelve days since I had held her, kissed and made love to her, and even as I thought of her, I knew she was more to me than the pretty thing named Alice. There's something wonderful when a mature woman just lets go and enjoys sex, free from the fear of conception. Sorry, Alice, 'her indoors' is pretty good and always gives one hundred percent between the sheets! Dear God, what was going on in my mind?

Hudson slept like a baby; the six Aussie Marines who had remained behind with us on the top of the Baba Mountain range were all awake. Syd, the one with a radio, had been awake all afternoon. His vigilance was typical of all the Aussie men. I admired them as much as I did our own Marines. Suddenly there was Bruce's voice crackling through the airwaves.

"Calling Zero Bravo, calling Zero Bravo, come in Zero Bravo," and so it started as Syd reported that we were all safe and had seen no one all afternoon; we learnt that the others had rescued the lost men and were heading back and would meet up with us in a couple of hours. Nothing was said about how they had found and rescued the men. Equally, there was no mention of injuries or fatalities. Nothing, it was all too good to be true, surely?

Two hours and a half passed before they began to appear. I held my breath and counted them all in; there in the midst of them was Ramin, and the other four missing men! The silence was deafening as each Marine chose a spot in which to sit and rest. Syd and the five, who had stayed to hold the base camp on the flat top of the ridge, had somehow been preparing hot drinks and food for all of the weary Marines. It was touching to witness their care for their dusty and blooded colleagues and for Ramin and the four who were obviously half starving and dehydrated. A great deal of Celox gauze was in evidence as the cuts and bruises were attended to and dirt removed from faces. As darkness fell, we knew we were trapped there for the night.

It was a dark and cloudy night; I saw no stars and wondered at the possibility of low cloud hampering our exit plans. Syd had been busy on the radio and we were all advised to kip down for the next six hours, until the Chinooks were due in. We maintained the silent mode; the watch was set and changed every hour. By four in the morning we were being roused and packing up all evidence of our presence. Cloud still hung low over the top of the mountain and the staff sergeant was debating the possibility of having to walk back down using the rope to protect the likes of myself.

Even as the cold misty cloud enveloped us and Hudson continued with fastening the rope around my middle, there was a sound that instilled fear in all of us. I dropped to the ground and watched as everyone's rifle was set to the ready position; too late, we were facing a complete circle of what appeared to be to be uniformed fighters, all hazy and indistinct in the white mist, with their firearms aimed straight at us. No one pulled at their trigger, both sides seemed frozen in time. Only eyes swiftly moving from one possible target to another gave an indication that we were all still alive. It was the silence that terrified me, it somehow indicated that they could taunt us, rather than just kill us straight out. Then the thought crossed my mind; were we about to be taken prisoner?

Suddenly their leader spoke, in a language I couldn't initially identify, and they all lowered their weapons; as he walked forward and stopped in front of the staff sergeant and said in perfect English,

"Hello, Bruce, sorry it took us so long to get here."

"At ease, men," the Aussie SAS man called Bruce said, as he held out his hand to the other, "say hello to our Pakistani friends."

With that he stepped to one side with the newcomer and we were unable to listen in to their conversation. But ten minutes later we understood.

They were not Taliban, but genuine Pakistani soldiers come to help us get back off their territory and returned to Afghanistan. An hour later as the mist blew away and as Syd directed Chinooks to our position, we found ourselves helped aboard by the smiling Pakistani soldiers. It was almost unreal, except that they seemed to respect us and understood that we were not there to attack them, even though we had strayed over the border and into their territory. Later, much later, I was to learn that their leader was originally educated in Britain and was not radicalised even though he was a devout Muslim. Bruce and Tony seemed more than familiar with him and I look back with gratitude for escaping what my own paranoia thought could have been a close encounter with the Taliban.

On the flight, I got my first hesitant chance to speak with Gareth Hughes, who sat with his mouth right against my left ear. We managed somehow in spite of the noise; it was an eye-opening account of their stupid attempt to track the Taliban back to their base, only to find that after the Taliban had led them on for some distance, they turned the tables on them, as they had entered a crevasse. By blocking them into the crevasse they were able to take them prisoner. So it was they were led over the border into Pakistan, and they found themselves imprisoned in a Taliban stronghold. The rescue began when Ramin escaped and found himself face to face with some Pakistani soldiers, the ones who had later helped us into our Chinooks. By the time that group had met up with our Aussie and Kiwi SAS men there was a sizeable fighting group available to storm the Taliban camp. Their delay in reaching us at the top of the mountain was entirely due to their need to clear out the remaining evidence of the Taliban from that camp and its surrounding area, before coming to escort us off their territory. But Hughes looked troubled about something, and yet reluctant to speak in the presence of the others. He indicated that he was tired and I understood, giving him a thumb up sign and mouthing 'later!'

Back at Camp Bartkowski, we were all immediately marshalled into a large meeting tent and left to await the generals. When they entered, all of them were stern-faced and obviously annoyed at the events of the past few days, but it was the British Brigadier Henry Fulton who lashed into the four from Williams's platoon for causing unnecessary risk taking.

"And let's be honest, our budget is not bottomless. The cost of the Chinooks alone has used up nearly half our budget for the coming week, and what have we got to show for it?" Fulton was almost red-faced with rage by the time he had finished speaking.

"Twenty four dead Taliban!" said a sneering Norcross.

"That justifies nothing!" shouted Fulton, "You were already on Pakistani soil when you were captured, we were just lucky that our Australian friends had contacts in the Pakistani military or you'd all be dead. Do anything as stupid again and you can go home."

I felt Fulton was just trying to put on a show of military discipline for the benefit of the American generals, because as he finished speaking he turned and stormed out. With a shrug of his shoulders General Raven followed him, before General Colbert turned to the staff sergeant, standing alongside him, with an "over to you, Staff Sergeant."

"At ease, men," followed and then we all sat waiting for instructions until I was called out by a gofer.

"You're to report to the office, sir."

I left the gathering of weary men and allowed the messenger to escort me to General Colbert's office. Entering, I found Fulton, Raven and Colbert laughing as they stood drinking hot coffee and eating some delicious American style cookies. It was then that I realised I was starving hungry.

Chapter Twenty-Six
FOB Bartkowski

The view was superb, helped by the fact that the sky had cleared of all clouds, the wind was negligible and the pilot of the Blackhawk helicopter was very aware of my requirements. It had taken less than an hour from when all the clearances were given by the JTAC, for me to be in the air and being flown over that part of southern Afghanistan earmarked as a possible route for an oil or gas pipeline. By the time we were back at base, I had taken hundreds of digital shots to add to the official aerial photos from earlier military surveys.

Landing back at Camp Bartkowski, I found General Raven and the rest of the Leatherneck/Bastion personnel had already left, including Hudson. It was my first experience of feeling truly alone in a foreign land since arriving at Bastion. However, after a hearty meal in the D-FAC and an hour with General Colbert, I was escorted to the carpool where I was introduced to a Humvee and its driver. We were to be part of a column of empty fuel tankers heading back to Camp Edinburgh at the end of their resupplying mission. I had been reassured of a reasonable journey, the expectation being that we would arrive before nightfall. From there the return to Leatherneck was to be organised on the Sunday.

I surprised myself by dozing off quite quickly and being surprised at being woken four hours later, I found myself in the centre of Camp Edinburgh, with its giant oil and petrol storage bladders, very similar to the ones at Camp Bastion.

Sunday morning a chopper came out for me from Bastion Airfield and on arrival, I first called in to see the Brigadier to thank him for his help. He was laughing and came out with a comment that had me nodding in agreement.

"If only you had been given authorization to explain your real mission, I could have sent you up to take a look, and you could have been home in less than a week. Politicians and desk-bound geriatric generals have some weird ideas about combat zones."

"Maybe," I said with a wry grin, "but I would have missed the adventure of the past fortnight."

"Is that what it felt like, an adventure?"

"Well, it does now it's over. I felt a bit nervous a couple of times, but more importantly I have learnt that it is time to retire. Some things are best left to young men."

"But wisdom improves with age and the older man makes a good teacher! Have you thought about that for a new career?"

"No, but I am interested in reporting back to the PM that spending money on killing people might be put to better use teaching them."

"Oh!"

"Well, look at young Ramin, he's been educated," I said, but the brigadier began speaking in a quieter voice, as if the outer office might be eavesdropping.

"To our way of thinking, he can speak, so we can understand him, so we think he is educated. But his cultural background is still there and is perfectly valid; I ask myself, have we educated him away from his own people? Does he feel alienated from them? My wife is a teacher and says we cannot impose all our systems on the Afghan."

"Democracy, hygiene, respect for learning, and valuing the rights of women might be good, for a start," I said.

"I know we can all quote the Taliban leader who said, 'the face of a woman is a source of corruption!' but others believe it as well, even amongst Christians."

"So men have no self-control!"

He shook his head and said,

"Which beggars the question, who is the teacher? Boys run wild here, not even the mothers are allowed to discipline them. As for some of the tribal leaders and fighting men, they abuse boys as young as nine or ten, when they've no women around to satisfy them."

"That's a universal problem," I said, "and we can't blame the women for that. It is an ingrained attitude where Afghanistan is concerned."

We each knew that we were talking to release ideas that sat heavily inside our weary brains. I thought of the peace of my home and how I honoured her, my wife and lover of thirty five years. Suddenly I longed for home, and said so to Fulton.

"Can't send you back for another few days, but we are aiming for Wednesday or Thursday at the latest. That OK with you, Matt?"

"Wonderful thanks." I smiled at Henry Fulton as he then advised,

"Three days to get your report written up. See the American photographer for prints, their equipment is better and faster than ours."

"Isn't everything?"

He laughed out loud and at that we parted. I headed off to see Williams. It took some time, finding he was released from detention, I still called into the NAAFI and got him some Haribos don't ask me why, but I did just that, sweets to cheer him up! It was in the NAAFI that I met up with Johnstone, who explained that the platoon was still having a rest day and then, thankfully, he directed me to Guy's billet.

What a shock greeted me when I tracked him down, to find him back in his sleeping quarters, looking tense as he sat on the edge of his cot-like camp bed.

"They let you out?" I asked with a smile, as I handed over a couple of bags of sweets, "I'll have the stars and the bottles, you can have the rest!"

At that he laughed and stood up grabbing at a bag, before ripping it open with his teeth and just pouring the small jelly sweets into his upturned mouth. Then he offered me what was left.

"They've sent her home," he said with a look that said it all.

"Why?"

"Norcross spilled the beans about our meetings. General Raven was so angry, you could hear him over half of Leatherneck. I was summoned to his office, and in front of Alice, he questioned me. It was a case of answer truthfully and she was dammed, lie and he wasn't going to believe me anyway. You know how you can tell when everything is stacked against you?"

"Why did Norcross tell, it was hardly likely to get Alice on to his side?"

Guy went to his Bergen and took out a letter Alice had written him during her time at Camp Bartkowski. It was touching and I felt her fears and sorrow in every word.

'My darling, Norcross has written to my uncle telling on us. I tried to deny it all, but you are going to have to face him, so he says. Uncle says he's sending me home tomorrow, after he's seen you. I've got to go and he says I will probably be let go from the military. McNaughton is gloating; she had been following us around taking photos. Don't worry about me, I love you, I meant it when I said, yes. I do want to marry you. I will write and tell you where I am, and when you

get back to England I'll join you. I love you and I'm going to miss you. Please don't stop loving me...'

I looked up and read Guy Williams's face; it said he would never stop loving the beautiful girl he had kissed behind the D-FAC, or was it the hospital cookhouse?

"She has gone?" I asked as if for confirmation.

"This morning, he sent for me and there she was in General Raven's office with him just looking at her with an expression on his face of murderous thunder. There was Captain McNaughton. You could tell she was delighted. I think she hated Alice. When I tried to jump in by saying, 'It's my fault, sir', I got no further, he looked from me to her and her to me, as he shouted, 'Well, you spoilt child, did you encourage him?' But her face was a picture and she looked completely calm and brave as she said, 'Yes, Uncle, I love him and I want to marry...' she got nowhere, he exploded. He picked up the phone and shouted, 'Send in the MP's now!' Two military police came in and the General told them, 'You have less than an hour, forty minutes, to be precise, get her things packed and she's on that plane that's leaving in forty minutes. If necessary drag someone off, but put her on, and strap her in, do you understand? She misses it and you are also in trouble, do you understand me?' Then they go something like a *'HOO-rah'*, as they do over there in Leatherneck and then she's marched out. Alice didn't even have time to look back at me; she was gone. Not satisfied with that he then he barks at the Captain, 'McNaughton, get her on that plane, do you hear me. Glue it to the runway until she's on it.' Well, the Captain was delighted and also did a big HOO-rah before leaving. As for the General, he looked at me, straight in the eye, as he shouted, 'Get out, boy!' The way he said 'Boy' spoke volumes, the man's a bigot, probably in the Klue Klux Klan, if the truth be told. I was marched back here, through the camps. But I stood outside and watched for the plane leaving. Then I found this, and I just know we will be together one day, I just know it, sir."

Smiling at him, and not wishing to crush his spirit, I hesitated for just a moment before telling him,

"I felt like that about my wife. I just knew she was the one."

"Thanks, that's comforting; so I'm not as odd as I was feeling a moment ago. Other people have felt like this. Good! Now, I'm glad Alice is away from here, she will be safe back home until I've finished this tour, then at the first chance I get, and I'll be over to the States and claim her. Norcross cannot win, sir."

"Are you out on patrol tomorrow?" seemed a sensible question, or so I thought.

"Yes, just half of 5 Platoon is heading towards somewhere; I think this is it!" He handed me an order paper and I read it with some eagerness.

The word Sangrin was all that registered with me; Guy explained that Sangrin base was in the middle of a bad patch at the moment, too many injured.

"It'll just be for a few days, taking twelve men. And it will get me away from here for a while. Too many memories of Alice, I keep thinking she will appear around the corner at any minute."

"Good God, man, you do sound lovesick."

"So, I am in love, what's wrong with that? You just said you..."

"Nothing, enjoy it while you can."

"Now who's being cynical, you tell me you love your wife and yet you sound as if you're not absolutely convinced that I love Alice. What's the matter? Hasn't it lasted?"

"It's lasted over thirty years, if you must know."

"Never tempted to get out?"

"Depends on what you mean by temptation. No harm in window shopping, just don't buy is my motto."

"I'll remember that!"

We laughed together and I felt the lad was one of the nicest of the young men I had met at Camp Bastion. If MI6 really wanted to recruit him, I'd say he should be ready in a couple of years; just keep a close eye on him.

Chapter Twenty-Seven
The Day It Happened

I woke feeling relaxed, the world outside seemed quiet, there was a distant screech of MERTs' sirens, but it was all so far away and being carried on a gentle early morning breeze, that I took no notice. This was my golden opportunity to get on with my report to the PM. Checking through the digital camera, I found I was happy with my efforts, and I knew that what I had to say in my report was going to be backed up by photographic evidence. Breakfast had seemed quiet, with no sign of Hudson. But using the tongue in my head, I managed to get the right directions to the photographic reconnaissance department from a young Marine; and just as Henry Fulton had advised, it turned out to be a magnificent set up with two cheerful technicians. I emerged an hour later with wonderful photos and retired to a sheltered spot with wooden picnic tables and benches, to write the report to go alongside the photos.

I must have spent another two hours on the report and finished comfortably by one o'clock. Being me, I was starving by then, and as I was alone I decided I wanted a totally British meal; no meatloaf, I wanted slices of real British beef. It was any easy choice, head for the hospital cookhouse. Having chosen the latter, I was delighted with everything that was put on my plate, finishing with a wonderful crumble and custard, which would have easily got my wife's disapproval. To finish the meal I filled a paper beaker with strong sweet tea, and then I walked outside to find a MERT with sirens blazing, heading for the hospital. I suppose curiosity got the better of me and I made my way into the reception area as a second MERT screeched up behind the first.

Sometimes we do things and we will we never be able to explain why; I stayed there and for the rest of my life I would wonder what made me do that. Was I psychic or had my heart heard his cries of pain, because by staying there, I was to witness the truth of his injuries; as he was carried past me, to be rushed into triage...

... I saw his bloodied face and hands

... I saw his legless body

... I heard his cries of pain

... I heard him call her name: Alice!

Lieutenant Guy Williams was to all intents and purposes near death, I felt certain of that, beneath the smeared blood on his face was the death mask of a bloodless body. Then, just as I had registered that idea, I had to immediately confront the sight of Gareth Hughes, on the second gurney, looking as if he also were dead. There was no sound as he was carried past me.

I raced outside and threw up.

If you live to be a hundred, you would have looked back at that moment and still have felt the full horror, such as I felt that day. I feel it even now, twenty years later.

I am ashamed that having looked at pictures of war-wounded on many occasions, I now realise how little reaction I have had to them; but on that day seeing two people I knew, in that dreadful state, only then I had reacted with real feeling, real pain coursing through me, my nerves felt like razor blades cutting me, all over and through my body. I have over the years since chided myself that I was until that moment impervious to other people's pain, because I felt detached from the sufferer. It was the sight of two people who were known to me which induced in me such a distressing and traumatizing state. I remember my aging mother speaking of the Vietnam War and commenting on the immediacy of the news, when compared with her experiences during the Second World War. She believed we were heartless, exposing every wounded person to the glare of the media. I argued that it was seeing it, as it happened, that turned the tide against the slaughter. Now I ask myself, have we become so accustomed to YouTube helmet cam recordings from the battlefields and the newsreel Instagrams, with their verifying of the truth, that we fail to see the pain endured by the injured, on both sides of the fighting? There is a 'once removed from reality' contained in every movie-like presentation; whether on a cinema screen, tablet, computer, IPhone or TV, it becomes barely distinguishable from any other film of violence. Remember Saving Private Ryan, or better still Christopher Walken in the Deer Hunter, winning an Oscar! It doesn't matter who gets shot at or blown to pieces one minute, because they are seen walking and talking their way up the red carpet, alive and well and signing autographs as they collect their Oscar or Bafta! War is real, but even when watching news on CNN or BBC we never get the sickening smell, the heart-wrenching sounds and the sight of real gruesome injury. I felt powerless to help and could only think that Guy and Alice would be finished as an item.

In the end, I wandered back to the hospital cookhouse and got myself a strong coffee and a jam doughnut, I wanted to rid myself of the taste of death which was still sticking in my throat. Sitting with my head in my hands, I tried to pray for the two injured men. Yes, I prayed that they would die now, if living with the results of such terrible wounds would be harder to bear at their young age. I wondered if I could face what they were facing, just yards away from where I was sitting. The shiver that went up my spine was for them and the hope that it would never happened to me. It was still possible, war wounds don't make a booking, and they are traumatic and affect you and those who love you.

Sorry, Alice, will you still love him? Then the worst thought of all came into my head; *who will tell Alice?*

Later I wandered back into the hospital and sat beside Guy's bed. He was unconscious and hardly recognisable beneath a variety of plasters and bandages around his face and arms, but it was the presence of a blanket support that screamed out to me. He had lost his legs, and I didn't dare ask the nurse for precise details. How much of each leg was now missing, I did not know at that moment. I didn't want to know until I could share the pain with him, hold his hand and comfort him as he came to realise the extent of his injury.

Gareth Hughes was in the next bed and still under the influence of the anaesthetic, but even as I wondered how long before I could ask him about the attack, in walked Norcross, Johnstone and Lewis. They stood in silence around the beds, before inviting me to join them outside. Craig Lewis, the quiet one, became the spokesperson and said,

"I expect you want to hear what happened?"

As we left, Surgeon Commander Peter Wallis was just coming out of the operating theatre. He saw me and said "Coffee?" So we gathered him up and took him into the hospital cookhouse with us. Tom Johnstone got coffee for all of us, and Norcross collected a plate of sandwiches. The silence of grief hung over all of us for several minutes until Peter Wallis obliged by recounting the extent of Guy's and Gareth's injuries, as well as a possible forecast of their future prognosis. He ended by congratulating the three men.

"And well done, lads, you definitely saved the lieutenant's life, it worked for definite and if the truth be told, probably also the staff sergeant."

"It worked?" was the enquiry in my voice and on my face.

"The tourniquets work; our proof is in the statistics. We are extending their use, we are going ahead, and training starts tomorrow. Don't be surprised if you are the instructors."

"What statistics?" I queried.

"The new tourniquet has definitely saved lives, more than ever before."

Johnstone came in with, "We were each carrying one, so we could shut off the bleed quickly."

"Guy tried to loosen it, sir," Norcross said to the surgeon, "But I sat over him and kept tightening it. I screamed at him, 'Do you want to bleed to death?' but all he could do was moan Alice's name and I kept saying, 'you'll walk again, Lieutenant, you'll walk down the aisle, I'll let you marry Alice', but he didn't hear me."

"Well done, man, you certainly helped to save his life. We know how much it hurts, that's why the unconscious cope better." Wallis was standing even as he spoke to Norcross.

He had heard the whoop-whoop-whoop! With his persistent state of vigilance for the sound of incoming wounded, he was alerted to the noise outside even before we were, and he left us to return to his duties. The four of us sat there in various stages of nibbling at the snack food in front of us, when Craig Lewis, ever the joker in the pack, said, "Perhaps you should have knocked him out!" They laughed at that and I could see them allowing themselves some light relief. As for me I did no more than crack a half smile, just to let them know it was OK by me if they joked about it.

I look back and I am amazed that I could eat, but my nerves were still shot to pieces and I felt the lack of sugar in my muscles.

I got the second round of coffee and as we drank I asked to be told what had happened. I am not sure you want to hear, but anyway it went something like this; they had set off, to drive up towards Sangrin to offer some back up to the FOB there. There were four vehicles, Guy was in the point vehicle, and the three of them were in the last one. Altogether between the four vehicles there were twenty members of the platoon.

"Usual story, sir," said Tom Johnstone, "we're out in the open and driving past a couple of trucks that seemed harmless enough, when we were forced to stop, what we can now say is that what looked like a man lying beside a broken down truck, trying to repair the exhaust pipe, was in fact a booby-trapped dead Afghan."

"You couldn't tell if he was wounded or dead, it really did look as if he was checking his exhaust, it was so well staged, believable, you might say. His back was towards us; his head seemed half under the truck." Norcross added, to make certain I had understood the tableau the Taliban had set up.

Craig then took over the story, "Like idiots we stop and the Lieutenant gets out; damn, he was stupid!"

"And so were we!" once again Andy Norcross extended the information to his satisfaction.

"We didn't look behind us; those innocent looking trucks had turned round and just one sniper was picking off the IEDs planted around the parked truck. Thank God the one nearest Guy's right side didn't go off, it was a damp squib. He only lost his right foot. He's still got most of his right leg."

"Yeah, but no left leg, come on, Andy, he's finished and we know it. We've seen it all before, man. He might linger a few days but then bingo, he's gone. Infection for a start, remember the mess that was blasted into the bleeding stumps? Don't tell me that you didn't see the grit and the dirt and probably camel dung deliberately put there just for the pleasure of infecting the poor buggers they intended to kill. No, he's a goner, I don't care what Wallis says." I could feel the anger building up in Craig Lewis. How to diffuse the tension?

"The wounded man, did you save him?" Well, I had to ask, they had said he was beside the truck. It was Tom Johnstone who took up the account.

"That's it, isn't it? The poor bugger looked injured and Gareth went up to him to see what could be done and as he knelt down to just turn the man's head towards himself, boom! Another f***ing IED, that's what took off half of Gareth's face. Bloody Taliban, they'd obviously killed the man, he had a slit throat, when we eventually got to look at him properly. Kill one of their own then and set the trap and dear God, Gareth is lucky not to have lost both his eyes, but he'll be disfigured for life, you can be sure of that."

After that outburst from Tom Johnstone, I was surprise to hear myself asking about the snipers who had driven past them.

"Oh, Lewis got them, their vehicle exploded as it tried to drive away," said Norcross, with an obvious satisfaction in his voice.

"I got the petrol tank as the driver tried to turn the truck back onto the road," claimed Craig Lewis. He didn't look triumphant, just sad at having killed, and then watching him, it seemed as if something exploded inside him. Veins that showed up dark and blue began protruding on his forehead, sweat poured out of him as his voice rose in anger. He was verbalising all the deep-seated anger out of himself, and it was shocking to witness.

I just sat there and listened, wishing I had the tape recorder to collect the sound of the man, to give to the PM. Hearing gives a better understanding of the emotions racing around that table that day.

"It's the dammed Geneva or even the bloody Hague thingies; we should have stopped the truck in the first place, but we can't shoot unless they point a gun first, but they can shoot whether or not we've got a gun pointing at them. Bang-bang and we're the bad guys, unless we are killed, then we're the good guys and everybody says how wonderful we are. There's no such thing as a live healthy hero, only disabled ones. I say we're the foolish guys. We are supposed to fight like a robot, watch our mates get shot up and then go home to be prosecuted for losing our tempers, or complaining about the wonderful injuries inflicted by Taliban, because of rules written before we were born. Come on, it was bad enough in Northern Ireland, never mind Bosnia, now this it's..."

He took a breath, I cut in; "You were never in Northern Ireland?"

"My dad was and he got a bullet in the back from a known sniper who has never been charged, and these guys would never be charged because they are the invisible Taliban. We go back out on the road to look for killers and one of us...yes, one of us ... us ... do you understand? One of us, not one of them, has to be fired on and probably be killed, before the rest of us can fire back."

283

Norcross and Johnstone had remained silent and still, letting Lewis offload his feelings. Now in the total silence that came when he had finished speaking, I realised that numerous other men and women had gathered around us, and suddenly the silence was broken as first one then another began clapping, until all were joined in an applause that almost frightened me. Embarrassed, Craig Lewis stood up and pushed his way through the gathered audience to the entrance, where he suddenly turned and looking straight back at me, he said,

"There's never been a war like this one. We don't plan attacks, we go walking about supposedly looking for the bad guys, but we can't fight them unless they attack first; that takes our fighting skills away from us. We are not fighters, we are mere defenders of the rights of the bloody Taliban, and we may only react to attacks. We are castrated by bloody Haigh-Geneva rules for gentlemen soldiers, written before the very idea of the Taliban was born. Please, I'm begging you, go home and tell them, terrorists are not gentlemen! I repeat, terrorists are not gentlemen, but all the so-called goody two shoes who wear red shirts and kick bloody balls about on a Saturday, they are the world's heroes, while we who get our balls kicked off every day as we serve our country, are disparaged and condemned for not acting like middleclass gentlemen in three piece suits! The Taliban are not westernised gentlemen, they are cruel, misogynistic, uneducated smelly animals who kill their own people without any qualms. Guy has lost his legs, so have hundreds and thousands of innocent Afghan kids!"

He looked at me long and hard, I could see the sweat on his brow and the trembling of his fingers as he pulled his rifle round to hold in front of him. For a moment everybody shifted as if afraid that Craig was going to fire into the gathering. He stood still, and then he lowered his rifle to his side, as Norcross and Johnstone walked towards him. They both put their arms around him in a real man hug.

Norcross said, "Well done, kid!"

With that the three of them left the cookhouse.

I took out my notebook and wrote and wrote as near as possible every word Craig had uttered. I looked up and saw I was being watched by others from 5 Platoon.

"He were right, sir."

I said nothing, just patted the nearest man as I stood up and looked at all of them, still standing where they had gathered around Craig Lewis, to listen to his outburst.

"You write in the America press, sir?"

"Em, well, yes, why?"

"Tell Obama, and then just maybe he'd tell Brown to get the bloody English press to lay off us, please, sir."

"Right, I will. I would like you to put your thoughts on one of my recorders. Would you?" They all nodded in agreement, I suddenly felt excited; I couldn't have wished for anything better to round off my reports for the PM.

"Wait here for me, I'll get my machine."

I took my leave and jumped on a passing bus to get back to Leatherneck. My head was thumping, my body felt as if it had been run over by a steam engine, but my heart wanted to let Alice know what had happened. I wanted to record those young men speaking it was just what Gordon Brown wanted. 'They were the words the generals weren't telling him.'

At my billet I found Hudson reading a comic; roping him in to drive, we were back at the cookhouse ten minutes later, and recording a massive amount of free speech from five young members of 5 Platoon. It was amazing to hear, I knew the PM would be moved by the expressions of loyalty mixed in with the anger at the feeling the country had forgotten them or why they were there.

Satisfied that I now had enough to add on to my earlier report plus all the details of Guy's and Gareth's distressing meeting with the Taliban, and the witness of their golden hour achievement, I thanked all concerned and left with a strong desire to find out if Alice knew what had happened to her love, Guy Williams.

Should I interfere or not, I asked myself? Questioning the wisdom of such an action, I headed for General Raven, who greeted me with the surprising news that he had already made contact with Alice.

"She's devastated," he told me in a quiet, almost reverential voice. "Fortunately Alice is already with her mother, my sister and they are both heading off for some place in Birmingham, England. Alice insisted that she wanted to be there. The Brits have ordered a flight; they will fly him out on Wednesday."

"I'm supposed to fly then," I told him.

"Then we'll make certain you are on the same flight, have a word with Fulton."

I looked long and hard at Mike Raven; something was bothering me and I just had to ask, "How come you knew so quickly about Guy's injury?"

"Because Fulton told me that they left after breakfast and had only gone about thirty miles. It only took a MERT less than an hour to get them into the hospital. Henry Fulton had sent me an immediate message, he knew about Williams and Holford. We're not heartless Matt. We just don't make the rules. It was Henry who advised me to get her to Birmingham."

"The Selly Oak Hospital?"

"Yes, that's the one."

"I'm going to email my wife and she can meet me there."

"Why?"

"I'm going with him."

My email to Cathy must have worried her. I could imagine her muttering to herself, and yet getting on with it, in that lovely way of hers, knowing she was helping me.

As I walked the long way back to my billet, I thought of all the times in my military career I had reasons to be proud of her. Every time I was away, it was her loyalty and stoicism that frequently gave strength to my own mission. She was my backbone, my courage and my reason to defend against all who would harm her world.

Chapter Twenty-Eight
Camp Bastion Hospital

Sleep had been fitful and full of dreams of IEDs blowing me up, or murdering people I knew and loved. The solution was to get up and go and check on Guy and Gareth. The walk would help, I felt certain of that as I managed to steer myself between the various tents and offices until at long last, by taking time to look at the map Alice had given me, I realised the shortest route was by the TOC and around D-FAC number five. Not stopping to eat, I had that endless walk to the hospital to face, until I managed to reduce it to two miles by avoiding the long market area and the food outlets. Somehow I managed to arrive at Guy's bedside by six thirty.

He looked colourless, deathlike; oh, I don't know the words to tell you, but truthfully he didn't seem to be breathing. Gareth Hughes was awake in his untidy bed and watching me carefully from beneath a massive bandage, covering the right side of his head and face. His good eye stared at me, as if expecting me to cry or shout with grief. But nothing came; I sat down and held Guy's free hand, the other was connected to a cannula drip. I could feel the warmth passing from my hand to his, as I gently caressed his freezing fingers, and without taking my eyes from Guy, I spoke across to Gareth.

"Did you sleep?"

His military humour had not left him: he joked at me,

"Yeah, shot through with morphine, but it wore off about an hour ago. I could do with some now, could you run out into the nearest poppy field for me? Don't go too far, I need the f***ing stuff."

With that he screamed out a loud distressed cry of, "Nurse!" and two nurses came running. I watched as they pumped a full syringe of morphine into him and pulled the curtain closed before tucking him back to a more comfortable position. They were talking all the time, as if they were mothering him back to sleep. I heard him murmur a thank you, as they pulled back the curtain.

One of them, noticing me, said, "Best if we let him sleep, same with the Lieutenant, let him sleep. Have you had breakfast? This is the best time for bacon butties; go on, sir, go and eat and come back afterwards. It'll be okay. We won't kick you out; you can babysit them for us. He's going to wake up talkative, and swearing blue murder, they always do." She nodded towards the silent Gareth, now looking peaceful in his tidied up bed.

I stood and thanked her and said, "I'll be back," which made me feel like an Arnie Schwarzenegger-mimicking idiot, but she laughed and I felt pleased. I was glad they were being treated by military nurses with an understanding of the situation.

For a few moments I felt like a sleepwalker, as I walked quietly down the corridor and out into the sunshine. It promised to be hot and I was aware that I hadn't taken in enough fluid to survive the day, so it was a full English breakfast for me, plus two half pint paper cups full of Yorkshire tea, plus half a pint of orange juice. That should have kept me going, but by eleven I was back for another top up. The heat outside was unbearable and I escaped it again, until late afternoon, by staying in the air conditioned ward, sitting beside Guy, occasionally rubbing his cold hands, wiping his brow with a cool damp cloth and following the instructions given by the nurse, I called her every time he seemed to moan with pain. His morphine was being given via a drip. I watched over his lips as they dried out and began to crack so I even moistened his lips with a wet sponge, and if I was lucky some of the cool water found its way into his mouth and onto his tongue. "Seems a bit old fashioned, using a sponge," said another nurse, "But sometimes the old methods are still the best."

I was to agree with her, when later I saw Guy's lips suck on the sponge, even though he seemed to be sleeping. It thrilled me; it was a sign of life, of hope for recovery.

Surgeon Commander Peter Wallis had visited the two invalids several times during the day, and seeing me trying my best to get water into Guy, reassured me that there was no immediate danger; it was chiefly the anaesthetic that was keeping him sedated. "It gives him time to heal," he said as he checked over the record of vital signs, "Em, they're both doing alright, keep up the good work." With that he left to see to the next patients, which we could guess were coming in on the noisy MERT blaring out its arrival, for all to hear. There never seemed to be a way of not hearing the rotors' whooping noise, it penetrated the whole camp site, nor the shrill siren of the ambulances noisily determined that everybody got out of the way of their precious cargo.

Guy must have heard, for I felt his hand squeeze mine and looking at him, I saw some rapid eye movement under his closed eyelids. The muscles around his eyes seemed to be responding; I squeezed his hand and whispered,

"You're OK, Guy; it's me, Matt Fleming!"

Do I say 'and Alice knows and is heading for the Selly Oak Hospital?' I decided against it; there was always a possibility she might change her mind when she heard of his injuries.

Gareth woke about three and begged for more painkillers, and he seemed more alert this time. The shout was for, "Tea, please, nurse!" By the time he had drunk two cups and eaten some toast, Gareth was looking more himself, the bandages had become familiar and they seemed to bother me less; whether they were less bothersome to Gareth, he never said. He was stoically uncomplaining, became the darling of the nurses and by eight o'clock that evening was sitting out of bed chatting to them, as they changed sheets and plumped up his pillows. He stayed up talking to me until nearly ten, when I needed to get back to my packing.

We were to fly out on the first flight tomorrow morning. Tom Johnstone had called in about five o'clock to reassure me the plane had left from RAF Lyneham and was set for a West Midlands Airport return and it would be a direct flight with in-flight refuelling, both ways. No hanging about when the injured need to be brought home.

He also confirmed that the FLO had informed Cathy of my arrival time at the old Selly Oak Hospital, the new Queen Elisabeth hospital was only just being built. Then he explained that the transport to Selly Oak hospital was to be by something called a 'jumbulance'. I breathed a tad better, knowing that and that it was being set up with stretchers for eight patients and several walking wounded.

The next morning I was up early and had a sentimental last look at the shower and bathroom facilities, remembering the little lady who had first introduced me to them. Then the last bit of packing before I walked over to the nearest D-FAC and, wonders of wonders, found Hudson sitting like a lost sheep looking down on a half-eaten meal.

"Hello, buddy," I said with as light a touch as I could manage.

"Missed you, but I just had to stay with Guy."

"I've got three weeks left, Matt, then I'm going home and I'm going back on Civvy Street. Don't look at me like that, please, but I kind of gotta leave this goddam awful place for good. If I don't get out I kind of know they'll gonna send me back here."

His voice was tight with nervousness, he seemed to be rambling from one thought to the other, but I reassured him that I understood.

"I wouldn't want to come back either, Hudson. There's no shame in saying you've done your turn and enough is enough. What will you do back home?"

"Going to join the police; already put my application in at the local police academy. Shouldn't be any problem, I've kind of qualified for the service."

"Glad you see it as a service, Hud. Well I wish you luck."

Hudson drove me to the hospital to check that our two patients were ready to be taken out to the plane, and then he took me onto the airfield. Johnstone, Lewis and Norcross were there with Williams Bergen and Hughes's one as well, everything packed and shipshape. Johnstone told me,

"The lads have put cards and letters in there for the Lieutenant, if he ever wakes up again."

"I'm certain he will," I said as reassuringly as I could and as I shook hands, thanking them for their help.

Craig asked to speak to me. There was so much noise we had to move to a room set aside for waiting crew who had travelled out with the plane, already kitted up with oxygen cylinders, ventilators, monitors of all kinds and sizes, pumps, as well as what was explained as vacuum mattresses to prevent sores, and a vast array of medications. They were using the bathroom facilities and rushing to be ready when they heard the MERTs arriving with the injured. Their turnaround time was one hour on the ground. Suddenly we had the room to ourselves.

Craig and I settled down and I smiled at him to relax him. I knew what was on his mind.

"Sorry about yesterday, sir."

"Pity, I had hoped you meant every word of it, Lewis. May I make a suggestion, write it all down and sent it to the PM, you know his address!"

The young man looked at me and slowly smiled as he asked. "Would he read it, sir?"

"Whether he does or not, you will feel better for having written it. I'll be writing to him as well, I'll mention you and the boys and how you saved Guy's life."

"Would you? I was afraid I would be up for the Tower for what I said."

"Not the Tower, man! Not unless you're talking about Blackpool Tower, in which case I'll join you. Write to me, all of you, let me know how this all ends for you, will you do that?"

"Sure, I'd like to keep in touch."

"As the Yanks would say, HOO-rah, or something like that, but I'm saying remember all I've told you, write and send to Number 10."

We laughed as we shook hands and went back outside to say goodbye to the others, sitting in the jeep and watching as MERTs arrived with the wounded and the teams of doctors and medics who were to travel with them, as they organised their settling into the centre of that enormous cavern, which was the body of the aircraft.

We shook hands again, as if reluctant to let go and I turned to board the plane, when another jeep raced up to the ramp and I heard my name being called.

"Hold on, Matt!"

It was Brigadier Henry Fulton and so I walked back down to greet him. We shook hands and he wished me a safe journey.

Then he handed me a memo giving me news of the arrangements made for Guy and Gareth. I was grateful and said so.

"Would be happy to meet up sometime, when I'm back," he said with warmth in his cultured voice that told me he was sincere.

"Me too," I said, "And thanks for your help."

We smiled and parted, each wondering if he would be able to survive the developing conflict. We both realised how much worse the situation was becoming in Helmand Province, how impossible it was to expect the same moral standards from guerrilla fighters who have never heard of any gentlemen's rules for war.

I turned and saluted Hudson and the men still watching. They saluted me back and for the first time since I had arrived, I felt like one of them.

I walked back up the ramp for the last time, or so I thought!

Chapter Twenty-Nine
Selly Oak Birmingham

The journey was very different from the one I had made just fifteen days ago. There was so much activity; nurses constantly checking on the wounded, changing the bags of blood and other drips, all being supervised alongside what one of the doctors informed me were called vital signs; blood pressure, temperature, heart rates. Several of the injured were sedated to keep them from feeling the pain and discomfort of the journey. Certainly it was no surprised to me that Guy Williams was 'out for the count'. He had arrived at the airfield looking as if he were sleeping, and once I had boarded the plane I stopped by his stretcher bed and realised there was to be no chance of a chat on the journey, he was heavily sedated.

I could not sleep and found myself being an irritating presence on board; I nosed around, checking out the action and talking to staff who really must have wished I'd shut up and go to sleep. One nurse offered to sedate me, but I survived without that humiliation.

By the time we touched down at Birmingham International Airport, I had sussed out that the plane and its medical crew had been given an arrival space of one hour by something they called the Aeromed Office. When the C130 touched down it was directed to a cargo terminal where once again I was amazed at the organization. For twenty injured there were four NHS West Midlands paramedic ambulances, a large double length military ambulance called a jumbulance and even a coach for the walking wounded, which apparently included seats reserved for Cathy and me. Cathy had been waiting in the cargo terminal with the other families. Turning my head, I saw several police escorts. I marvelled at the efficiency that had returned Guy home just forty-eight hours since his injury. I tried to add up the numbers who had striven to save the life of just this one man! Then multiply it by the rest of the wounded and you realise how wonderful millions of anonymous blood donors and the vast military frontline medical personnel teams truly are, in saving broken lives.

I began the count with the platoon members who had rushed to tourniquet his wounded legs, to prevent him dying by bleeding out within the Platinum Ten minutes, they initially saved his life. But so did the Chinook crew who rescued him while being guarded by the Apache crew, then there were the MERT crews on the Chinook, and in the ambulance that rushed him to the triage at Camp Bastion, to the countless doctors and nurses at the Camp Bastion Hospital and to all the one hundred and twenty blood donors from England's blood service, whose blood gave life back to Lieutenant Guy Williams. Then I added on the pilots and Medevac crews that transported him four thousand miles home to England, to be met by Sergeant Tye and his team, who rushed the patient to the English hospital in the jumbulance, so that he was now into the care of the staff at Selly Oak Hospital, to the makers of prosthetic limbs and then to all the physiotherapists and staff at Headley Court.

Nearly three hundred people would be able to say they had been directly involved in the repair of this Humpty Dumpty called Guy Williams.

How many others have had as many reasons to be grateful to so many invisible and visible helpers, just to get their loved ones home alive? What credit has to be given at that point; but does the wonderful system that came out of Afghanistan's war continue once they are home?

It was as if Churchill himself would probably say,

"Never was so much owed by one man to so many."

There were not many good things that came out of that dreadful conflict, but this was one of them. People had shown that they cared, even if it was just in the giving of a pint of blood.

My wife Cathy had driven down to Birmingham the day before and had spent last night in a Birmingham hotel, and thanks to help from a kind lady responsible for family welfare arrangements, was waiting at the airport to greet me.

She had rushed at me with her arms open and her breathing almost choking her, as her nerves registered that first sight of me still wearing my American Combat fatigues' and looking wide eyed as I struggled against the weariness of the journey.

There is something meaningful in that first hug; every returning soldier will tell you the same. It speaks of her gratitude for your return, it shouts with relief that her days of fear and worry are over; it is the moment when your aching body can at last relax against the softness of her loving breasts, as she surrenders herself into your hungry arms. Your heart sings and your eyes shine with tears of joy, until you remember those who were injured and those who had died.

Cathy's first hug said all that to me. No words were needed, it was all there as I felt her soft breasts push against me, felt her hands rubbing at the side of my face and the warm wetness of her lips as they opened mine to a deep and satisfying kiss.

My heart thankfully rejoiced to be back in her arms, I swore that I would never leave her again, sorry Prime Minister, my service is over. This is where I belong, with my wife.

Eventually we walked arm in arm into the hospital and knowing we could not follow Guy onto the ward until he was settled, we made our way to a corner with a drinks machine. The wait did not worry us, we realised what was going on, and we just stood, arms around each other, before ending up outside the ward, waiting to be told when we might enter and sit with Guy. A pleasant nurse took a moment to speak with us; she assumed we were Guy's parents, "He's fine, sleeping peacefully." I laughed and asked, "Does he know he's home?"

Suddenly, I heard her, I knew it was her high heels clip-clopping along the corridor and when she turned the corner and saw me, Alice Holford yelled with pain and joy all mixed in her voice.

"Matt, Matt, thank God you're here, how's Guy? Does he know I'm here? What happened, Uncle Mike says he's lost his legs, and he said he was blasted by an IED, how did he manage to survive? Tell me, Matt, tell me..."

Standing behind her daughter, there was her mother leaning so close it looked as if her jutting chin was resting upon Alice's shoulder. I was suddenly presented with two faces looking at me with the same deep blue-eyed intensity.
One anxious, the other angry beyond words!

I put my arms out to Alice, who shook her mother off and literally flew into my arms. Cathy walked past me and I heard her say in her usual gracious way, "Hello, I'm Matt's wife, Cathy. You must be Alice's mother."

"He'll be OK, sweetie, he's sedated or sleeping, I don't know which."

Then I heard the hardness in her mother's voice as I cradled a sobbing Alice against my weary body.

"Yes, I'm Naomi Holford. What's going on? Please, I couldn't let Alice come alone; we have been given practically no information from that wretched brother of mine."

The pitch of the voice was hard. It was the physical likeness between the two women that was amazing, one of those cases where you could say to your son, 'Marry the girl, she will always look like her mother'. That was until you had realised the mother was acting like a monster, and no recommendation for the character of the daughter.

Even as we gathered there outside the ward, other relatives arrived for those who had been on the same flight, and they were allowed in, but we were still held back until another half hour had passed. Obviously Guy needed more attention than most, so I took the opportunity to explain what had happened in more depth.

There came a moment when Alice went to visit the 'bathroom' and Cathy went with her. In the silence that ensued, I witnessed that angry expression once again cloud Naomi's face. It seemed to demand a response from me. So I asked as gently as I could,

"What is it, Mrs Holford?"

"She can't marry him now; her father will never allow it. I'm to take her home as soon as she's seen him and told him."

"Has he asked for her hand in marriage?" I pretended ignorance.

"Yes, seemingly that young man has done so!" There was a pause, then with a straight back and a steely glare she looked at me as she added,

"Her daddy won't give his permission, and he's told her, no!"

"Is there any reason why he is saying this? Does he object to his being a soldier?"

"Soldier, don't be ridiculous, he's no legs and probably lost his…his… you know… you know what I'm saying. We are an old family and … we want grandchildren. I want grandchildren, my husband wants grandchildren, and we own a vast farm and… and we…" she came to a shuddering stop which sent all of her body into a spasm she couldn't hide.

I realised that she imagined his private parts were blasted away by the IED. I tried not to sound judgemental, so I softened my voice.

"But he's only lost his legs," said I, looking and feeling somewhat stupid, before adding,

"Hundreds of people walk again with artificial limbs, and there was no mention of his wedding tackle being damaged."

But it didn't work; her voice was now raised in an angry attempt to correct what she saw as my lack of understanding. I tried to look kind and gave a half smile, to let her know it was alright to be angry, to grieve.

"I beg your pardon, wedding tackle, is that what you call it? I'm thinking about my girl wasting her life looking after a cripple."

The whole hospital must have heard her; I felt an anger growing inside of myself and tried to calm my feelings as I said,

"You can't say that, Mrs Holford. I know many people who live normal lives and you would never know they were wearing artificial limbs."

"We would know, and I just couldn't bear the idea of something so imperfect being part of our family. 'No son-in-law of ours will enter our home unless he is as God made him,' that's what her daddy says. That's what her daddy demands, she's to say goodbye to the young man and come home with me."

Mrs Holford did not see Alice returning with Cathy, and standing back listening to those last hurtful remarks.

"You can go home, Ma, I am going to marry Guy. He's not a thing; he's the man I love. Go home to your perfect life, in your perfect home, with your perfect husband. This very imperfect woman is going to marry her imperfect lover."

"Lover? You haven't... you haven't? Oh, dear God, are you pregnant? Your uncle was afraid you might have jumped the gun."

Everyone stood silent; we were already weary of the cruel direction in which Mrs Holford's angry attitude was trying to take us. It was Alice who changed things.

"Please, Matt, when can I see Guy?"

At that, I took pity on her and appealed to the ward sister to at least let Alice in to see her beloved.

"She's desperate, Alice is his fiancée," I said and seeing a further hesitation, I added,

"She's just arrived from the States!" That seemed to do the trick.

"We usually say only two at a time, he is in a very poor condition, no tiring him now, let him sleep until he wakes naturally." The admonition was said with a smile and we all nodded in agreement.

But the four of us were allowed in and taken to a curtained cubicle, where Guy lay flat on his back and with a cradle lifting the covers off his injured legs. He was in a King's Fund bed and it was lowered at the head end and raised at the foot end, obviously to help stop too much pressure on the stumps of his legs. Even so his face was somehow a paler shade than usual; it was almost as if there were layers of white paint beneath the tan.

We sat some time in silence, all except Alice who knelt close and could not resist putting her hand gently on his. His eyes were shut and yet they seemed to be holding a look of pain, so tense were the muscles around them. It also showed in the jumpy, twitching muscles around the mouth. He was suffering, we could all see that.

I felt disappointed that Cathy's first real sight of Guy was devoid of his handsome youthful look; Alice and I knew that he had the face of a romantic hero, his eyes deep blue and constantly lively that everyone whoever met Guy would afterwards comment upon them. His light brown hair cut short for military life, was capable of curling over his forehead to annoy him but to delight the girls. Guy Williams had always had a star-struck following of young ladies, eager for his attention. University and Sandhurst had been the training grounds for more than his intellectual development. Girls loved the very kindness of him, the gentle polite manners that knew how to listen to others. His six foot frame was held straight with his shoulders back, his head up and his chin held modestly back. He did not hold his jaw jutting out as some military men do. Alice loved everything about her fiancé and she cared not what the rest of the world was going to say, she was determined to marry the man she loved.

Mrs Holford sat with a look of fear or hate, I could not decide which, and I just hoped Guy would never see anyone look at him in that manner. Surely coming from a farming community, she was familiar with injury from tractor accidents, from horse riding accidents, from car and motor bike accidents? She kept making a noise which I can only describe as a 'huffing sound'. Cathy tried to stop her, but it was no good; eventually it did disturb our dear Guy.

He slowly opened his eyes and looked immediately into Alice's smiling face, now inches from his own, but he couldn't smile; he lifted his left hand up to touch Alice's sweet face as she knelt beside the lowered end of the bed, so as to kiss him.

It was a passionate and uninhibited kiss. We all sat silently as the young lovers then spent time whispering sweet nothings to each other, between barrages of lighter kisses. She explored every nook and cranny of his face and neck until he gave a laughing gasp before saying,

"I love you, Alice, thank you for coming, but I need to breathe a bit."

Speaking quietly she said,

"Darling we're getting married as soon as you can sit up in a wheelchair."

"Oh, Alice, I'm so sorry, I can't let you think like that. I've no legs!"

"I'm not marrying your legs, I'm going to marry you, silly, I love you and I am going to marry you!" She enunciated it word by word, and loud enough for us all to hear.

Mrs Holford's face was a picture of stony anger; her eyes were blazing with hate, even as Alice's shone with love. It reminded me of the truth that there is less than a sheet of Bronco between love and hate.

Cathy, bless her, seeing the situation, decided to get the mother out of the ward. No easy task, and yet I could see it was for the best.

"Mrs Holford, we should wait outside, Guy needs his rest, and the sister did say only two at a time." Putting her arm across Mrs Holford's back, she began to pull her up off the chair and steer her away from the bedside.

Three steps later Mrs Holford stopped and turning, looked Cathy straight in the eyes and in a voice loud enough for the whole ward to hear said,

"What will you do for money?"

The crassness of the woman was unbelievable. I don't know what came over me, but at that point the dam burst, or the worm turned, I don't know which, I only remember I moved to stand in front of the woman. The whole ward heard my outburst.

"Mrs Holford, you may have a bad opinion of the British, but we have a Welfare State which includes a National Health Service and such things as war pensions! And what's more, Lieutenant Guy Williams is still in the army, and has not been drummed out of the services. He may not wish to do a complete Douglas Bader, but if he did, nobody would stop him, he will be a soldier for as long as he wants to be."

If I was puce with rage, Mrs Holford was white with anger, as I watched her stomp out of the ward with Cathy the peacemaker running behind.

I felt ashamed and pleased all at the same time. I felt cleansed somehow, of all the tension I had felt, ever since Monday. From now on I just knew I would watch over the young lovers, I would be their friend.

Returning to my chair, I sat and watched my temper subside, as with each inhale and exhale of my breathing I relaxed muscle after muscle and let go of my time in Afghanistan.

Every now and then I glanced up at the lovers. It was as if Alice saw none of the drips, or bandages, and it was noticeable that Guy was looking less tense with pain. I smiled at him and winked as I asked, "Guy, are your parents going to get here?" His face went back to its white look.

"No family, Matt. Oh dear God, Alice, your parents will be horrified; I was adopted, but they're both dead now. No family, no legs. What did your mum say to you, 'as God made' well, I'm what an IED made of a man with no family. How can I marry you?"

Then one of those miracle moments came about, as a voice from beyond the curtain said,

"For better or for worse is part of true love, married or not."

I pulled the curtain aside to see a cameo of a young couple, heads held close together and smiling into each other's eyes.

"Sorry," I said, feeling the blush rising up my neck and onto my face, "So sorry, I thought you were speaking to us."

"I was," the young woman replied, still smiling, and looking at Alice she added, "I was speaking to you.

I heard your mother; mine was the same, when Dave was injured ten years ago. We're only here because Dave is having his annual check-up."

"Copped it in Iraq, mate. Hi, I'm Dave and this is the missus, Charlene. Take it you've just stepped on an IED. That seems to be the order of the day, these days. You'll get yer legs, no worries. I'm quadriplegic, I got a chair, but she still married me, no worries."

"You use a wheelchair?"

"What wheelchair? I'm so used to it I don't see it, and it's powered, so he can out-race me any day." Charlene was laughing and looked the most contented woman imaginable.   Then Guy, seemingly having lost all his inhibitions somewhere in Afghanistan, bluntly asked,

"Are you working, Dave?" The friendly-faced young man, who must have been in his thirties, but like his wife, looked years younger, just laughed and smiled back at Guy. I stayed silent as he explained.

"I was an engineer, took a sniper's bullet in the top of my spine. I'm what they call a C6. Retrained as a book keeper, I enjoy it, work for a local company and the boss is great, so long as I do the reconciliation at the end of each month, he never complains if I have to have hospital appointments in between times."

The four young people seemed oblivious of me, sitting watching and marvelling at their lack of shyness about their personal affairs. It was clear to me, that I could liken what was happening to the joining of a new club; the more senior and experienced members helped you understand the rules and helped you avoid the pitfalls. As I listened, I knew that Guy and Alice would be fine. They had just made their first new friends: together as a couple, they would survive.

But he was an orphan and she was about to disobey her parents, and rightly so, I felt. Such an attitude to disability was monstrous in my eyes. I would befriend the young couple and help them on their way.

Plans for the future seemed to flood into my mind. Into my heart as well; here was a job I could cope with, here was my new future. Cathy came back onto the ward at that moment. She was smiling and signalled to me to join her outside. We left them alone, lost in their dreams for their future life together.

Chapter Thirty
Lower Peover, Cheshire

Picture the party, we were celebrating in The Bells of Peover, the meal had been just perfect, the weather had been warm all day, Guy and Alice had not stopped laughing since they had arrived from Headley Court.

Cathy had cried at the sight of Guy walking into our home on his prosthetic legs. He had stood up straight and proud, until he wobbled when bending forward to kiss her. Then his arms grabbed hold of her and Cathy changed the tears to laughter; and that set the tone for the rest of the day.

The house we were viewing was everything the young couple had imagined of an old Victorian parsonage. Big rooms, high ceilings, what the estate agent called *features,* but to Guy they were what he called 'fireplaces and fancy bits on the ceilings' and he liked them every bit as much as the garden and the garage, all of which pleased him. The stair treads were wide and each riser was no more than four inches. Alice loved the bannisters and the volute at the bottom step where the newel post was positioned. Cathy laughed and chided Alice with admonitions of "No sliding down the bannisters!" to which Guy cried, "That's an idea, shall I try now...?" The chorus of protests were all good natured.

Cathy and I watched them as they explored and planned their new life together. The decision to buy was easy, they had received an excellent survey of the building and thanks to the family liaison officer assigned to him, who had help Guy sort out his disability pension, and he was able to apply for the mortgage that very day.

Thinking back, the day we had found the house was one of those days when you woke and just knew that everything was going to turn out alright. The sun had risen early on that September day, five months after our return from Afghanistan, and several months before Guy's release from Headley Court, the rehabilitation centre for the military wounded. We all accepted the separation, Headley Court was two hundred and fifty miles away down south on the Epsom Downs, but with each visit to see him, we all accepted it was the best place for him to be; he was walking again, swimming , exercising and getting his fitness back. By now, Guy was able to walk for a couple of hours each day and was already talking about a trip to Stoke Mandeville Sports Centre. He announced that one of his new dreams was to win a handful of gold medals in the next Paralympics; swimming, table tennis and archery were his first choice. He had laughed and said, 'running can come a bit later'.

We had also celebrated when a military ROSO G1 helped him talk through his future in the army. Guy was so impressed by the help he had received, he asked to be considered for a position as a family liaison officer himself. Little did we know at that point that he dreamt of returning to Afghanistan as a serving officer, he had met up with others who had done just that and who had inspired him to face the future bravely.

Alice, meanwhile, had taken the advice given and was planning their wedding and the setting up of their new home. The decision to move in with us until she had fulfilled her brief was easy. We lived a reasonably convenient distance from Birmingham and she had been able to visit Guy most weekends throughout his recovery there. It was harder for her once his rehabilitation had begun, but most weekends we drove her down to see him. We would pick Guy up and have him to ourselves for several hours each weekend. Staying in a clean and cheerfully run B and B near Headley Court, we were able explore England south of the Thames; Alice loved the visit to Windsor Castle as much as visits to Brighton or walking with Guy in the New Forest. Cathy was fascinated by Alice's excitement at the quaint little tea rooms that litter the tourist areas of England, laughed at her getting dreamy over thatched cottages and she shared Alice's admiration for the well-kept gardens of so many homes. The 'neatness' of it all was a wonder to her and she talked endlessly of her plans for making Guy's life happy in his English castle. The months passed quickly, we were all busy focussing on the future, there was little time to sit around regretting what had happened to Guy; to us he was still Guy, even though he had suffered a traumatic injury.

Sometimes when we were driving back from Headley Court, the two girls would fall asleep as I drove up the M1. Alice would nod off first, she didn't like motorways, and 'Boring roads!' was her complaint; whereas my Cathy was often tired from worry and overwork. The car journey became for her a trigger which allowed her to doze off to the rhythm of the engine, and the noise of the tyres hitting the road.

As I drove, I enjoyed the peace; to me, my Evoque was a place of silent peacefulness, a place to think. I found time to examine my own attitude to all that had happened, thinking about how my life had changed, simply because I had said 'Yes' to the Prime Minister.

I thought about when we had eventually returned home to Cheshire, two days after we had all arrived at Selly Oak Hospital, Cathy and I had brought Alice back with us. The hospital did not want us there twenty-four-seven, Guy wasn't dying and his treatment would progress better without the distraction of any of us. We saw Naomi Holford off to the States, via Manchester Airport. Alice shed no tears, it was her mother who wept when she was quite rudely told to go home and tell Alice's father that she wasn't ever going back to that ghastly farm, in the middle of nowhere. For a moment I felt sorry for the woman, she must have been about my age, and here was her only child telling her goodbye, probably forever.

Alice settled in the guest room remarkably quickly and was content that we could visit Guy in two weeks' time as agreed with the doctors; "Give us two weeks and you'll see a remarkable change in him."

I remembered how I had sat in my office and looked at all the material I had brought back with me. I had then set about rewriting my report, before sending it off to 'C' and to the Prime Minister. A week later I was summoned to Vauxhall Cross where the questions got fired at me like bullets out of a machine gun. I stood my ground:

"You can never have too many birds in the air, and the hospital did a great job, sir, the golden hour or the platinum ten minutes, say how you will, if they can get the soldier to the hospital, they do their darnedest to save him! Don't blame the medics; get the patient to the hospital." I pleaded for more birds in the air.

'C' was flustered; birds cost money and the PM hadn't got much spare, was his argument. I disputed his facts and pointed out that since 2001 the MPD had wasted millions with eight Chinooks in cold storage because of disagreements with the manufactures of the computers used in them. I never got a return visit to Number 10 Downing Street, the PM was too busy. Sitting there in a motorway tailback, I reasoned to myself, *'he only sent me out to cover his own back.'* Brown had wanted something to help him out of the financial pickle he was immersed in, I didn't give him any rope to hang himself with, and neither did I give him a lifeline. As far as I could see, my trip was a waste of political capital; the only good that came out of it was meeting Alice and Guy.

So life had gone on, Alice had little money, but we happily fed and housed her. However, she was a girl with military discipline in her, even though she had disobeyed Directive One. Two weeks after she had arrived, Alice was spending her days stacking shelves at Tesco's, and pulling pints at The Bells of Peover, five nights a week. Naturally her pretty face and toned figure attracted a great deal of attention and several local lads were regularly chatting her up; their disappointment at her constant rejections made me smile. Their shock that she had 'stood by' her injured soldier was almost offensive, if it hadn't been laughable. *Par for the course,* I said to myself. Cathy and I had witnessed several ignorant expressions of prejudice towards the disabled, in the months since I had returned home with the news that Guy and Alice were to live with us, at least until they were married and had a home of their own.

Having heard nothing from her parents for over six months, not even when she had sent the wedding invitation, Alice relied on Cathy in such a way that

Cathy eventually said to me, "Alice is the daughter we never had!"

Now, I'm a man and cannot tell you about wedding plans. Mine to Cathy was plotted and planned in secret, my whole life has revolved around secrets and Cathy understood, especially during my active MI6 time. Being part of the Royal Navy meant that the title of Commander covered a multitude of absences from home, without too many intrusive enquiries from gossipy neighbours and other curious people. So it was Cathy who did the entire donkey work needed and I just turned up on a shore leave, to find my wedding organised for the day after next. I wore my uniform and we had a quiet wedding at St Oswald's, the lovely church, by my favourite pub; we ate in the pub and left for a honeymoon on dry land! Yes, I liked my wedding; but Alice is an American and she was a tad younger than my Cathy had been, when we had married.

But women being women, Cathy showed Alice the wedding album and that settled it, she wanted to marry in the same church, St Oswald's, Lower Peover and she would have everything the same, except for the colour of the bridesmaids' dresses. I suppose I should have been glad, it saved considerable time, no traipsing around trying to find the dreaded reception venue!

Apparently it was to be a traditional British wedding and I was to wear the full morning suit and a cravat in the same colour as the bridesmaids' dresses, a colour I almost hate, but I kept my mouth shut and wore it anyway. My only input to the decision-making for the event was that I opted to carry a silver-grey rather than a black coloured top hat. My Cathy looked beautiful in a light coloured blue dress and jacket with a pretty brimmed hat and matching shoes and gloves. That night I teased her about looking like royalty; she hit me and said, "So long as you don't mean the Queen Mother!" "No dear, she's been dead these nine years." That warranted another swipe and I retaliated by chasing Cathy around the house and up the stairs. What happened next made up for the disappointment I was going to have to swallow at the church! It is best if I begin at the beginning.

Naturally, Alice was a miracle of loveliness in creamy lace and carrying pink flowers to match the bridesmaids' dresses, and my hated cravat! The church at Lower Peover was decorated with ribbons and flowers; the churchyard was in full autumn bloom with colourful dahlias, russet reds, golden yellows, white and shades of purple. Every shade of coloured chrysanthemums showed off the beauty of the graveyard surrounding the ancient church. With the Hughes's section making up the four groomsmen, there were plenty of smart uniformed men to please Alice and her military friends, plus a military guard of honour of Lancashire Fusiliers who had arrived ready to line up after the ceremony, as the newlyweds left the church. It was going to look fabulous.

We were ready and waiting for the car to take Alice and me to the church. We stood looking at each other, she was a picture; I couldn't help myself, I leant forward and kissed her forehead, saying,

"I am honoured that you asked me, Alice."

Then the texted message came thorough, all was ready; Guy wearing his uniform looked smart beyond words, and Cathy wrote that she was nearly crying at the sight of him.

The car drew up at the door and I prepared to escort Alice to the church and down the aisle to marry the man she loved. I felt a pride I cannot explain, a childless man allowed a privilege few ever get offered.

It was a body blow I will never be able to explain; we drew up at the church to find Alice's parents standing outside, dressed in full wedding glamour as befitting a wealthy American farmer and his wife.

My Cathy was looking pale in spite of her make-up; she could not smile as she watched the photographer take a picture of me helping our Alice out of the hired and bedecked Bentley. Together Alice and I walked arm in arm towards the waiting group, when Alice suddenly let go of my support, and ran with hands outstretched to her parents; who realising her forgiveness was there for the taking, opened their arms to her, and the three of them hugged and kissed and Naomi cried out in her loud voice, "Forgive me, Alice, forgive me!"

Well, there you go! I never got to walk Alice down the aisle, but I did get to make a speech and had the joy of meeting up with Gareth Hughes, with skin grafts healing on his face, with Craig Lewis, Tom Johnstone and Andy Norcross, all dressed up in uniform and acting as a group of best men!

The most surprising revelation of the day came after a lovely meal in the pub; the vicar asked Alice's father if he was related to their Holford.

"You are a Holford?"

"Well, no not exactly, but the Holford Chapel was built in the late eighteenth century. It's the chapel at the east end of the north aisle."

That did it, after the meal the vicar began chatting with Olli Holford, yes, he was now well inebriated and telling everyone to call him Olli, he preferred it to Oswald, he said as he worked the reception and thanked everybody for being so kind to his daughter. Then Olli declared that his known family tree began with the arrival of the first Oswald Holford in Virginia some considerable time before 1800, and all he knew was they had come from Cheshire. Olli Holford was beside himself; his name was Oswald and yes, he believed his Alice, knowing her family history, had searched out St Oswald's deliberately to honour her family. In fact it was her great grandfather four times removed who fled to the New World.

Later, the parish priest and the verger helped flatter Alice's parents by giving them a tour of the church and a long and happy browse of the parish registers for birth, marriages and deaths. By the time the day was over and the only thing left was the clearing away of the glasses and the remains of the wedding banquet held as planned in The Bells of Peover, Olli and Naomi Holford were beside themselves with joy. They believed they had come back to their Holford roots.

Knowing how much alcohol they had drunk that day, I warned everyone to go along with their happy news and let them sleep on it. Tomorrow when they were sober again would be time enough to prove or disprove the legitimacy of the hoped for connection. They had booked into a hotel in Knutsford, and there they stayed for the next ten days, until Alice returned from the honeymoon, after which they moved in with Alice.

With Guy back at Headley Court and learning to drive his newly adapted car, Alice got on with finishing the decorating of the old vicarage and set her parents to do what they could do well, under Cathy's tutelage; give their daughter the English garden she wanted, and also set raised beds into the area set aside as a vegetable garden, so that Guy could have an easier time planting out. She was determined that they would eat home grown food, "Just like home, Daddy!"

she said. And Daddy obliged and planted out a winter crop of onion and cabbage, enough to feed the village.

More importantly, Olli and I went off to a local gardening centre to choose a suitable green house. I was rightly impressed with the man's ability to spend money. He excused his behaviour with, "Well we didn't bring over any wedding presents." I told him that his surprise presence at the church was gift enough for the happy couple. Being grateful that he hadn't come to harm his daughter or Guy, I had long since accepted his presence in our lives, as well. We were sitting in the cafe at the garden centre and downing strong coffee and croissants.

"Naomi would call this a second breakfast." He was laughing as he tucked into the food. Olli was a big man with a big appetite, and like many a big man he had a jolly personality, once he got used to you.

So I was pleased when he suddenly announced,

"I feel bad about what I said about Guy, before I'd even met him. You see, now I look at him moving about, well I find I clean forget he ain't got real legs!"

"Me too, he's pretty darn good. Did he tell you he's staying in the army?"

"He's not?"

"Yes!"

"Lord help us, he ain't going back fighting, surely not fighting?"

"Well, I can't answer that; I think he has to wait until he has finished rehab at Headley Court and he has passed all the tests to prove he is fit. You know the sort of thing."

"He wants to work; do you think he could manage my farm?"

"Olli, I was waiting for that question, difficult one!" I paused and he watched as I took a long slow sip of my coffee and a mouthful of a croissant, before saying,

"Sometimes I believe he feels he can't do much else. I mean he talks as if the things that made him a good soldier don't fit in with making him a good non-soldier. Do you see what I'm trying to say?"

Then Olli bowled me over as he spoke.

"Sure, sure, I hear yer. he don't realise how valuable a commodity a man is who knows how to be loyal to his boss and to his workmates, who is a good time keeper, ain't lazy, has respect for others, skill with machinery, endurance of hard work, suffers different climates, has a respect for different cultures, a strong spine, and an ability to learn new skills and all that, and he still has a pleasant and companionable nature; he's a gift to any employer. I mean any boss would value his talents. I'd hire him any day; he's a gift, he's a talented and valuable gift. Yep, I'd employ him."

"You and I both, Olli, he's a hundred per cent employable."

We both laughed and I felt totally comfortable with my new friend. We sat in silence for several minutes and I knew Olli was building up to something, I wasn't certain what, but when Olli was thinking he had a funny way of letting his lower lip jut out and cover his top lip. I was right, he was thinking.

"Yer know, Matt, it's like this, I could leave the farm to run itself, say with a manager in place, but can you guess what Naomi and I were talking about in bed, last night?"

"I've no idea, Olli, what were you talking about?"

"Selling up and moving back here to where our real roots are, live here in Cheshire. I'm nearly seventy; the farm really gets to me, especially when the winds blow. Alice will never come back, not to the farm, there are no other young families about, it's very isolated and even Naomi doesn't miss that, she's pleased our gal has given us the idea of moving. She says it seems providential that Alice found our roots. There are no more of us over there. We are the last of the Holford line, as far as I know. I'd like to see my days out peacefully and end in the churchyard near a chapel built by an ancestor. What do you think?"

"What did Naomi say?"

"Oh, she said yes, she said it's would be great not to be stuck in the middle of hundreds of acres and her nearest neighbour over a mile away." He went quiet and again I sensed something momentous was brewing.

"We're looking for a home here, we went to a, what do yer call it here when buying a house?"

"An estate agent?"

"That's it, in Knutsford, and Naomi fancies Knutsford, near enough, but not on top of our Alice, she says, and the idea of living near a store that she can say is within walking distance, is just magic! Sure, she loves the way the ladies here have shopping bags on wheels and just 'pop out' for a loaf or a pint. She says she loves it here and Knutsford is right cute. She says Knutsford is a right cute village."

I made a note to explain that in British terms it was considered a town, but for now I let the lesson slide. Could we all cope with them living so near; when Olli suddenly came out with,

"And guess what the darling said? 'How about we buy a Winnebago and set off and see places we've never been to'."

Nodding my head and silently giving him thumbs up I waited, and then had to ask,

"Do you think you'll get a buyer for the farm? I mean grand plans cost money."

"Got one already, got a neighbour who has been after it for years."

I knew I enjoyed his company; I was not too sure about Cathy, but Cathy never complained and together with Naomi, she helped Alice get all the curtains sorted and put up, as each room was newly decorated in colours chosen by an excited Alice.

At the weekends, one or other of Guy's army friends would come and stay. Norcross was particularly attentive and apologetic. He came at least twice, making himself most useful when the hall and stairwell were being decorated. His height was a great help with all the ceilings.

There came a time when I was able to ask Norcross why he had behaved as he did over Alice.

"Jealousy, Matt. Bloody-minded jealousy! Now I'm glad they got to know each other before it all happened. Don't worry, I'm not chasing Alice; I've taken up with a girl in the Lancashire's, she's from Bury."

"Make sure we get invited to the wedding,"

He smiled and said it wasn't likely to be before the next spring, but he wouldn't forget us.

By late September the weather was still warm and very much what we in England call an Indian summer. Norcross on one of his visits helped me introduce Olli to Manchester City football club, and explained the game much more reasonably than I could.

Meanwhile Naomi and Alice were shown around Liverpool One shopping centre and a trip to the new Liverpool Everyman Theatre with its total accessibility. They had been stunned when the usher informed them that people in wheelchairs could even access the lighting rig.

Then Alice's parents went back to Illinois for Thanksgiving and to finalise the sale of the farm, promising to be back in time for a very English Christmas. Two containers loaded with their furniture and things were packed up and sent off to be shipped to storage near Knutsford. It was to take six weeks, but there was Christmas to enjoy in the meantime, and surveys and exchanges of contracts to be got over, before their things arrived the second week in January.

But every idea for our future together was to hover in the ether of Guy's progress at Headley Court and the success of his rehabilitation. We all agreed that must wait upon the hopes and dreams of our dear boy.

It was Olli, who watching Stephen Hawkins speaking on TV, suddenly announced, "If that lad can do what he does and he's that disabled, our Guy can fly to the moon, drive a train or build a house, if he wanted to, I'd sub him any day. I'd give him the wherewithal to follow whatever his dream is."

I wanted to believe him; I also wanted to follow Guy's dream.

Chapter Thirty-One
Headley Court

It was spring again and with one month to go before he was to leave Headley Court, Guy phoned me; by now he treated me as a surrogate father and I could tell he was stressed because for the first time he actually called me so.

"Dad, please come down and see me on my own, alone and without telling Alice."

When a grown man trusts you as if you're his surrogate parent, you know he's desperate about something.

I thought I could give Cathy the excuse of being called in to explain something contained in my Afghan report. If she didn't believe me, Cathy wouldn't have said anything to indicate she was bothered. Seven months married and Alice was pregnant! All our weekend visits had achieved what Cathy and Naomi had most desired; they were in seventh heaven, suddenly they had hope in their hearts, a

Meanwhile Olli and I had learnt to jog along together, a couple of times a week we would go off playing golf, and I knew he was the one who would be disappointed at my news. In the end over a pint in my local, The Bells of Peover, I took him into my confidence, and we plotted like two naughty schoolboys trying to deceive their parents.

I took him with me, pretending we were going off on a week's golfing trip to various sites down south. If Naomi and Cathy suspected anything, they said nothing; no more than when Olli and I took ourselves off to visit the Fusiliers Museum in Bury. That visit alone had convinced me that Oswald Holford was a history buff; and on that day he had without my probing revealed that he was in fact a Vietnam vet.

We had again resorted to the comfort of a local pub for lunch. Two pints in, he suddenly opened up about his time as an twenty year old who had lasted only six months, thanks to a bullet in his groin, made worse because it was from friendly fire! Also he was injured right at the end of the conflict and spoke of being grateful to have got out alive.

"It was a bad time. Sometimes ending a war is worse than beginning one. Matt, I was shot by a rogue bullet from one of my own platoon, the guy was and is still a friend of mine, but he got trigger happy when he mistook me for a Vietcong. Left me with a load of problems; Naomi and I tried for a baby for nearly twenty years, until when we had finally accepted that it wouldn't happen, out popped Alice."

"Is that why you were angry at Alice for saying she would marry Guy, no matter what? You were afraid they'd find it hard to conceive their own child."

"Yes, and I'm ashamed of what I said."

"Don't be, I've no proof that I wouldn't have reacted in the same way."

Olli was a great driver, he had a big car and with his generous spirit he never quibbled over petrol money. We did share hotel bills, I insisted on that and he was as excited as I was at having Guy to ourselves, to talk 'man to man' for the first time in months.

The journey was easy, I had begun to enjoy Olli's way of thinking; he was pragmatic and yet funny. His direct and 'straight to the point' view of life had grown on me as the weeks and months had passed and now, just months since we had first met, we were happily comfortable in our friendship.

In order to cover our tracks with the wives, we booked into a golf club an hour away from Headley Court. That should look good if they phoned, or snooped around our desks looking at credit card statements. That was Olli's idea; he said Naomi had a thing about checking his American Express statements. When I asked why, I was treated to a fabulous account of Olli's misspent youth, after his accident with the bullet in the groin.

"Naomi still calls it sowing my wild oats, but I tell her she was the best, being the final ripe corn I gathered in!"

"Is that why you call her a-maize-ing?" I asked with a play on the word 'maize' at which Olli laughed so much, I wondered he didn't have a heart attack. We were still laughing when we walked into Guy's room at Headley Court, to find him looking thoughtful and anxious.

He looked at me as he spoke, but I think he was really trying to say something to Olli. It was as if he knew I would understand, but he needed Olli to be the one to explain things to Alice.

"Dad, I'm going back, I have to."

Both Olli and I remained silent; we waited and waited until Guy felt ready to explain the details. When they came I was only slightly surprised at his reasons; knowing his honest heart, I knew it wouldn't be for any chauvinist macho reason, he was a man with a sensitive spirit. He was troubled by what he had left behind in Afghanistan.

"I'm going back to check on Ramin, and I want to make sure that they didn't kill that poor girl."

Neither Olli nor I could speak. We both understood the implications of that simple truthful direct statement of intent. We both knew our boy was torn by guilt over something that wasn't his fault and we respected his scrupulousness in telling us the truth; he gained more respect from Olli by being direct and coming out with the real truth, than if he had made us wait to find out.

"What do you want me to tell Alice?" asked Oswald Holford with great dignity and in a quiet voice as if he was battling with himself. I suspected he wanted to shout and say, "Don't go, you'll get yourself killed!" or something akin to, "Think of your wife!" But he didn't, he just sat waiting patiently for Guy to speak.

At last Guy turned his face towards his father-in-law and allowed himself to look into that face that I had come to respect, and see what I saw every time I looked at Oswald Holford; a man as open as he was direct in his speech. The only way to deal with Olli was to be truthful.

"Remember when Norcross set me up with Ramin and those two new boys on a training exercise in the Baba Mountains? Well, Ramin sensed it was a set up, so, once he had clocked the coincidence of the Hughes section and myself all being there, at the same time, he told me that there was a drug run due through there that day, and the Taliban were intending to use the route you and the section were to take later on. Remember the route other people didn't use because of the crevasse where tribesmen trapped and stole off each other, when cornered in that crevasse? I admit I was weak, but Ramin did what he did to save me from what he believed was Norcross's treachery, he hadn't realised we were at loggerheads over Alice. Such a concept was alien to him, young men choosing their future bride. We'd seen your cars coming from over twenty miles away; we had half an hour to make our plans. Sorry, Dad, I'm truly sorry, I hadn't realised you were going to be in the cars with the men. That's why I was so mad with Norcross, but firstly I had to get those young inexperienced men out of there. Once I'd sent you up the side of the mountain, I drove them to the nearest checkpoint, which was about thirty miles away, where I literally dumped them on the captain in charge and gave a feeble excuse about their being in his care, until I could return for them."

He stood up and hesitated before saying,

"I lied to you when I was in detention, I'm sorry. I'd known all along that Norcross had set me up. Anyway when I got back to the checkpoint, Norcross shot at my leg in total rage, he believed I'd been trying to run away from the fight."

"The same accusation you were trying to avoid making about him and the section?" I asked.

"Precisely; I was beginning to see the reason why the army said no fraternising, it's not the fraternising. It is the jealousy that goes with it."

I stood up and gave him a hug and said, "You're not responsible for Norcross's emotions. Where is he now?"

"They are back at Bastion."

"They, you mean the section, or the whole platoon?"

"5 Platoon is back at Camp Bastion and they are there; even Gareth Hughes, his skin grafts took well. He aims with his good eye and Johnstone wrote that the others always set themselves on his blind side when fighting, when marching."

At that point, Guy handed me a letter and after reading it I handed it on to Olli. We saw the news, that the boys hadn't seen hide or hair of Ramin.

So that was what had triggered this unrest in Guy!

Olli and I sat down and looked at each other. We felt for the lad, but we realised that whoever was leading 5 Platoon was not going to want Lieutenant Guy Williams coming in and kicking him out of his ranking position. We both knew that rank matters even to the most modest of serving men. The silence that ensued was lengthy and punctuated with frequent shifting about in the uncomfortable chairs provided. Eventually I came up with a solution; it went something like this.

"OK, if you're going back, so am I!"

"Good idea, think I'll come with you," said Olli Holford, before rising to his feet and saying, "Pub lunch, you idiots?"

Good old Olli, it worked; we trudged down to the local, all three of us walking with our hands in our pockets and with laughter and insults very much the order of the day. By the time we reached the Dog and Whistle, Guy was jubilant; it was the longest walk he had achieved with his hands in his pockets, he viewed that as an indication that he had at long last mastered his balance on his walking legs. By now he had four pairs of prosthetic legs, two pairs of walking, one with just metal rods and one pair with what he called his sexy designer calves, one pair for swimming and a pair for running. Olli was joking about Guy having to have an extra baggage allowance, if he intended to return to Afghanistan.

The meal was one I will always remember, if only because it was Olli who said at the end of it; "Can anyone stop us going to Afghanistan as tourists?"

The deepest silence I have ever known followed that remark.

Then Olli said, "OK, Guy, I'll come with you, we fly to Kabul Airport, reason; to investigate setting up village schools for girls in Afghanistan, as a charity, as a gift from the countries that fought the Taliban. Then we get permission to travel as an official delegation to that village, the one you went to, find the answers about this Ramin fellow and the girl who was locked up. How does that sound to you?"

"Perfect!" Guy said, visibly excited and pleased at his father-in-law's idea.

Chapter Thirty-Two
Kabul One Month later

We flew via Frankfurt to Kabul on the Afghanistan-owned Safi Airline. Olli was thrilled to be able to join us on our adventure; we were equally pleased to have someone rich enough to sub it.

It would be dishonest to say we lied about our trip; it was our intention to at least look at the possibility of starting a school in the village of Karvelk. If it never materialised it would not be our fault entirely, considering the terrible attitude of Afghanistan males to the teaching of girls and women in general.

Getting there was the easy part of the planning; before we set off, we had three women of our own to convince that we had 'to do what a man has to do' and as Cathy said, 'don't give me all that cowboy crap!' Surprisingly it was Alice who defended us once she realised our true intention. Cathy and Naomi never really accepted our leaving for such a war-torn country; we at least obliged by handing over all details of our insurance policies and instructions for our funerals. We became deliberately over-morbid, until Cathy laughed and ordered us to go, to give them some peace.

"He's teasing me, the way he did for years while he was being attacked by drug barons and gun runners and God knows what else. No, he knows what he is doing and I promise you, Naomi and Alice, he will probably bring them back with Ramin in one pocket and the girl who has disappeared in the other and set them up in our garden shed!"

Olli sorted sufficient funds to keep those at home and those travelling in reasonable comfort for a month. We had set that as our time limit. If we hadn't found Ramin by then we were coming home, disappointed but believing we had done our best for Ramin.

Once through customs at Kabul Airport, we got a taxi to the large Intercontinental Hotel, where by some miracle we had managed to pre- book a suite of rooms. Showered and smartly dressed, with cameras around our necks, we tried our best to look like charitable men on a mission. Next stop was a visit to the British base on the outskirts of the city, where we negotiated a visit to Camp Bastion. It took two days, but eventually we got there, flying out on a half-empty Chinook, which had just delivered ISAF soldiers from Holland returning home via Kabul and Frankfurt.

Camp Bastion airfield seemed busier than ever; so much so, that I felt almost guilty for adding to the workload of the base staff. But as with the army rules of courteous respect for visitors, we were seemingly expected and quickly housed in a vacant prefabricated box-like room, one covered as usual with a canopy of camouflaged sheeting. Settling in, we enjoyed a short rest before setting off for the cookhouse first, and then to obey instructions, we were to report to the British brigadier. With several miles between the different sites, we managed to get the bus to the cookhouse, cadge a lift in a jeep to the brigadier and then we walked back to our billet to crash out for the rest of the day.

And crash out we did after an hour with Brigadier Thomason; Guy was almost angry to find that Brigadier Clitheroe was no longer at Camp Bastion, we had missed him by a couple of weeks. Looking back on that disappointment, I realise Clitheroe couldn't have been any more use than Thomason; maybe a better vehicle, maybe a couple of escorting military with a machine gun or two; as it was we were going to have to stand on our own two feet!

If I say that Brigadier Thomason believed we were mad, I am at the very least moderating his opinion of us, for even dreaming of returning to look for one he considered a rogue interpreter. We kept quiet about the missing interpreter Ramin, and talked instead about Wasima, the girl who had inspired our mission and our desire to give the village a school. Thomason was a red-faced man at the best of times, by the time he had finished with all three of us he was puce with the effort of trying not to yell at us. I distinctly sensed that he was going to give us trouble. What he did give us was a nearly clapped out modest little jeep, normally used to get around the camps. It carried no protective grilles or means of defence, such as was carried by the foxhound vehicles, but we didn't complain; we expressed more than sufficient gratitude, so much so that Thomason changed down from puce to a glowing red. I won't tell you what Guy said about the man, it was unprintable.

As ordered we were tagged on to the end of a column of about fifty different vehicles heading past the village of Karvelk. I was pleased about one thing; it was a Friday and the market should be in full swing by the time we got there.

Olli was quite comfortable with the wide open spaces either side of the river, he hardly glanced at the mountains in the distance. As he sat with his jutting lower lip more pronounced than ever, I knew he was thinking out his next move. I was driving, Guy had not yet passed his driving test; I felt certain it wouldn't matter out here, but we decided to obey the brigadier's rules, and keep to the letter of the law.

I drove right into the centre of the village and parked just metres away from Mohammed's compound. The benches were there, the gate was open but there was no sign of anyone living there, no washing on the line, no children playing, no market stalls. The place was bare, it was a ghost village.

Guy made his way around the compound, checked the rooms and the cell where I had seen the girl imprisoned, before coming back to join Olli and me still sitting in the jeep. He said only one word; "Taliban!"

We sat in silence, afraid of the shadows until we realised that we were alone, miles from anywhere and having been given instructions to wait for an escort back to Camp Bastion four hours hence, we sat feeling nervous but ready for anything. We were dressed as civilians and carried no weapons. Realising how vulnerable we were, that four hours was a long wait.

The ration packs were eaten and a fair amount of our water ration was gone, as sitting in the shade along the wall of the compound, we realised that the escort was late, the sun was setting and we were stranded.

As darkness fell I heard a noise to the right and gently touching the other two I alerted them to the approaching company. We all held our breath as I prayed that it was our escort; but my mind said it was the Taliban on a night patrol, probably to plant IEDs.

About fifteen or sixteen Taliban surrounded us with weapons pointing straight at us.

"We're not armed," I said in English.

"Karaar, karaar khabaree kawa," said Guy, standing and looking the leader straight in the eye. Years later he told me that he had simply asked the man to 'please, please speak more slowly.'

The only phrase he could remember from the army issue phrase book. It obviously had the desired effect because, whoever the leader was, he nodded and lowered his weapon before ordering his men to frisk us. They obviously enjoyed removing our timepieces, wallets and passports, which were all handed over to the leader before they thoroughly frisked us. But when they came to Guy's legs it would have been funny in any other circumstances, but on this occasion it was frightening. As the man got below Guy's knees he almost jumped back with horror! Looking up at Guy in disbelief, he struck the metal shin with the barrel of his rifle; the noise of metal on metal made all of them jump back in absolute horror or was it revulsion, I couldn't tell.

But Guy, cool as a cucumber, bent over and rolled his jeans up until they were level with his knees, exposing his metal legs. It was the first pair he'd had, when at Headley Court. Then he began walking around laughing at the men looking in disbelief, as he taunted them.

"Thought you'd kill us, did you; we've worked out how to walk again and we are all going to come back to get you." He was laughing like a madman, I was afraid that if just one of these men spoke English, we were done for, the end of us!

The leader did understand. In faulty hesitating English he said,

"You will come with us, you filthy foreigners."

With that he then spoke in Dari and ordered his men to tie us up. The realization that he was probably a War Lord rather than a Taleban crossed my mind and allowed me to breath once more. Well, I know that's what he said, because that's what they did; tied us up. Later we all became familiar with certain Dari words, and both Olli and I cautioned Guy not to speak out in English when in a temper, because many Afghans have smatterings of English, sometimes repeated with a clear American accent.

They took the jeep. They put us in the back of a truck and whisked us off into the vast plain that was Helmand. By now we were feeling tense and that first night none of us could sleep, as they drove on and on through the night. We were grateful in that we were kept together and just before dawn, we were thrown into a locked cabin, somewhere mountainous and cold. They didn't give us our backpacks; there was no water and no food. The only saving grace was that because it was cold Olli reasoned that we shouldn't die of thirst.

I didn't laugh, my mind centred upon why hadn't the escort team arrived and how soon would we be missed? I really didn't mind if it was initially the loss of the jeep that indicated our disappearance, and we would be landed with a bill for its replacement, just so long as somebody missed us. Guy reasoned that we were likely to be ransom material because we were in civilian clothes.

"You mean if we had been in uniform they would just have shot us?" asked Olli.

"Yes, that's exactly what I mean," replied Guy.

The next night they loaded us back onto the truck and we were driven further away. Sitting exposed to the night sky and nothing impeding our view of the countryside we were travelling though, it was hardly surprising that Guy could reckon we were being taken northwards, nearer to Uzbekistan; he believed the region was called Mazâr-e-Sharif.

"They can call it what they bloody well like, I ain't giving them any of my money!" said a very belligerent and hungry Oswald Holford.

It was many miles and possibly twelve hours later, when in that grey darkness just before dawn we drew up at a large compound of farm buildings, with a distinctive smell of animal dung in the air and the noise of a baying horse suddenly intruding into the otherwise silent enclosure. In the very centre was an almost familiar dwelling; the influence of Russian architecture could be seen in the painted carved wooden shutters and the arches all around a wooden veranda, for a moment I thought it looked like a film set for Doctor Zhivago.

Dragged off the truck, we were marched across the wet and muddy floor of the compound before being pushed into the building rather roughly, almost as if they suspected we might make a run for it.

Once inside we were walked through several rooms, each one led off the other, like some seventeenth century English stately home, built without corridors. Five rooms later we arrived at what we realised was the end of the building; a large high-ceilinged space with several windows, all shuttered against the cold air of the mountains outside. Was it possible that it was nearly seven in the morning? I found myself disorientated in time and space. My knees felt weak from hunger and lack of water, but I tried to stand as erect as possible.

We were confronted by several elderly men sitting around the walls on large cushions and low couches. With Guy in the centre, the three of us were forced to stand facing what we would later describe as a council of elders. I thought I recognised Mohammed sitting to one side, obviously here he was not the Mullah; had he accepted the loss of his village, was he also a prisoner being held to ransom by more powerful men?

As I just said, we were so hungry and thirsty it was a wonder we could stand, but they kept us standing, until Olli began to sway. Guy reached out to prevent him falling, but Olli was out cold, he fell taking Guy with him and I turned to help, but violent hands grabbed at me and held me away from both my friends.

A voice spoke from behind me; "What is the matter with you, you spineless Brits?"

"He needs water," I said, "We haven't had a drink in twenty-four hours. We'll be no good to you if we die of thirst."

At that the man sitting in the centre of the elders waved his swish to send a fly off his face and looking directly at me, he addressed me in a sneering tone with, "What you think you worth to us?"

"Money?"

"Money; OK, you give me money for me? What you worth?" He was still sneering at me.

"What's the usual price?" I sneered back at him, almost mimicking his voice. It had the desired effect; he stood up and came so close to me I could smell his bad breath. It was revolting; he stank of bad teeth, of an unwashed body and grimy clothes. His beard was matted and dirty.

"Every pound or you are dead, Englishman, you are dead."

Then speaking to the men behind us, he ordered them to take us away and lock us up.

"We sort ransom later."

We were dismissed and led down to the basement, to be locked in a large room with dirty cushions all around the edge; there was one table in the middle, where a loaf of bread and a jug of water were deposited before they left us, and we heard the door locked behind them. The next minute the door was wrenched open and our backpacks were thrown in behind us; I was amazed that the Taliban hadn't raided them, but I was to thank God they hadn't, I had medicines in mine. Once the door was slammed shut a second time, I held my breath until I realised they weren't going to leave us in darkness. Even better, I noticed a light switch beside the door. Good, I grabbed the jug and moved to Olli to give him a drink, but he laughed and straightened himself up as he said,

"After you, matey, after you."

Guy looked at him in astonishment; "But you were dying a moment ago, what the hell?"

We all had a drink, and Guy reached for the bread, pulling it apart, but Olli, proving he had once been trained as a soldier, said,

"Only eat a bit; we don't know when we'll get another."

Refreshed, if you could call a few sips of water and two mouthfuls of stale bread refreshment, Olli smiled and said,

"Sorry about upstairs, but I guessed they didn't know how to get rid of us. The old boys all looked a trifle gaga, so I thought a good dramatic faint would stir things up. It worked!"

"Probably all doped up if you ask me," I said, trying to convince myself that if they were all junkies, we should be able to deal with them.

We sat there leaning against the wall, after hiding our extra bread in our pockets, another of Olli's ideas; it might persuade them to give us a bigger loaf next time. Or so he thought.

After allowing ourselves some recovery time, we stood up and walked about looking for some means of relieving our bursting bladders.

I found the buckets, one empty, and one of sand with a small trowel, presumably to cover the deposits.

Satisfied and comfortable once more, we journeyed on. It was dark down at the far end. The room was easily sixty foot long, maybe longer for it went the whole length of the house, with wooden pillars holding it up at a number of strategic points, which obviously were supporting the crossbeams holding up the floor above. The whole house was wooden, that much we gathered, and we could see narrow beams of light through the floorboards above.

So busy were we touching the wood and its carved decorations, we almost fell over the body stretched out along the very far end of the room.

Who was it?

Was it a male or a female?

Were they sleeping or dead?

Nothing moved, there was no sound so bending down I touched the hand I could just about see, when I felt its icy coldness suddenly clutch at my thumb and at the same time I heard it; it was a whispered, "Matt."

The three of us carried him to the light and placed him, pillows and all, on the table. Ramin looked as if he had been beaten to within an inch of his life. Even as I assessed his injuries, Olli was putting the jug of water to Ramin's mouth. He couldn't drink; remembering Guy in hospital and how I had helped him then, I got a swab from my backpack. Olli was instructed in how to gently moisten Ramin's lips, until he was able to suck on the swab.

Meanwhile Guy and I raided our backpacks for any first aid goods we had with us, and with military precision we cleaned and dressed Ramin's bleeding wounds. I had a large supply of Celox plasters and Guy had bandages and swabs. Finishing, we then gathered as many cushions as we could find and made a comfortable bed, and laid the wounded Ramin down to sleep.

For the rest of that night and all the next day we took it in turns to sleep and to watch over the beaten and wounded wreck that was once a vibrant Ramin.

Chapter Thirty-Three
Somewhere in Mazâr-e-Sharif

For five days we lived on water and the daily ration of a loaf of bread, which we now shared between four, as Ramin's strength returned and he was able to eat without vomiting. It was pushed into the room through a barely open door.

Then on the sixth day, without warning the door opened wide and two Taliban men held us at gunpoint, while a veiled woman followed them in, to place a large bowl of food on the table, and a second woman placed a jug of steaming hot water, a bowl, towels and mercifully a roll of toilet paper on the floor just inside the door.

We looked at each other in surprise and a momentary fear; were we being fattened up for the kill? Then Olli laughed and said; "If they want to ransom us, we must look good or we're worth nothing!"

We laughed and tucked into the pot of potatoes, which had been cooked with sugar beets to sweeten and colour them, and were dressed up with the protein value of nuts. Nuts of all varieties, chopped raw onions, and a variety of seeds, some we recognised as sesame seeds, others we just hoped were edible. By the time we had emptied the bowl, our hands were filthy and coloured by the beet juice.

Filling the second bowl with the still hot water, we now stood around the table and took it in turns to wash. From our rucksacks we found flannels and travel towels, deodorants, shaving gear and hairbrushes. It felt wonderful to wipe our faces in hot water; the Wet Ones had kept us going, but we all appreciated the water, it's that feeling of cleanliness especially around the eyes. Between us we washed Ramin and redressed his wounds before setting down to sleep, this time we opted for a two hour rota of watch and sleep. Guy, our first watch, relaxed after the first hot food in over a week, slept through and beyond his watch, so that we all slept the whole night, nothing disturbed us. The contentment that came from the potatoes and a good night's sleep was magical.

All woke refreshed and by now slightly bored with the situation, it was Olli, who asked,

"You took some beating, Ramin, what happened?"

At first Ramin just shrugged his shoulders and refused to look at Olli. But Olli persisted, he was horrified at the beating Ramin had taken and kept asking him why it had happened. In the end, with nothing else to do, Ramin began to open up about what had happened when the Taliban had attacked Karvelk.

"The wife of Mohammed, she died."

"You're saying she is now dead? The lady I saw in the compound, hanging out washing?"

"No, she was his sister. Mohammed has had several wives; they were all young and died young. The Begum is dead, the last one she was only fifteen and pregnant, then she died giving birth to a girl child about three years ago. Mohammed was furious and sent one of his men to visit other elders to find him a new bride. He only wanted a girl, not a woman."

"Dear God, he must be seventy if he's a day, has he no heart?" cried Guy, horrified at the thought of the old man with a young girl.

"No, you don't understand."

"You're dammed right, I don't understand," Guy said vehemently.

"Sure thing, neither do I," Olli chimed in with his two cents worth.

I stayed silent and just watched Ramin, afraid that we might over-tire him; we were going to need him to translate for us, if we were to be interrogated.

"They believe only a pure woman, a virgin, is good enough for them. It's their religion and Mohammed wanted an heir, he wanted a boy child. The Begum had been promised to him when she was nine and she had been part of a debt settlement they call Baad. She died giving him another daughter."

"Same old, same old story; we've seen it all over the world, Ramin, they must have a boy," Guy whispered under his breath.

Ramin heard him and replied, "But Mohammed cast his eyes on Wasima, my girl, and because her mother had died Wasima lived out there, with her aunt, who was supposed to prepare Wasima for her marriage to me. I had asked for her. She was promised to me. I had a trunk full of gifts for her dowry, I even had jewellery and silks, we were to be married, that's why she was staying with her aunt in Karvelk. But Mohammed's agent offered her father a better deal. She tried to escape, but she was betrayed. Matt, you saw what happened, you were there, and her aunt was trying to help her and other girls to escape."

"Where is Wasima now?" I asked, with some suspicion that I wasn't going to like the answer. I was right, I didn't like the answer.

"She's dead, I believe she's dead."

We all remained silent, while Ramin seemed to collapse in grief and anger. His face was distorted with rage as he continued,

"Guy, you remember the girl who gave you a piece of paper and it was taken from you?"

"Yes, and she was locked up."

"That was Wasima."

The silence was almost unbearable, but Ramin was determined that we should hear the rest of the story. He stood up and began walking rather stiffly about the table, using it to steady himself, when grief or physical weakness overwhelmed him. I offered him a drink. He refused the water, before finally calming down enough to sit rocking backwards and forwards in a more subdued state.

"That night he raped her, he raped my Wasima and locked her up again before sending for her father, that monster upstairs. It was her own father, that monster, who held her down, and ordered Mohammed to cut her nose off for trying to run away, and I had to watch, tied to a chair, unable to help my girl, I screamed, but no one helped her. I swear she died of fright in front of us all. That bastard Mohammed believes he was doing God's will."

"What f***ing God demands the mutilation of a beautiful woman by a sexually perverse man, married or not?" Guy cried out in pain at the thought that he had been part of the scene that terrible day.

"He will never face justice; they will say it is Taliban law!" Olli mused to himself, his face distorted in anger.

"They threw her body out into the field. Then we were all rounded up and moved here," Ramin cried out in anger, "I was tied up and brought here in the back of a truck. I was beaten and starved for a week, and then they gave me bread and water, and still beat me every few days. Since you are here they have left me alone. I please to see you, Matt."

I kept silent for tears were in my eyes, and this time they flowed down my cheeks with the anger I felt for that wee girl, and for Ramin.

"Did nobody escape?" asked Olli.

"Yes, some did, but I don't know how many. They're probably in the caves now; that's where we usually went to hide."

I got up and went to put my arms around Ramin, cradling him as the tears flowed, and we all silently shared the pain that would remain with him for the rest of his life.

Meanwhile Guy was pacing the length of the room, and every now and then he was touching the walls as if trying to push through the wood. Four times Guy circumnavigated the space, his face solemn and set as I had seldom seen it before. Olli watching him, realised that Guy was looking for a way out of this prison, suddenly jumped up and quite literally raced to the far end of the room to join Guy in a whispered conversation.

They told me later that Guy had felt the full horror of what had happened to Wasima, and was trying not to believe that his taking the note from her had been the trigger for her death. Olli apparently supported Ramin's take on the whole affair, that Mohammed was intrinsically evil and misogynistic in his treatment of women.

"I thought he was your father?" I chimed in with the need to know if it was to be a possible extra difficulty, should I choose to kill the monster, Mohammed.

"Sorry, no, I lied about that; at the time I thought it sounded good. I've no parents, I'm an orphan because my father died fighting the Taliban, and my mother was stoned to death for going out on her own without wearing a burka, back in 2001."

"Forgive me, but why were you living in Karvelk if Mohammed was a Taliban?" Olli asked.

"Because when my mother was killed, that's where it happened. I buried her in a spot only I know. It's not as if the place is sacred to me, but it is special, because she is there, and I met Wasima there when we were children. We were to be married." Ramin reiterated the fact as if he was uncertain of our appreciating his truth. But we all nodded in accord, we shared his pain and understood his reasoning.

Then it was Oswald Holford who voiced our silent, developing thoughts with complete accuracy when he said,   "We need a plan, we need a plan that will work and we need a plan that leaves that lot dead and the four of us safely back in Camp Bastion. Ideas wanted, folks, think along those lines."

I liked Olli more than ever after that; he was prepared to do the worst if he had to, and fight like a soldier. We talked for hours until Ramin, remembering something that made him say, "Earthquake!" suddenly came up with the idea that if we followed him around the room tapping the wall, we could come across a change in sound that we would find interesting, but about which he would like a second opinion.

Afraid that too much noise might bring trouble from above stairs, Guy decided that only Ramin would tap at the wall. He walked immediately to a panel set between two supporting timbers on the far end of the room. Tapping the panel to the left and then the one to the right, before tapping the central panel, he was able to produce a completely different sound. Olli immediately rushed back to his backpack and returned with a small wallet that contained a quarter-sized tool wallet of screwdriver, rasp and a Stanley knife and other small versions of useful items.

Impressed with his forethought I praised him, as he responded with, "Never travel without it, Matt,"

Within moments he had unscrewed a door-sized panel to reveal access to the great outdoors. Why there was a door half buried we had no idea, until Ramin repeated the word earthquake and told us of a legend that more than two hundred years ago there had been a major earth tremor that had caused subsidence over several areas of the Province of Mazâr-e-Sharif. He believed that at the time whole buildings that were without proper foundations had sunk into the ground; this house probably only fell three or four feet, but it covered what was probably the original doorway, which they had then panelled on the inside and subsequently forgotten. The apparently raised veranda, he explained, was most likely the original balcony of the first floor, and the enormous room in which we were being held as prisoners was once upon a time believed to be the village community assembly hall, hence its size.

Basically the lower part behind the panel was compressed earth and impossible to move, the top part could be opened to the elements, if we pushed at the top, where a smaller second piece of wood was filling the space above the dirt. Olli moved it with his weight, until he created a gap just wide enough for us to slide through on our backs.

Then Guy took over, as if he were again controlling a platoon; we were ordered to collect our backpacks, barricade the door with the table, and then we began by passing first one pack through the opening, no reaction, so he ordered us to send through the other two, before he told me to go for it. So I was first, followed by Olli, who needed both Ramin and Guy to push him, one leg each, while I pulled him from on top, Then Guy sent Ramin up, before he cleverly balanced the panel to one side of the opening. Carefully he lifted himself through, then turning round he gently and cautiously pulled the panel back in place. With any luck it might give us a few minutes or even an hour's advantage, once our absence was discovered.

It was dark, there was little moonlight, and even in the darkness of night we could see heavy rain clouds suggesting an imminent downpour. Guy looking about and smiled; with no light coming from shuttered windows and the possibility of rain, we should be able to make our escape and the rain would wash away our immediate footprints.

Ramin, the lightest in weight of all of us, moved away first, crossing the open space to the edge of the courtyard, now minus all cattle, they were obviously being sheltered in a barn. He stopped and looked up at the house, cracks in the badly fitting old shutters revealed some dull light in some of the upper rooms, but there was no obvious sign of people. As he waved them forward the other three quickly moved, until all were beyond the perimeter and at least half a mile from the house and farmyard.

Pausing for breath, we didn't seem to mind the now teeming rain, or the newly arrived thunder that was crashing all around us. Opening our mouths they let the rain quench our thirst. A short walk further on and we found a shelter beneath a rocky overhang. A conflab was decreed necessary by Ramin; he was given the floor as the rest of us stood in front of him and listened to him.

"Let me go back and kill them."

We stared at him in disbelief.

It was Olli who said one word.

"How?"

"Fire; let me torch the place, simple solution! Didn't you see those petrol cans, I checked they are full. Give me half an hour, you rest here, I'll be back."

"Let's all go," Olli said with supressed excitement in his whispered tones.

"No, you have homes to go to, I just want revenge, and then maybe my people could live in peace. Not possible while they live. Let me free myself. Let me rid myself of their evil, their power, for there is a veil between life and death and I want to close it for ever."

We all nodded, we knew why he wanted to get his revenge and not one of us was going to stop him. Barely ten minutes after he left us beneath that rocky outcrop we witnessed a blaze so brilliant it rose with terrifying speed thirty feet up into the night sky. There were crackling sounds, as that ancient wooden mansion was rendered to ash; eventually as dawn broke the house imploded into the hollow beneath the house, and continued to burn, in that very place that had been our prison.

There was a feeling of satisfaction, such as I will never be able to describe; I said to Guy and Olli watching beside me, "That'll teach them to stop cutting noses off young girls who don't fancy them." I know it must seem a childish remark at this distance from the event, but it summed up my revulsion at the evil that was the Taliban and the War Lords of Afghanistan.

"Not just them, all those who ill-treat the women who bear our children," said Olli as if trying to show his disgust at the terrible abuse that we all knew about, from reports in the news.

When Ramin returned he was quiet and extremely tired looking, I gave him some of my bread and a drink of water. We sat waiting for him to rest himself before deciding what to do next. Whatever he did or however he did it, he had achieved his victory over the men who had killed his love. We could wait to find out the details, when he was strong enough to tell us.

We rested, waiting for the sun to rise to daylight to aid our journey.

It was Guy who asked Ramin where the nearest phone might be, and how did he suggest we get to it.

Olli argued for Uzbekistan as the safest haven.

I pointed out that we had no passports.

Ramin said, "Quiet, someone's coming."

At that we moved to hide behind some bushes, and just in time as a Foxhound light protected vehicle from the US Army went driving past and heading for the fire still visible for miles around, as it consumed the house. We hadn't had time to react and, uncertain as to who was driving it, we stayed low as three more vehicles followed on.

One could have been a stolen vehicle, four Fox hounds definitely not; it was a US patrol. We rose up as one body and were running behind them like jubilant madmen shouting and waving our arms, as we laughed with relief, until the tail end Charlie stopped and Norcross stood up, pointing a gun straight at us.

His first comment was, "Bloody hell, you've lost weight!"

The debriefing back at Camp Bastion was difficult, but we all spoke the truth, and the military police and the generals who gathered to question us were in the end satisfied.

We were all cleared of any possible charge; we were praised for uncovering the information that the leak out of the camps was via Mohammed's devious contacts with the Taliban during market days.

We were exonerated over the deaths that lay in our wake and we were praised for saving one of the best interpreters the ISAF used and wanted to continue to use. They had been mystified when the Taliban had kidnapped Ramin; they couldn't believe he had been duplicitous and they expressed their regret at the terrible punishment the Taliban had inflicted upon him.

Chapter Thirty-Four
Karvelk

We all decided to help Ramin rebury his mother. We felt it was a good way of saying thank you to the young man for all his help and support. There was Norcross, Lewis, Johnstone and Hughes who together with Olli, Guy and I made up the work party.

Taking shovels and flowers we dug a proper grave for her in the centre of Mohammed's large compound, now claimed by Ramin as his own. Then reverently and with care, we dug up the remains, we interred them and built a monument over them, so that Ramin could feel that at long last he had honoured his mother properly. Other villagers were there, having begun to return from the mountainous caves to which they had escaped. All rejoiced in the news of the death of their Taliban tormentors. We had a little ceremony to bless the grave, before planting the sturdy flowering bushes around the monument. Later we helped Ramin refresh the rooms around the compound, and repaired the locks.

Olli immediately set to work organising a school house and with the help of ISAF found teachers for the village children, boys as well as girls. Ramin was beside himself with joy and promised to keep Olli informed of its progress. By the time we were ready to leave two weeks later, every compound and house had been reclaimed, the Friday market was once again open to all and Ramin had been elected as village head man, he refused to be called an 'Elder!'

All of us found the Afghan people initially somewhat shy of us, until they realised the promises were not hollow and that eventually they had the chance to rebuild their lives in a time of peace. Olli and I liked the way the men were gradually more relaxed with us, taking their cue from Ramin.

That young man had aged in the past year; he seemed ten years older than the man child I had seen squatting under the bush waiting to kill Taliban. Frequently during that time before we returned home, I heard him telling Guy how much he missed Wasima, and how as the new man in charge in the village, he intended to put a stop to child marriages.

What happened next now lives in my memory forever; even if I wanted to, I would never be able to erase what I saw.

The day before we were leaving I went to say my goodbyes and without difficulty I persuaded Guy and Olli to come with me; as we walked from the excellent Jackal we were allowed to use to get us there and back in one piece, we stopped and stared at a bundled-up figure peeping around the open gate to Ramin's home. Only her eyes were visible, but Guy knew who she was; hadn't he said, "I'll never forget her eyes."

He knelt down beside her before she could fly off, his hand placed gently on her back felt the shudder of fear go through her, as he said,

"Welcome home, Wasima, this is Ramin's house now."

Wasima looked at him with eyes wide and tearful, what was she to believe? Ramin, hearing Guy's voice, came out of one of the storerooms and stood watching Guy lift Wasima up, she was as light as a feather. Her half-starved frame spoke volumes of her sufferings, it more than hinted at her rejection by others, and of her fear of others' reactions to her, because of her deformity.

I watched as Guy placed the diminutive figure in Ramin's outstretched arms and the veil fell away to reveal the hole where once she had had a nose. Ramin never wavered; he kissed her mouth and held her close until she lifted her arms around his neck. None of us needed words to understand what was going on in front of us; we just knew they would be together as lovers, for the rest of their lives.

Epilogue

No doubt, dear Reader, you want to know what happened to Wasima. Yes, Oswald Holford paid for her to come to Chester and for her face to be reconstructed privately at the Countess of Chester Hospital. Ramin stayed with Alice and Guy and visited us here in Lower Peover, while Wasima had her surgery. You cannot imagine the party we had before they returned to Afghanistan. Cathy called it a belated wedding feast; and it was just that, for Ramin and Wasima had married in Karvelk soon after they had been reunited.

All of us celebrated the growing awareness that out of the tragedy that was Afghanistan, all ambulance services and the NHS accepted the improved medical practices which were saving those with traumatic injuries. The tourniquet became widely used and to some of us it was privately known as the Platinum Ten Tourniquet, greater than the Golden Hour in helping to save the lives of our fighting boys. Some civilian workers, especially the likes of farmers, began to carry them when out alone on tractors. Others called it the one-handed tourniquet; Guy said, "Call it what they will, it saved my life!"

Frequently, I also gratefully think of all those anonymous blood donors who helped to save his life and would never know what they had done for him.

The Platoon kept in touch with one another, Guy made it his job to organise an annual re-union and they were all well attended. We met up with their growing families and shared news of new careers and hurdles overcome by dogged perseverance. They were times of renewal and remembrances. A great help to all the lads. Only Bryn Jones seemed to be missing until Guy set off to find him and bring him back out of a period of deep PTSD.

Guy continued to work for the army and he and Alice had four lovely girls. All of us happily watched them grow to girlhood and prepare to gain university places. Cathy and I joined Oswald and Naomi in sharing grandparents' duties; baby-sitting, bath-times, and holidays together, when I taught them to play cricket and Olli taught them baseball. Then the happiest of all the seasonal celebrations when we kept Thanksgiving with Alice and Naomi in charge of the food, and then Christmas, with Grandpa Holford always as Father Christmas, on the grounds that he was big and jolly and did a better ho, ho, ho than I ever could, claiming that as I was so skinny I didn't have the lung capacity. How we laughed and how we cheered when years later we watched our boy win medal after medal, at Paralympic Games, Invictus Games and Commonwealth Games.

Before he died, Olli reminded me of how wrong he had been about Guy marrying Alice; he said, "Matt, I frequently remember how mistaken I was, about our lad; if he's disabled he's a perfectly normal disabled person, who is more able than people with two whole legs!"

I laughed and agreed and said, "There's life after injury if you are prepared to live it and to bravely accept it. That's not easy, but he was lucky, Olli. He always had a home and a job; and a woman who stood by him, not all the boys were as lucky, many had no home to go to, no job and with their health ruined, they never find the right woman."

There was a long pause; again I saw that lower lip jut out as he thought of her. Did I also get more pompous with age, I think I did, but he was right when he said,

"I still think of Wasima, poor wee lass that she was. I'm glad she and Ramin are so happy, and their family growing around them, and all well-educated."

Olli wouldn't have had it any other way, he organised the funding of the school and watched with delight as it grew and grew until it became the largest school in the Helmand Province of Afghanistan, sending girls as well as boys to universities all over the world.

Olli loved his life and he revelled in it, growing old with a calmness and dignity, until after twenty happy years surrounded by his girls, he passed peacefully away and was laid to rest near his ancestors, in the graveyard of St Oswald's, Lower Peover.

Is Olli in heaven? I never thought of him as a religious man, he was too pragmatic to be superstitious. You had to be able to see it, understand it, plant it, grow it and harvest it; otherwise Olli had little interest in it. His grandchildren and the children in Karvelk were his harvest.

The years have been kind to me; I'm ninety now. I still wonder if Gordon Brown ever read my report; did I personally do anything to improve things? I doubt it. For more than six additional years the statistics kept coming as coffin after coffin carried brave young men and women home, and yet the miracle was that those same statistics showed that because of a clever little tourniquet and a better understanding of the nature of human blood, combined with the most dedicated workers in that medical trauma unit, ninety percent of those injured by blasts from IED were able to survive. I look at Guy sitting there, healthy, working, married and a father, and in my heart I thank all of those involved who made it happen for him.

Guy still calls me Dad, and we often sit in total contentment putting the world to rights, over a pint of the best, in the sunny garden of the Bells of Peover, and I lift my glass towards the church and tell Olli, all is well with the family, that Wasima is still alive and healthy and living in Helmand with her loving husband, and her daughters growing up reading and writing, and with their glowing faces fearlessly turning to greet the hot Afghanistan sun, as Ramin leads the way in the fight against the ancient tradition of child marriage.

[The next book by Pelham McMahon is due out by the summer of 2015 and concentrates upon the recovery and subsequent story of Bryn Jones.]

Also available to buy on Amazon the Digital Edition of Platinum Ten

10187668R00206

Printed in Great Britain
by Amazon.co.uk, Ltd.,
Marston Gate.